D0062214

BESTIES

FIND THEIR GROOVE

BESTIES

FIND THEIR GROOVE

BY KAYLA MILLER & JEFFREY CANINO
ART BY KRISTINA LUU

CLARION BOOKS
IMPRINTS OF HARPERCOLLINSPUBLISHERS

Based on the Click series, created by Kayla Miller.

Clarion Books is an imprint of HarperCollins Publishers.
HarperAlley is an imprint of HarperCollins Publishers.

Besties: Find Their Groove
Copyright © 2022 by HarperCollins Publishers
Library of Congress Control Number: 2022934063
ISBN 978-0-35-852116-7 hardcover
ISBN 978-0-35-856192-7 paperback

Inks by Victor Martins
Color by Damali Beatty
Lettering by Lor Prescott
Illustrations, additional inks, and additional color by Kristina Luu
The artist used Clip Studio Paint with digital brushes to create
the illustrations for this book.
Typography by Stephanie Hays
22 23 24 25 26   GPS   10 9 8 7 6 5 4 3 2 1

First Edition

For Mom, who helped me weather many formal wear—related crises —K.M.

For Katie and the Potato Sisters —J.C.

For Milo, my fluffiest best friend— rest in peace —K.L.

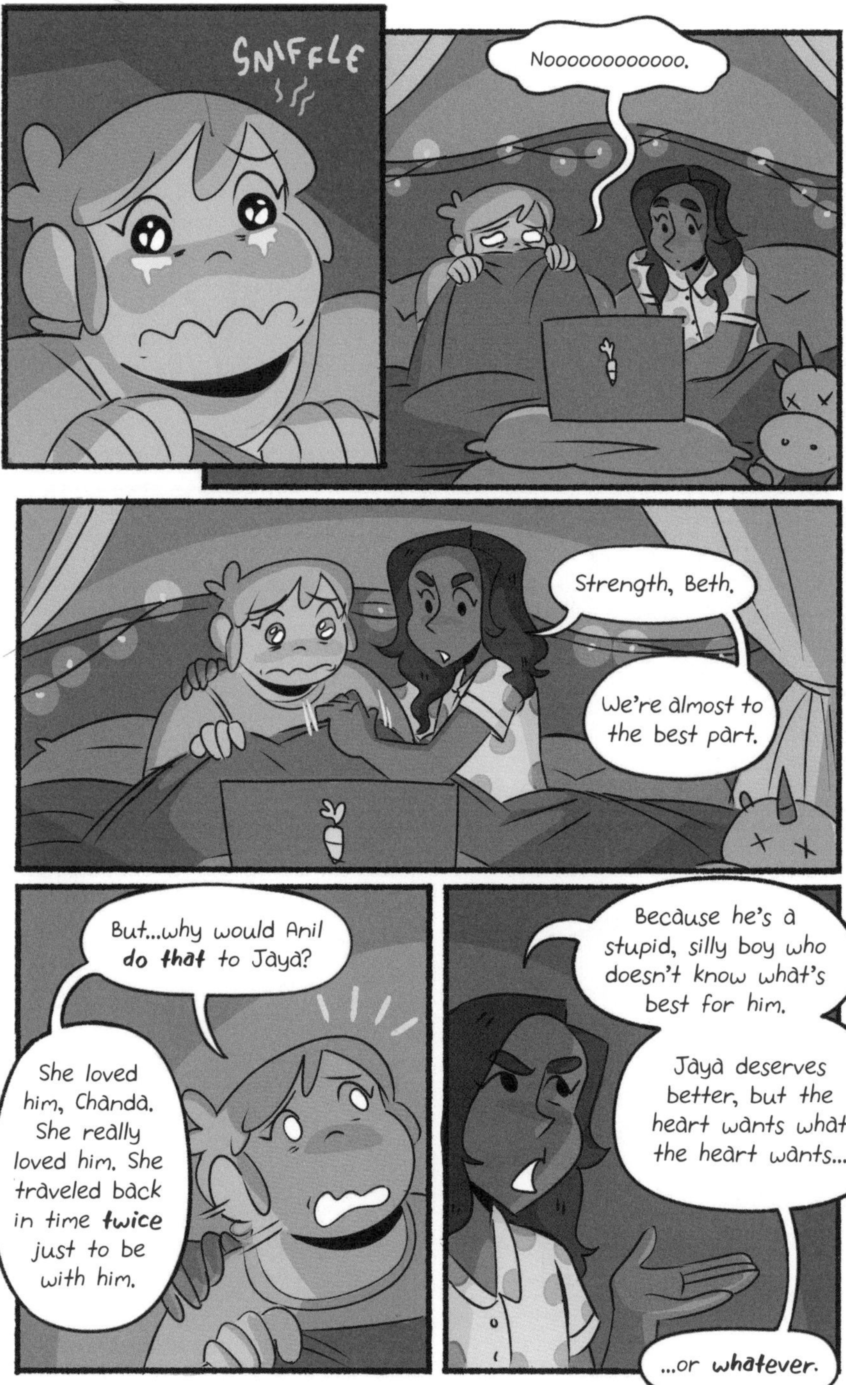
SNIFFLE
Noooooooooooo.
Strength, Beth.
We're almost to the best part.
But...why would Anil **do that** to Jaya?
She loved him, Chanda. She really loved him. She traveled back in time **twice** just to be with him.
Because he's a stupid, silly boy who doesn't know what's best for him.
Jaya deserves better, but the heart wants what the heart wants...
...or **whatever**.

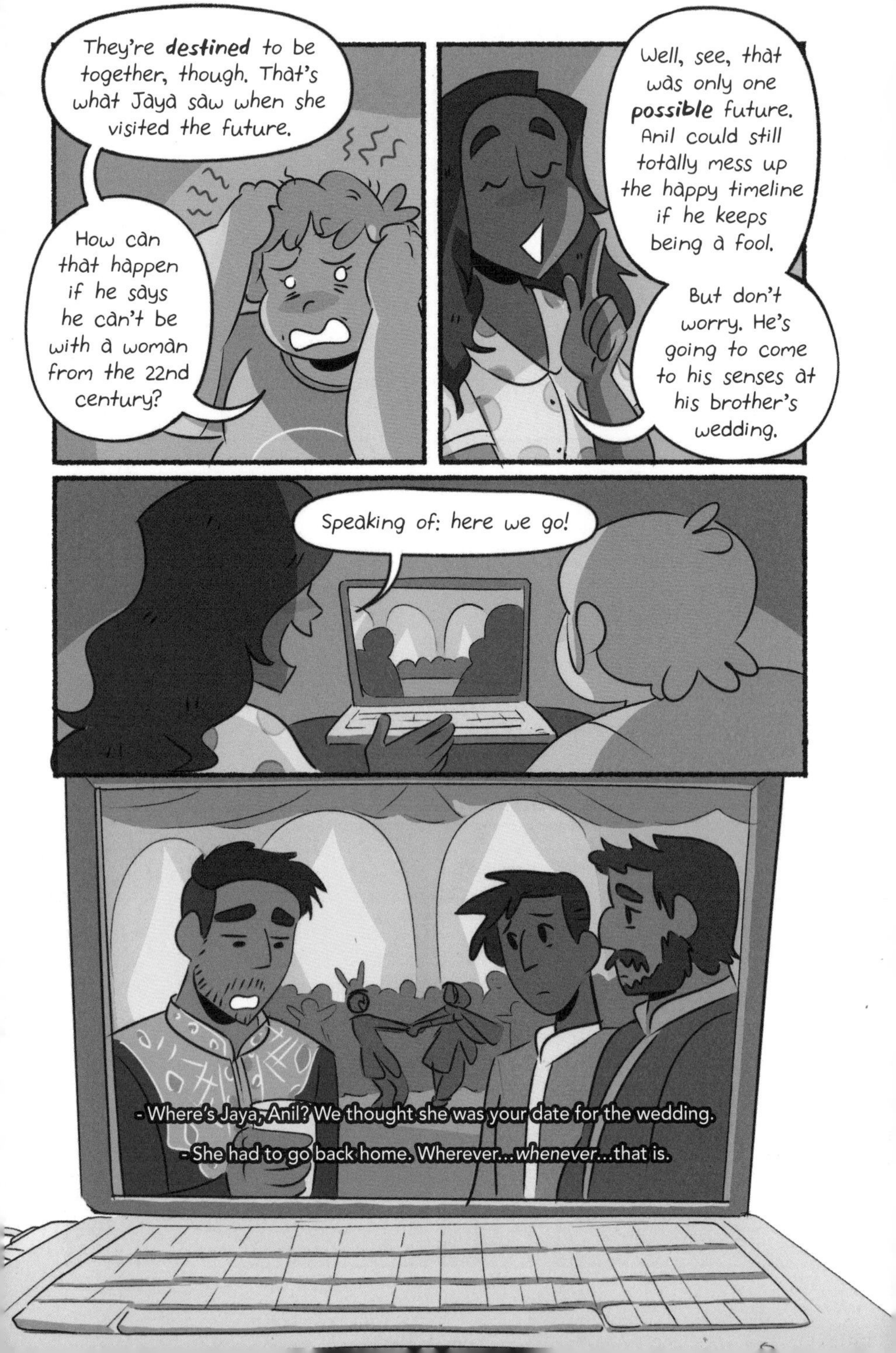
They're **destined** to be together, though. That's what Jaya saw when she visited the future.
How can that happen if he says he can't be with a woman from the 22nd century?
Well, see, that was only one **possible** future. Anil could still totally mess up the happy timeline if he keeps being a fool.
But don't worry. He's going to come to his senses at his brother's wedding.
Speaking of: here we go!
- Where's Jaya, Anil? We thought she was your date for the wedding.
- She had to go back home. Wherever...*whenever*...that is.

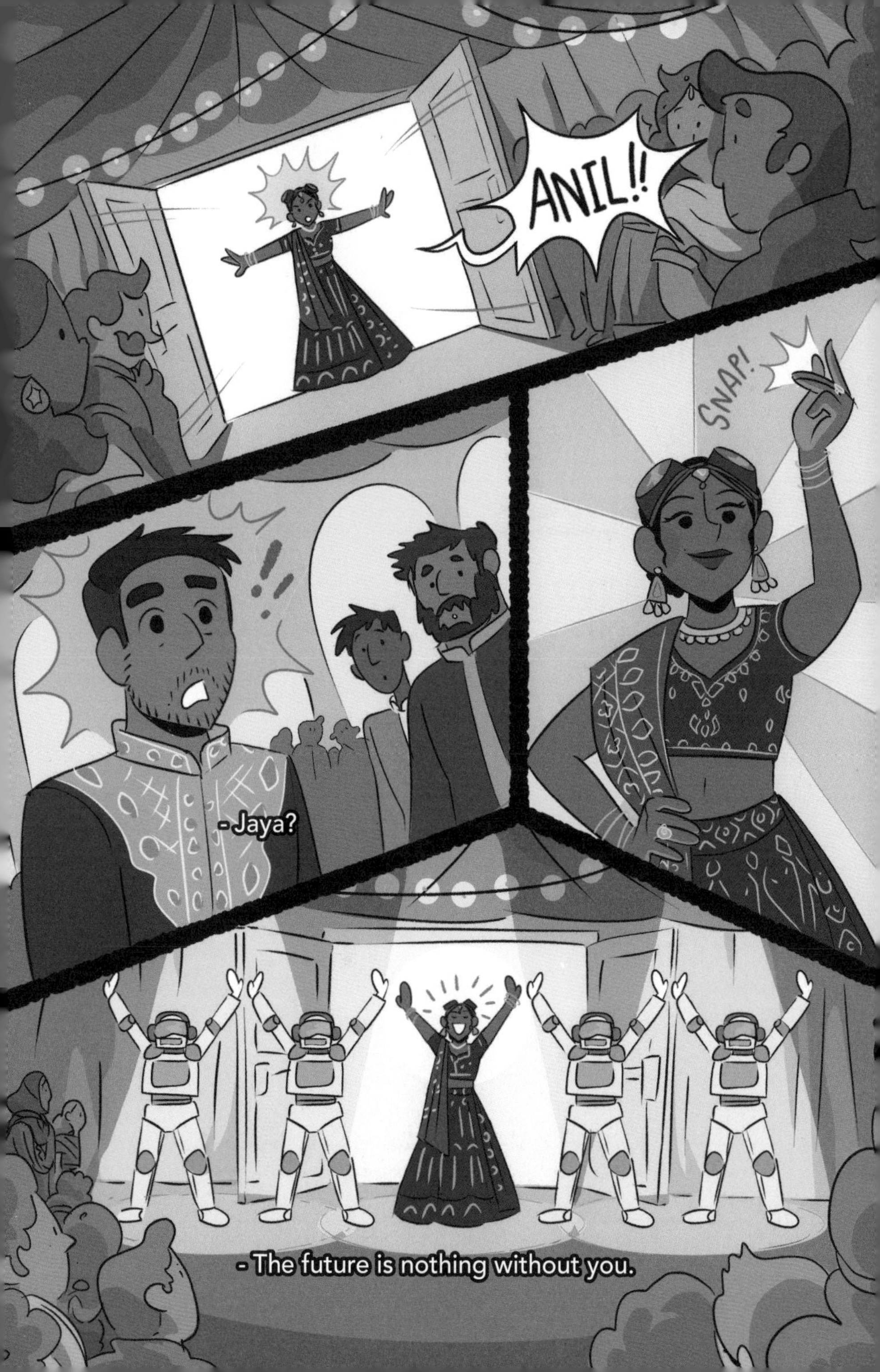
ANIL!!
SNAP!
- Jaya?
- The future is nothing without you.

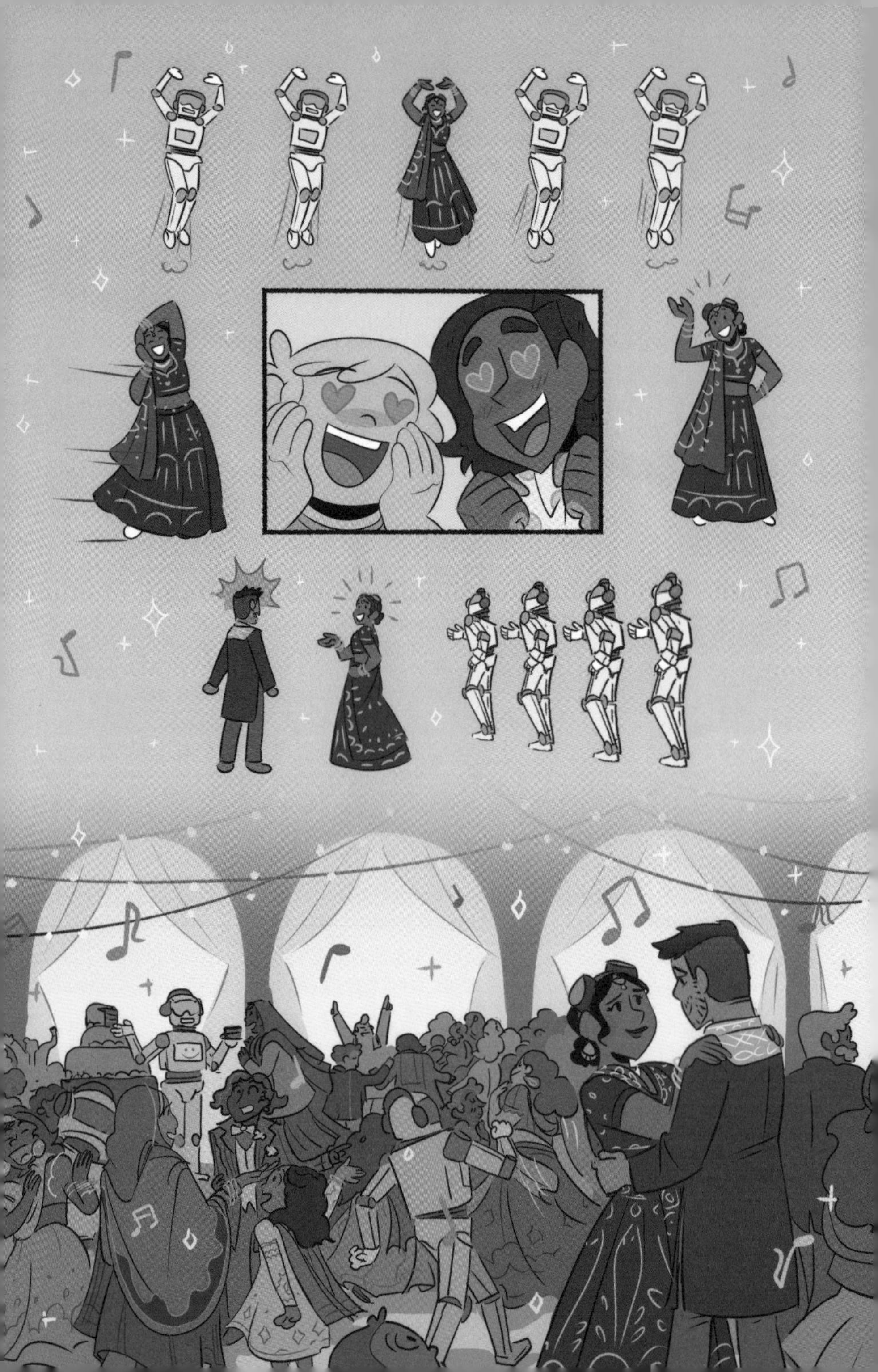

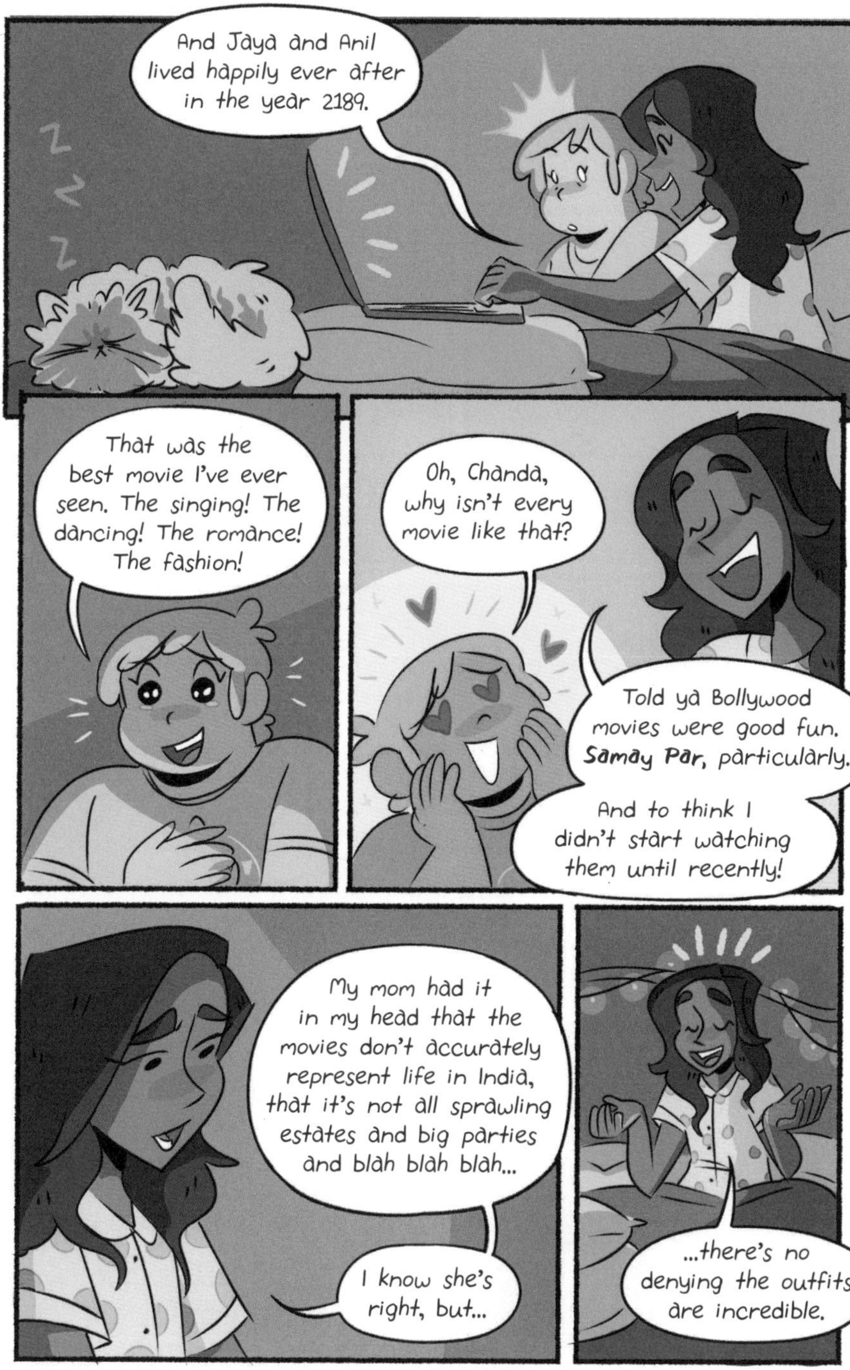
And Jaya and Anil lived happily ever after in the year 2189.
Z
Z
Z
That was the best movie I've ever seen. The singing! The dancing! The romance! The fashion!
Oh, Chanda, why isn't every movie like that?
Told ya Bollywood movies were good fun. **Samay Par,** particularly.
And to think I didn't start watching them until recently!
My mom had it in my head that the movies don't accurately represent life in India, that it's not all sprawling estates and big parties and blah blah blah...
I know she's right, but...
...there's no denying the outfits are incredible.

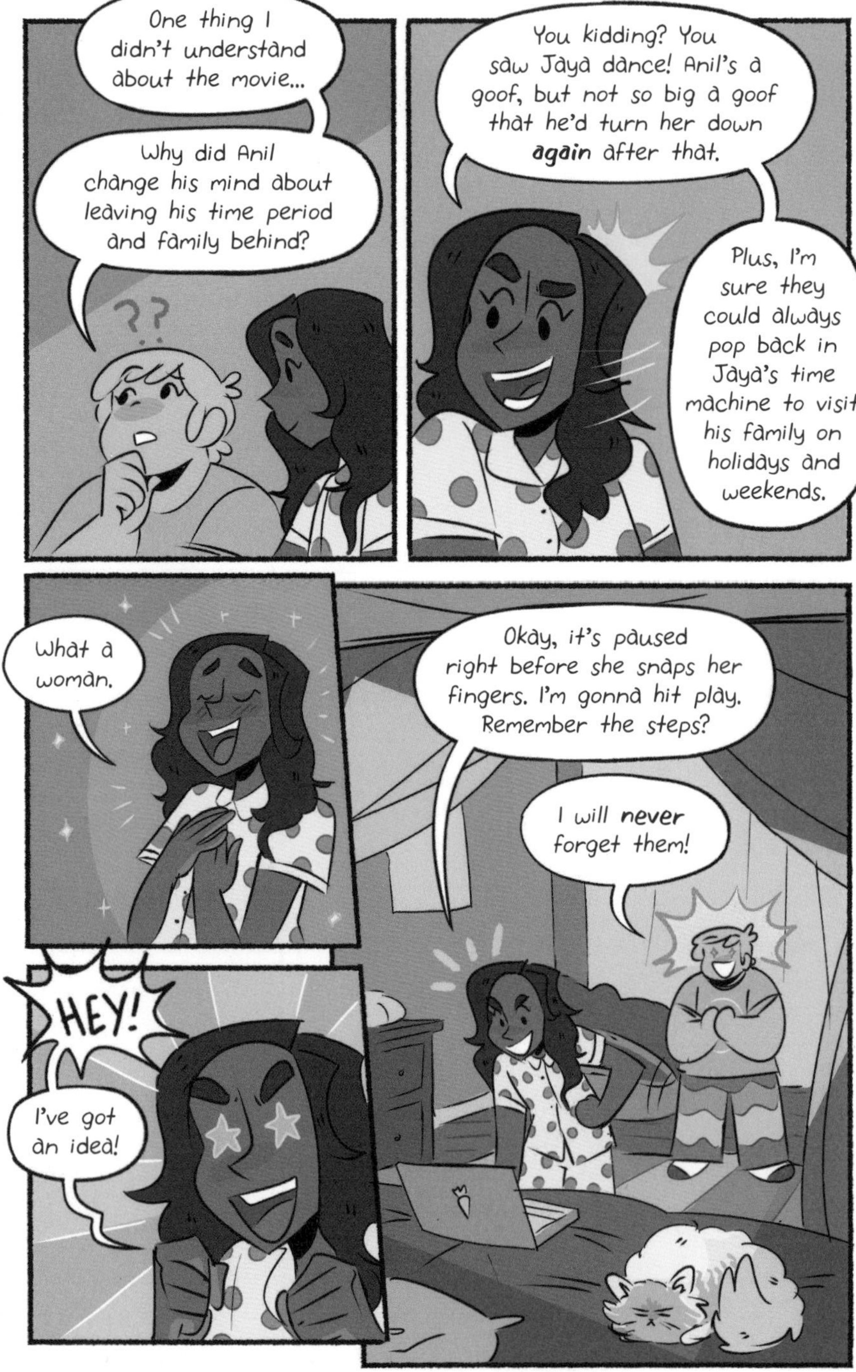
One thing I didn't understand about the movie...
Why did Anil change his mind about leaving his time period and family behind?
??
You kidding? You saw Jaya dance! Anil's a goof, but not so big a goof that he'd turn her down **again** after that.
Plus, I'm sure they could always pop back in Jaya's time machine to visit his family on holidays and weekends.
What a woman.
Okay, it's paused right before she snaps her fingers. I'm gonna hit play. Remember the steps?
I will **never** forget them!
HEY!
I've got an idea!

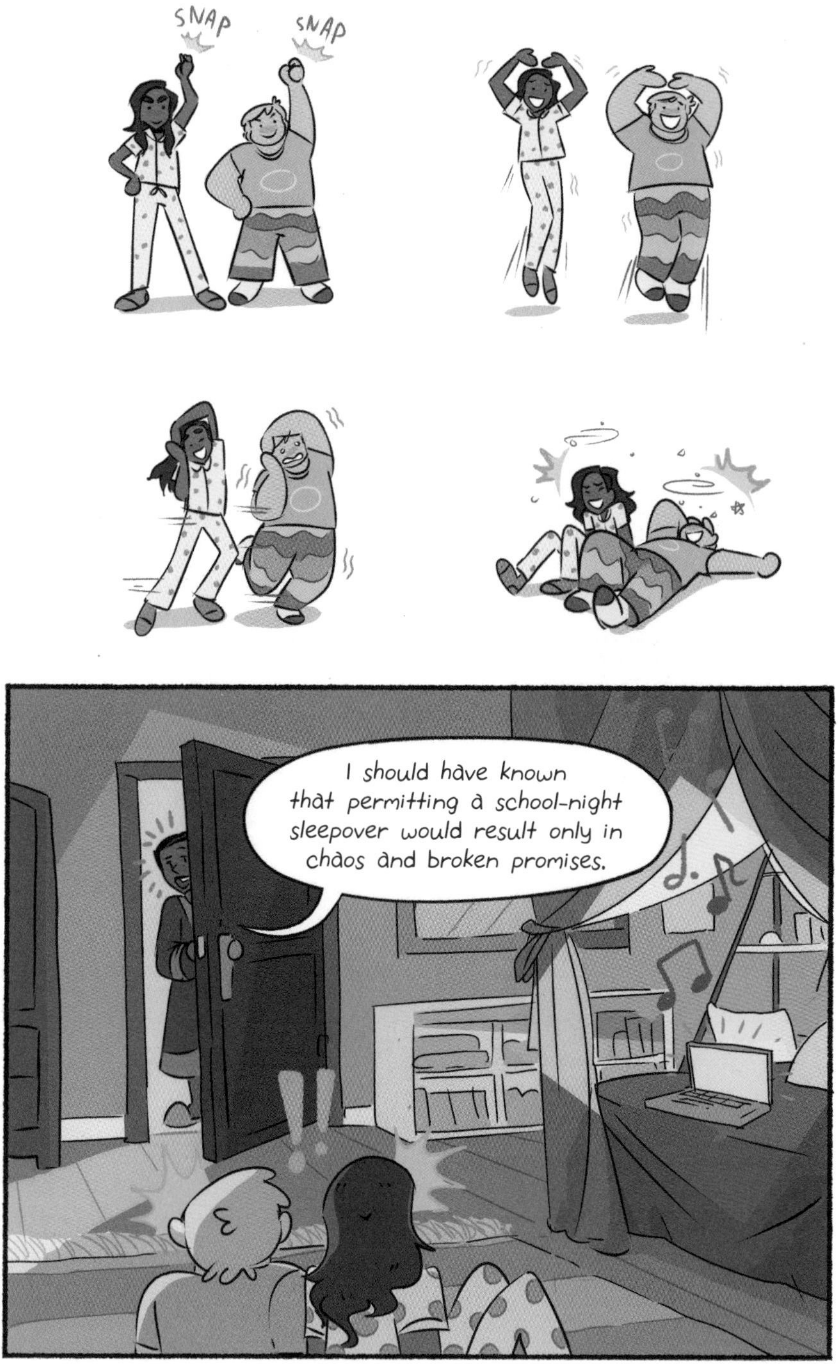
SNAP
SNAP
I should have known that permitting a school-night sleepover would result only in chaos and broken promises.

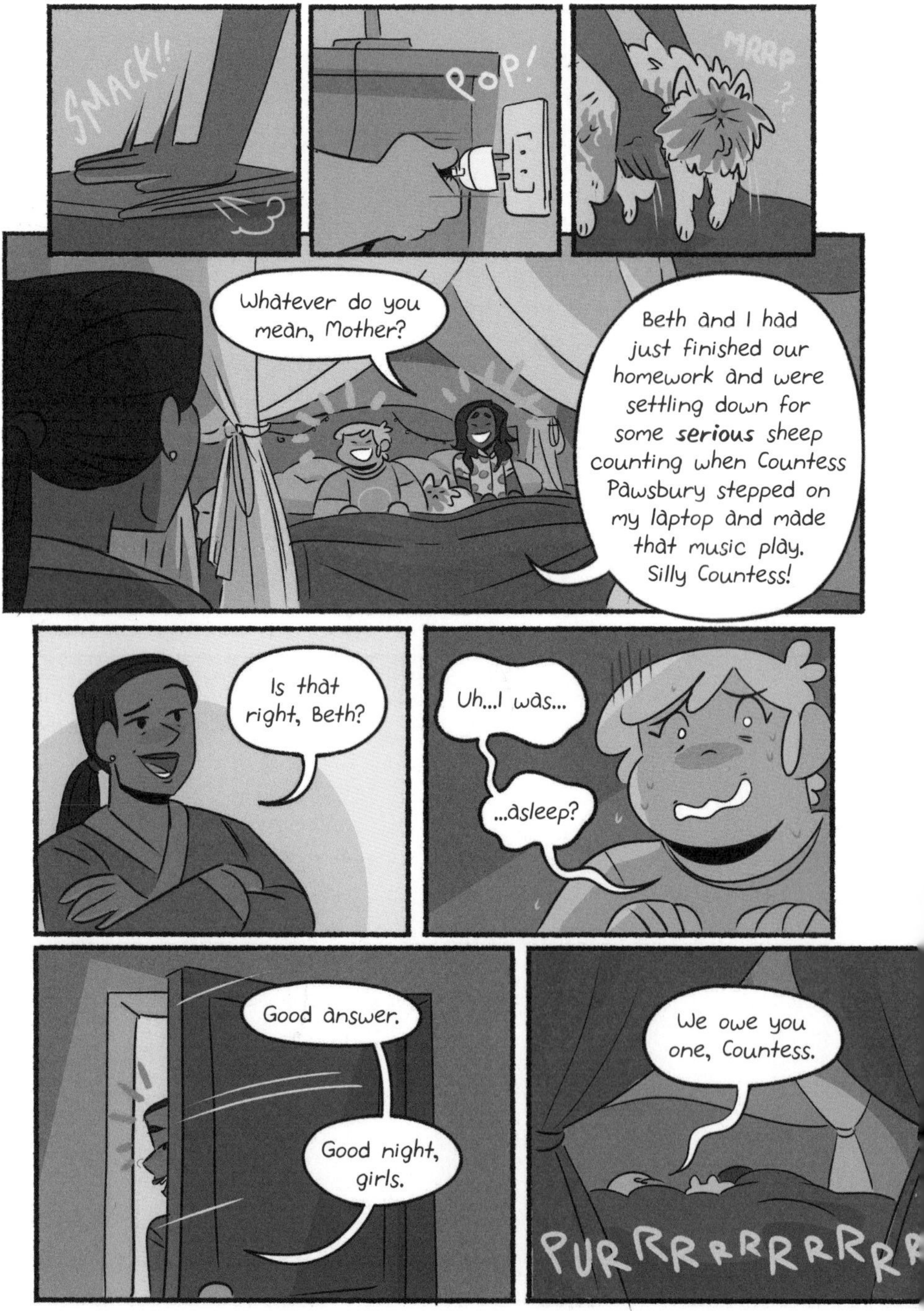
SMACK!!
POP!
MRRP
?
Whatever do you mean, Mother?
Beth and I had just finished our homework and were settling down for some **serious** sheep counting when Countess Pawsbury stepped on my laptop and made that music play. Silly Countess!
Is that right, Beth?
Uh...I was...
...asleep?
Good answer.
Good night, girls.
We owe you one, Countess.
PURRRRRRRRRRR

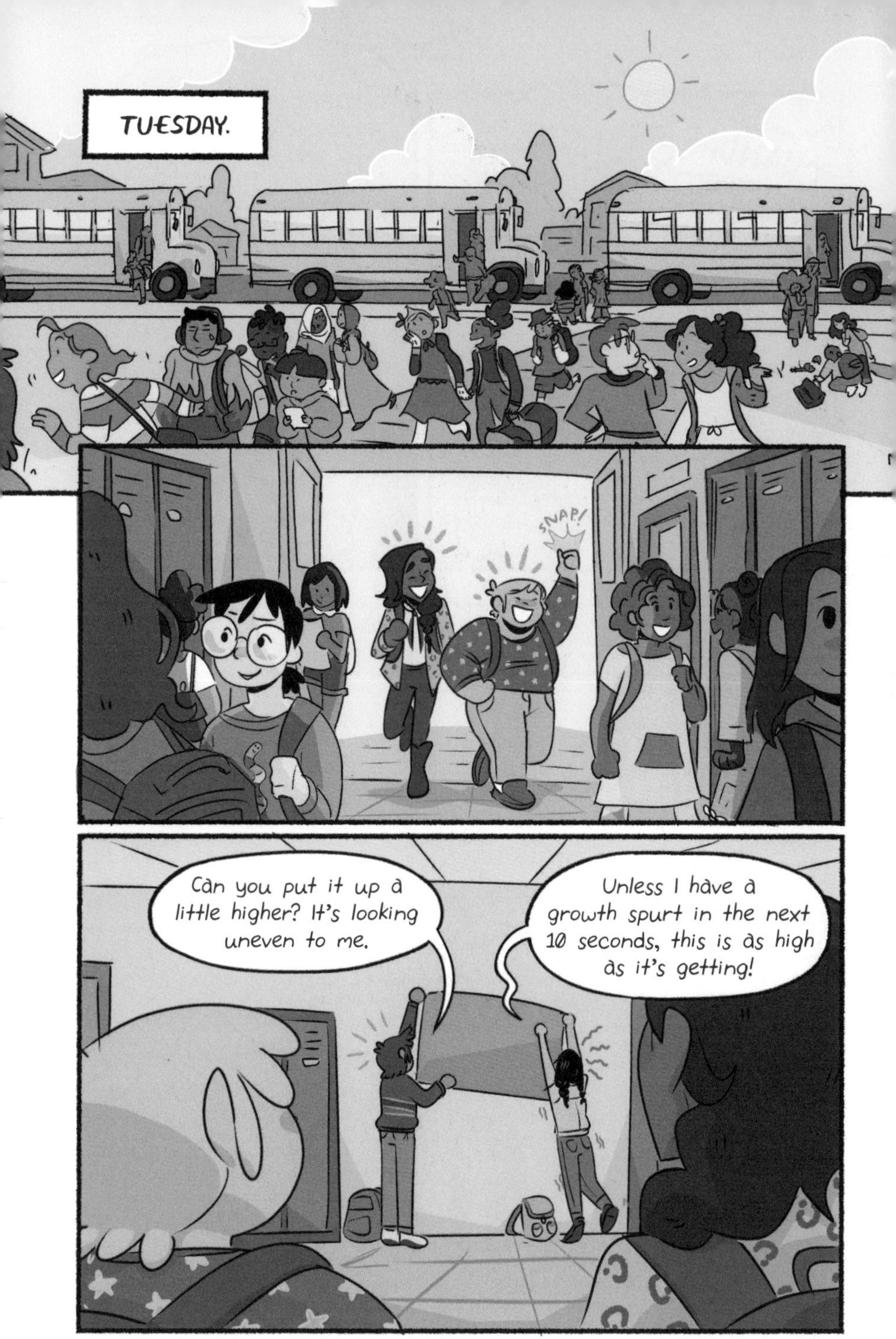
TUESDAY.
SNAP!
Can you put it up a little higher? It's looking uneven to me.
Unless I have a growth spurt in the next 10 seconds, this is as high as it's getting!

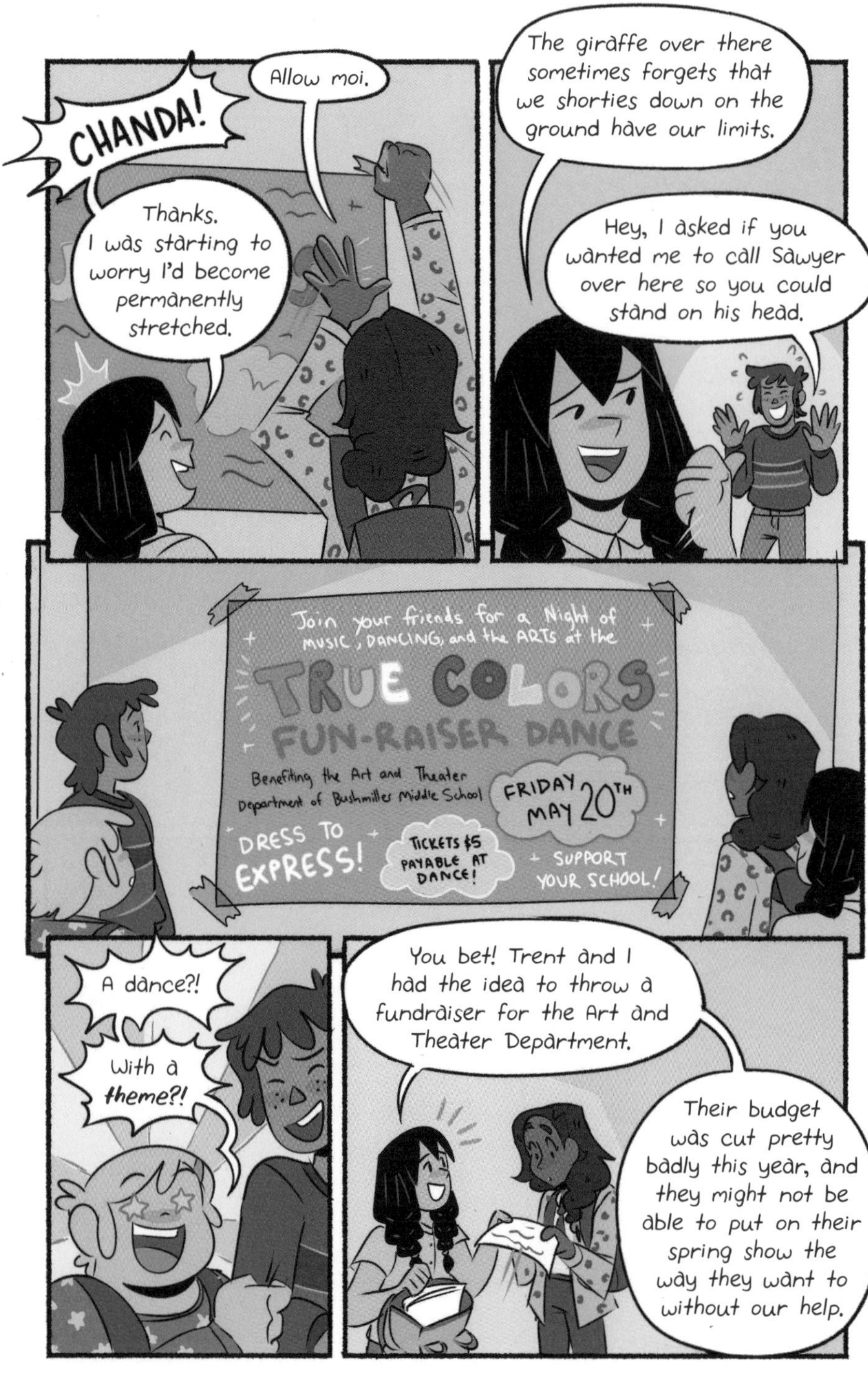
CHANDA!
Allow moi.
Thanks.
I was starting to worry I'd become permanently stretched.
The giraffe over there sometimes forgets that we shorties down on the ground have our limits.
Hey, I asked if you wanted me to call Sawyer over here so you could stand on his head.
Join your friends for a Night of MUSIC, DANCING, and the ARTS at the
TRUE COLORS
FUN-RAISER DANCE
Benefiting the Art and Theater Department of Bushmiller Middle School
FRIDAY MAY 20TH
DRESS TO EXPRESS!
TICKETS $5 PAYABLE AT DANCE!
SUPPORT YOUR SCHOOL!
A dance?!
With a *theme?!*
You bet! Trent and I had the idea to throw a fundraiser for the Art and Theater Department.
Their budget was cut pretty badly this year, and they might not be able to put on their spring show the way they want to without our help.

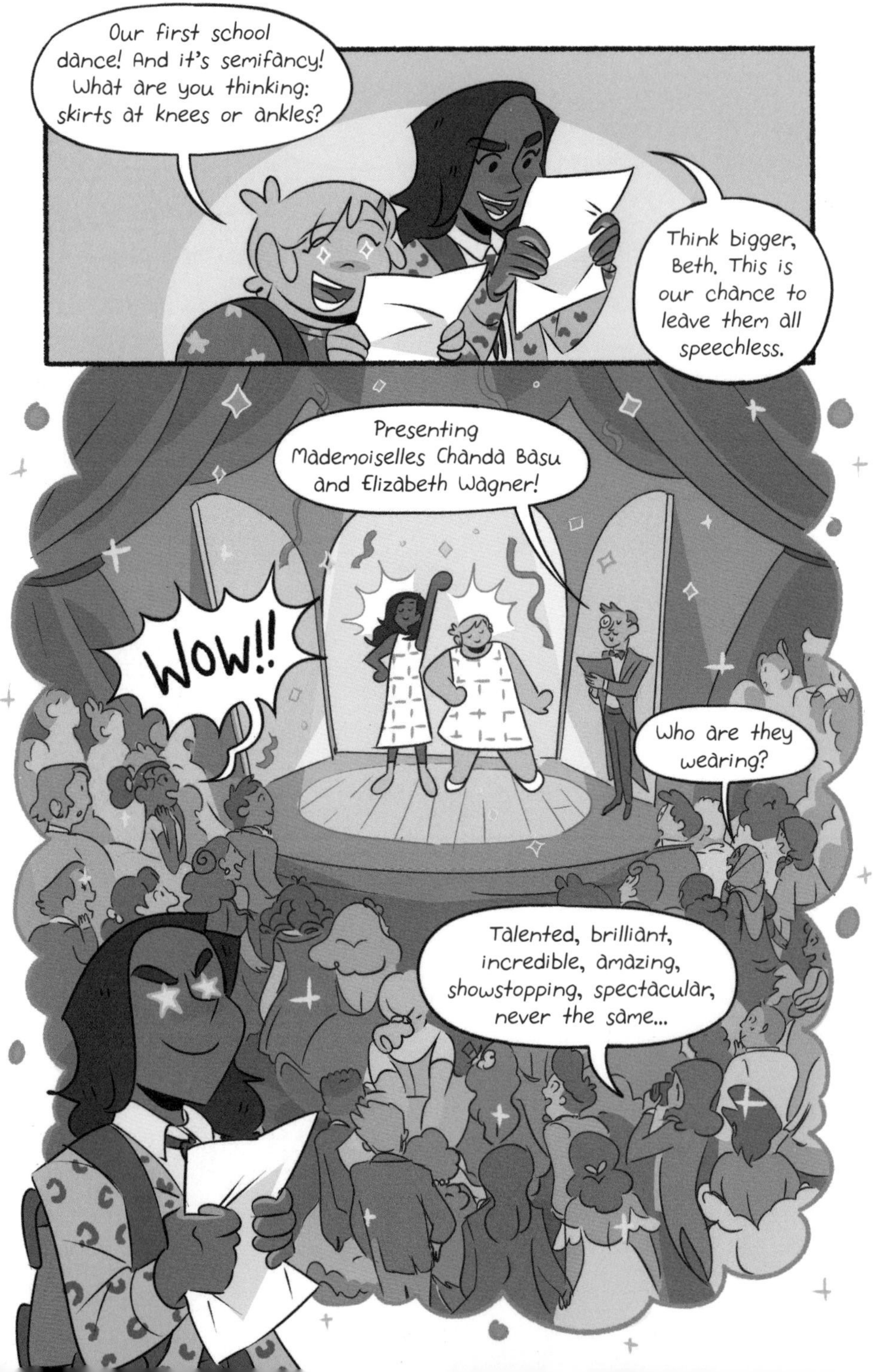
Our first school dance! And it's semifancy! What are you thinking: skirts at knees or ankles?
Think bigger, Beth. This is our chance to leave them all speechless.
Presenting Mademoiselles Chanda Basu and Elizabeth Wagner!
WOW!!
Who are they wearing?
Talented, brilliant, incredible, amazing, showstopping, spectacular, never the same...

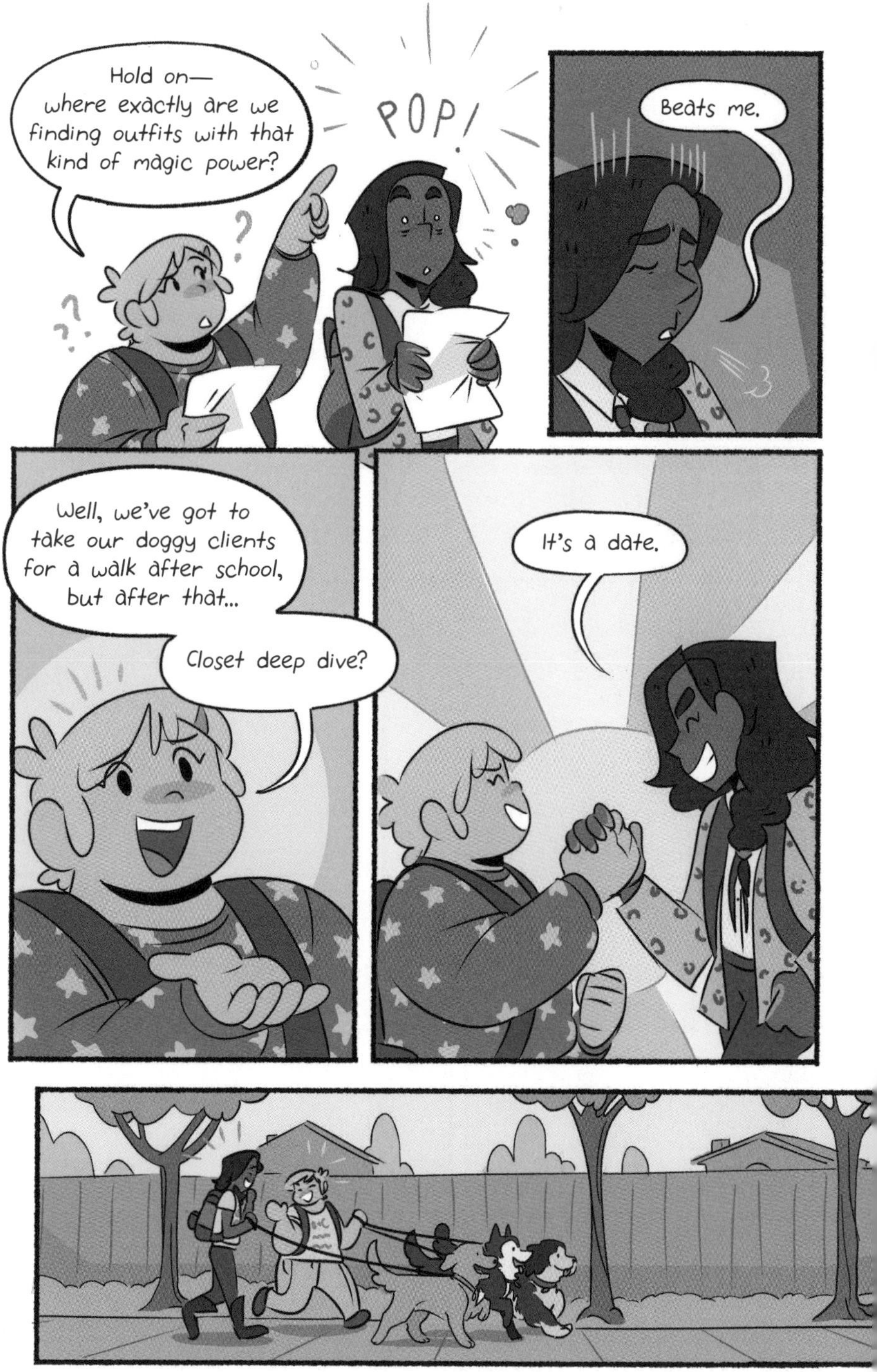
Hold on—
where exactly are we finding outfits with that kind of magic power?
POP!
Beats me.
Well, we've got to take our doggy clients for a walk after school, but after that...
Closet deep dive?
It's a date.

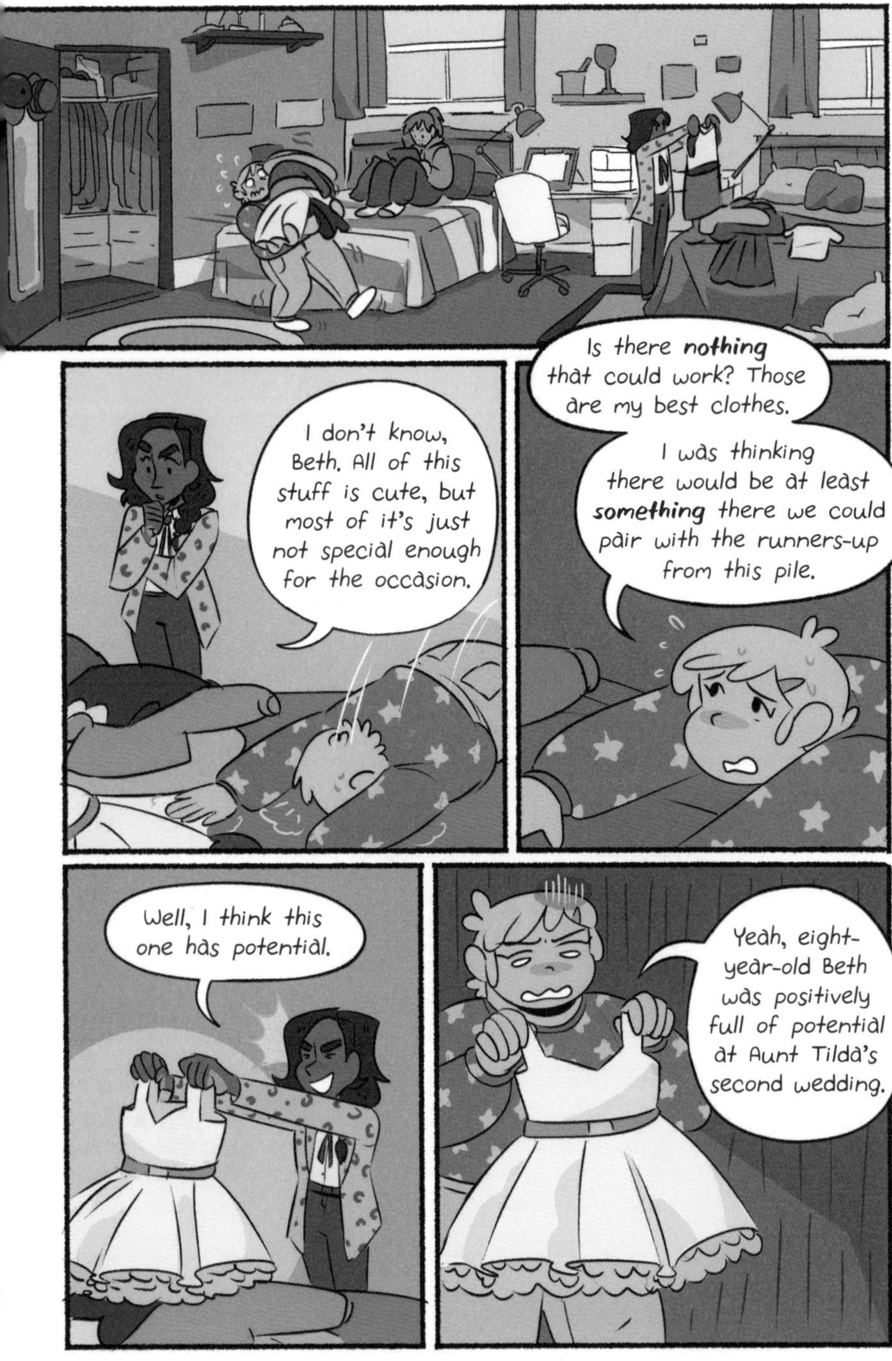
Is there **nothing** that could work? Those are my best clothes.
I don't know, Beth. All of this stuff is cute, but most of it's just not special enough for the occasion.
I was thinking there would be at least **something** there we could pair with the runners-up from this pile.
Well, I think this one has potential.
Yeah, eight-year-old Beth was positively full of potential at Aunt Tilda's second wedding.

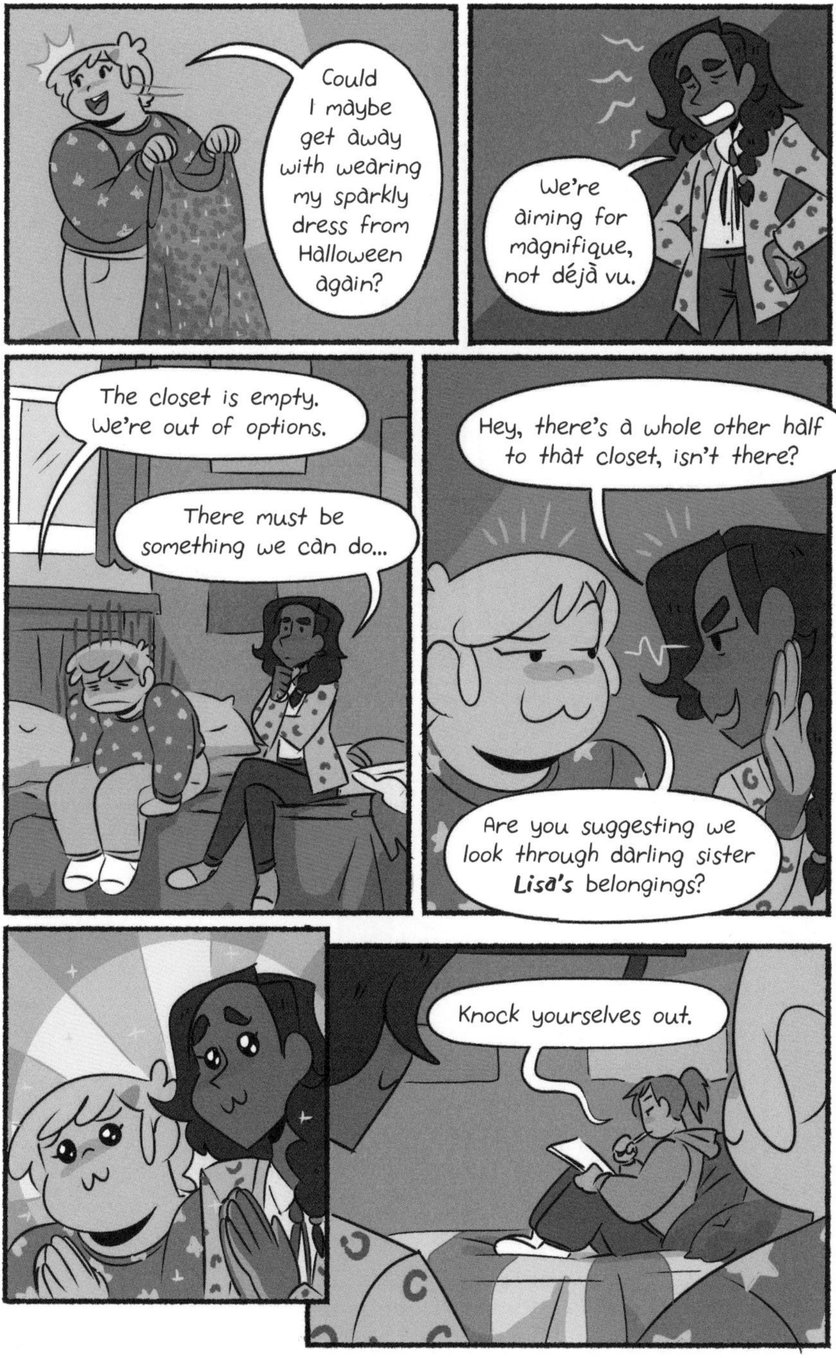
Could I maybe get away with wearing my sparkly dress from Halloween again?
We're aiming for magnifique, not déjà vu.
The closet is empty. We're out of options.
There must be something we can do...
Hey, there's a whole other half to that closet, isn't there?
Are you suggesting we look through darling sister **Lisa's** belongings?
Knock yourselves out.

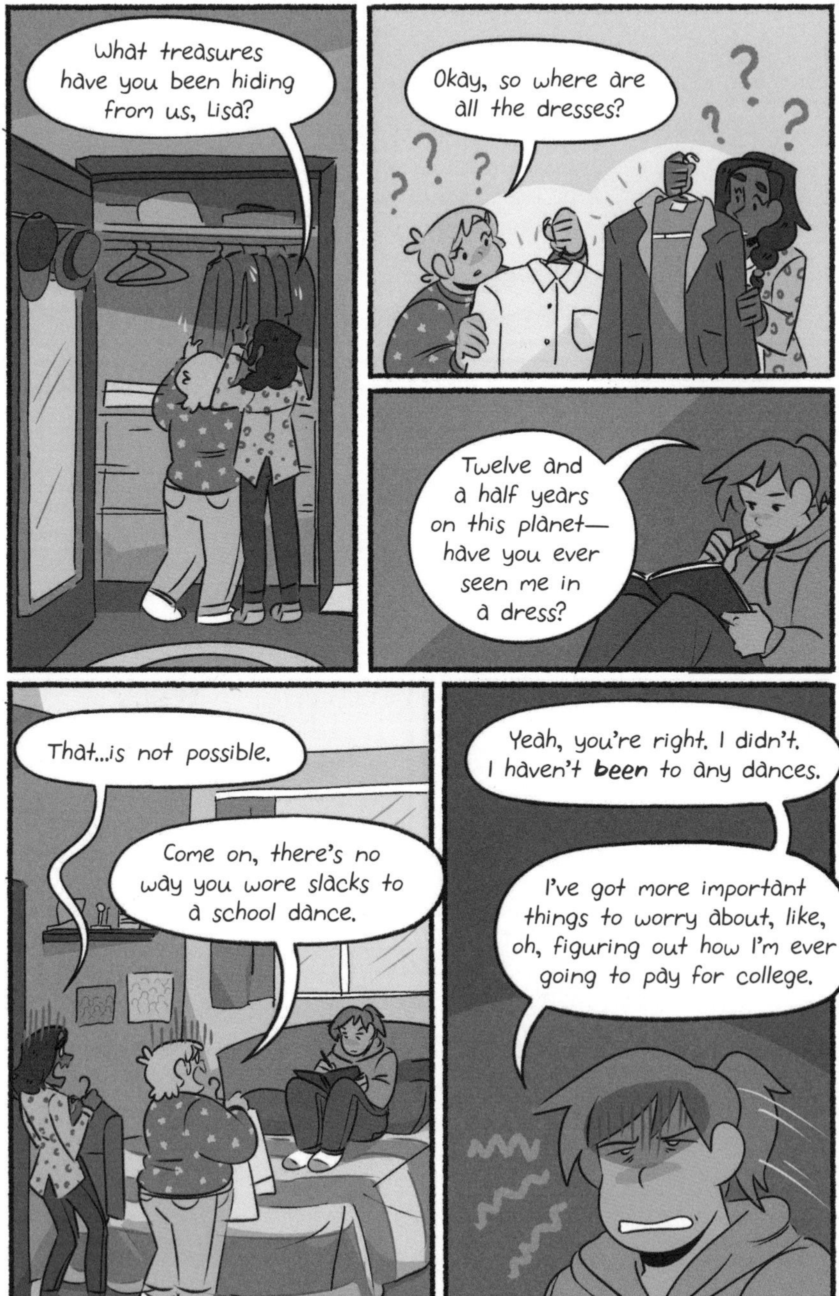
What treasures have you been hiding from us, Lisa?
Okay, so where are all the dresses?
Twelve and a half years on this planet— have you ever seen me in a dress?
That...is not possible.
Come on, there's no way you wore slacks to a school dance.
Yeah, you're right. I didn't. I haven't **been** to any dances.
I've got more important things to worry about, like, oh, figuring out how I'm ever going to pay for college.

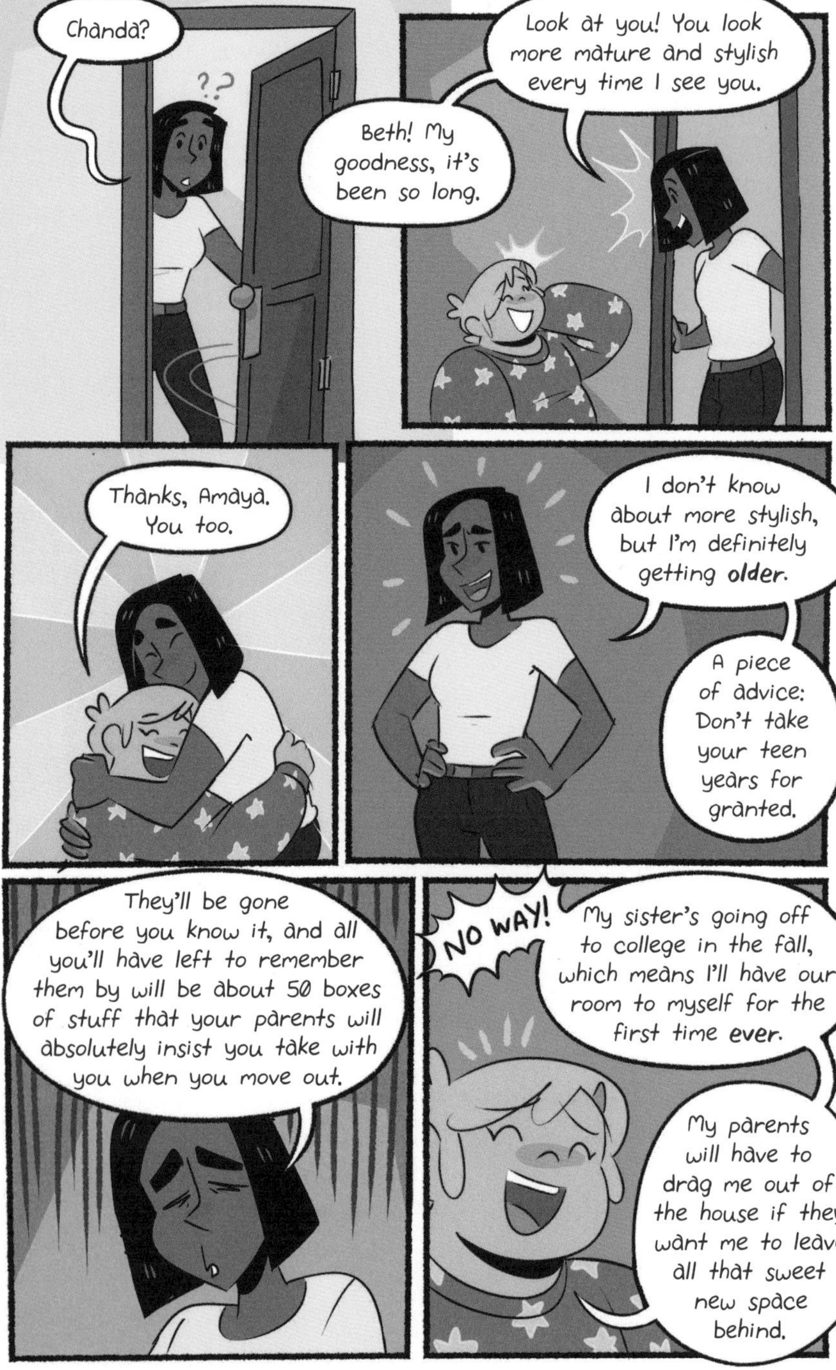
Chanda?
Look at you! You look more mature and stylish every time I see you.
Beth! My goodness, it's been so long.
Thanks, Amaya. You too.
I don't know about more stylish, but I'm definitely getting **older**.
A piece of advice: Don't take your teen years for granted.
They'll be gone before you know it, and all you'll have left to remember them by will be about 50 boxes of stuff that your parents will absolutely insist you take with you when you move out.
NO WAY!
My sister's going off to college in the fall, which means I'll have our room to myself for the first time **ever**.
My parents will have to drag me out of the house if they want me to leave all that sweet new space behind.

22

25

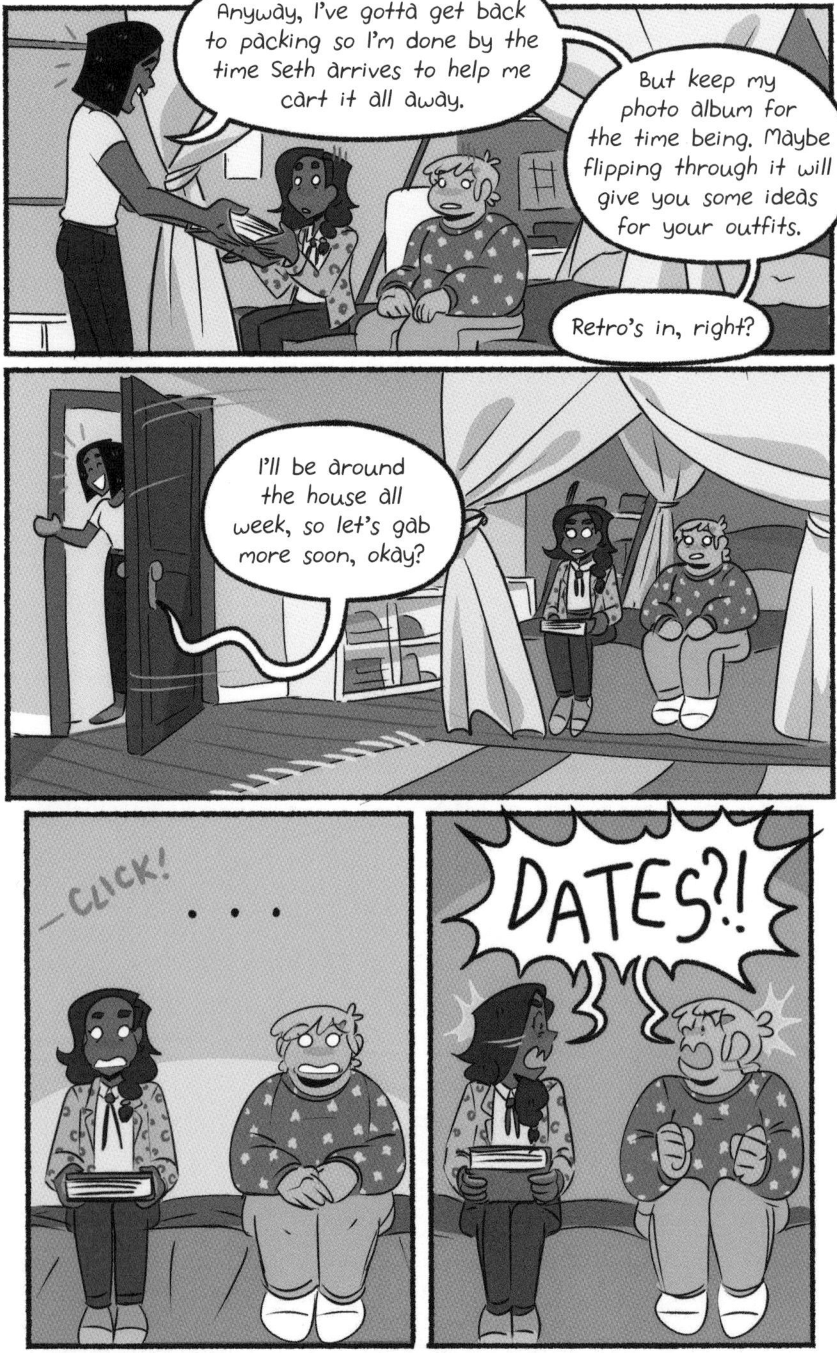
Anyway, I've gotta get back to packing so I'm done by the time Seth arrives to help me cart it all away.
But keep my photo album for the time being. Maybe flipping through it will give you some ideas for your outfits.
Retro's in, right?
I'll be around the house all week, so let's gab more soon, okay?
CLICK!
. . .
DATES?!

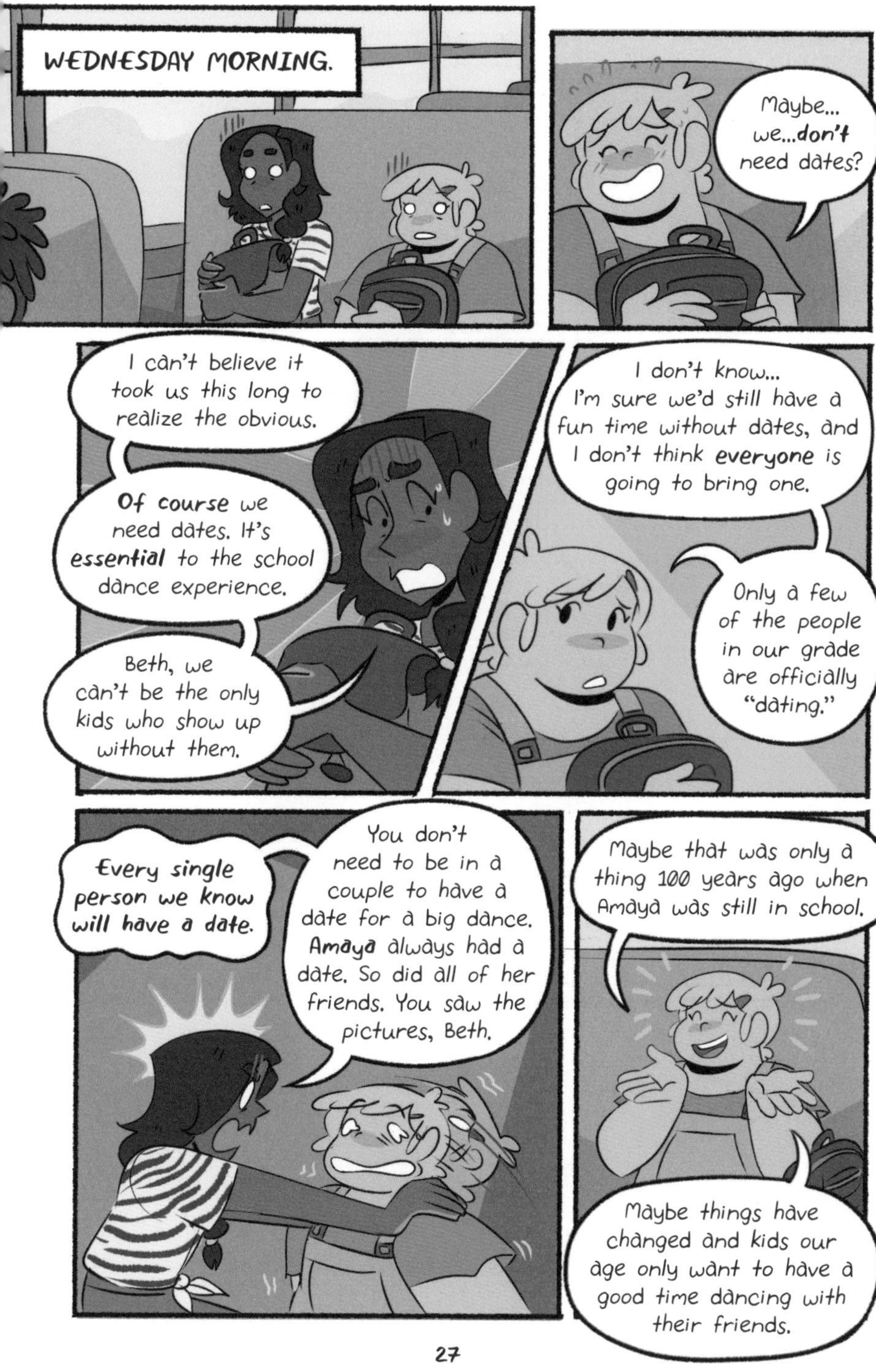
WEDNESDAY MORNING.
Maybe... we...**don't** need dates?
I can't believe it took us this long to realize the obvious.
Of course we need dates. It's **essential** to the school dance experience.
Beth, we can't be the only kids who show up without them.
I don't know... I'm sure we'd still have a fun time without dates, and I don't think **everyone** is going to bring one.
Only a few of the people in our grade are officially "dating."
Every single person we know will have a date.
You don't need to be in a couple to have a date for a big dance. **Amaya** always had a date. So did all of her friends. You saw the pictures, Beth.
Maybe that was only a thing 100 years ago when Amaya was still in school.
Maybe things have changed and kids our age only want to have a good time dancing with their friends.

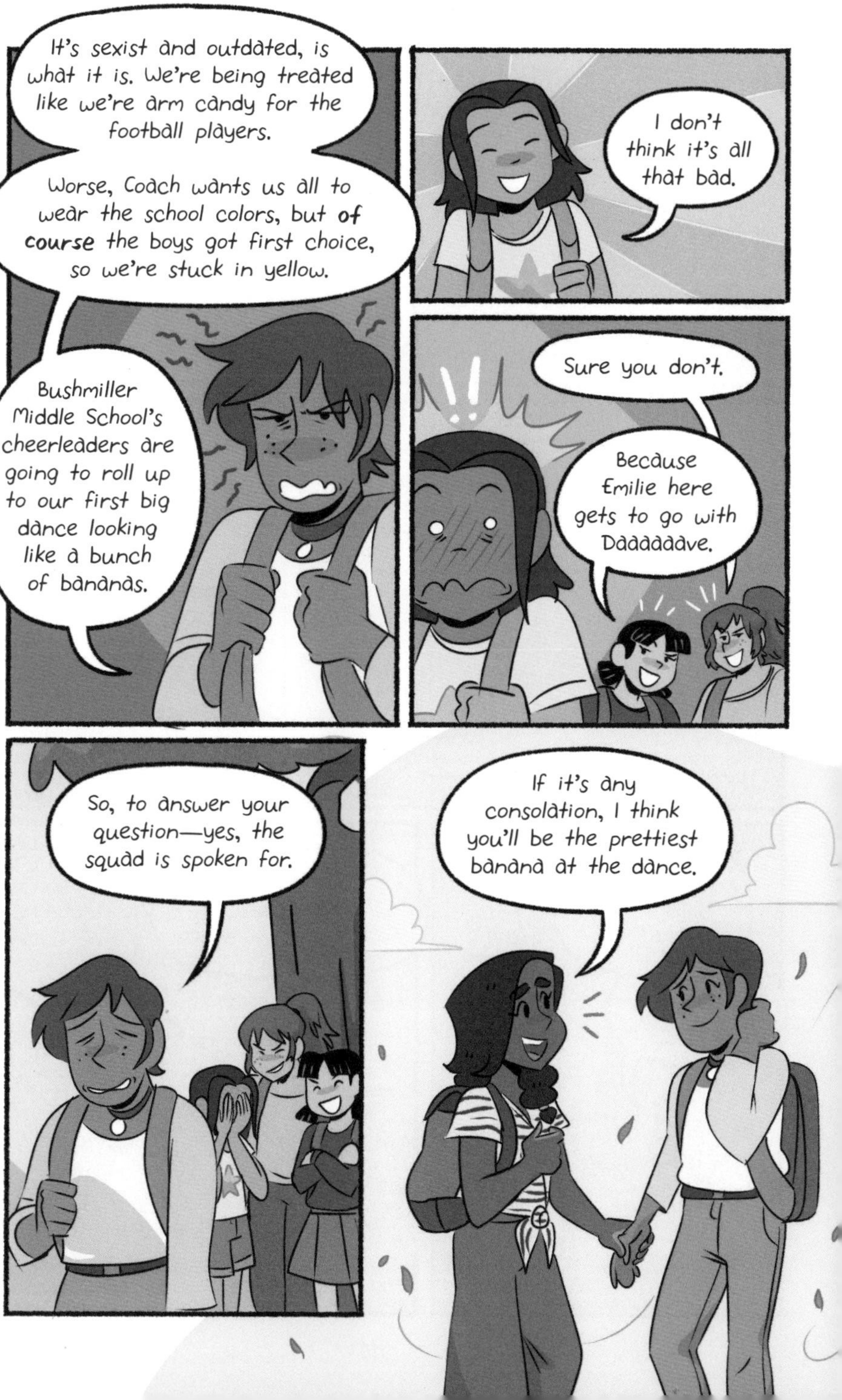
It's sexist and outdated, is what it is. We're being treated like we're arm candy for the football players.
Worse, Coach wants us all to wear the school colors, but **of course** the boys got first choice, so we're stuck in yellow.
Bushmiller Middle School's cheerleaders are going to roll up to our first big dance looking like a bunch of bananas.
I don't think it's all that bad.
Sure you don't.
Because Emilie here gets to go with Daaaaaave.
So, to answer your question—yes, the squad is spoken for.
If it's any consolation, I think you'll be the prettiest banana at the dance.

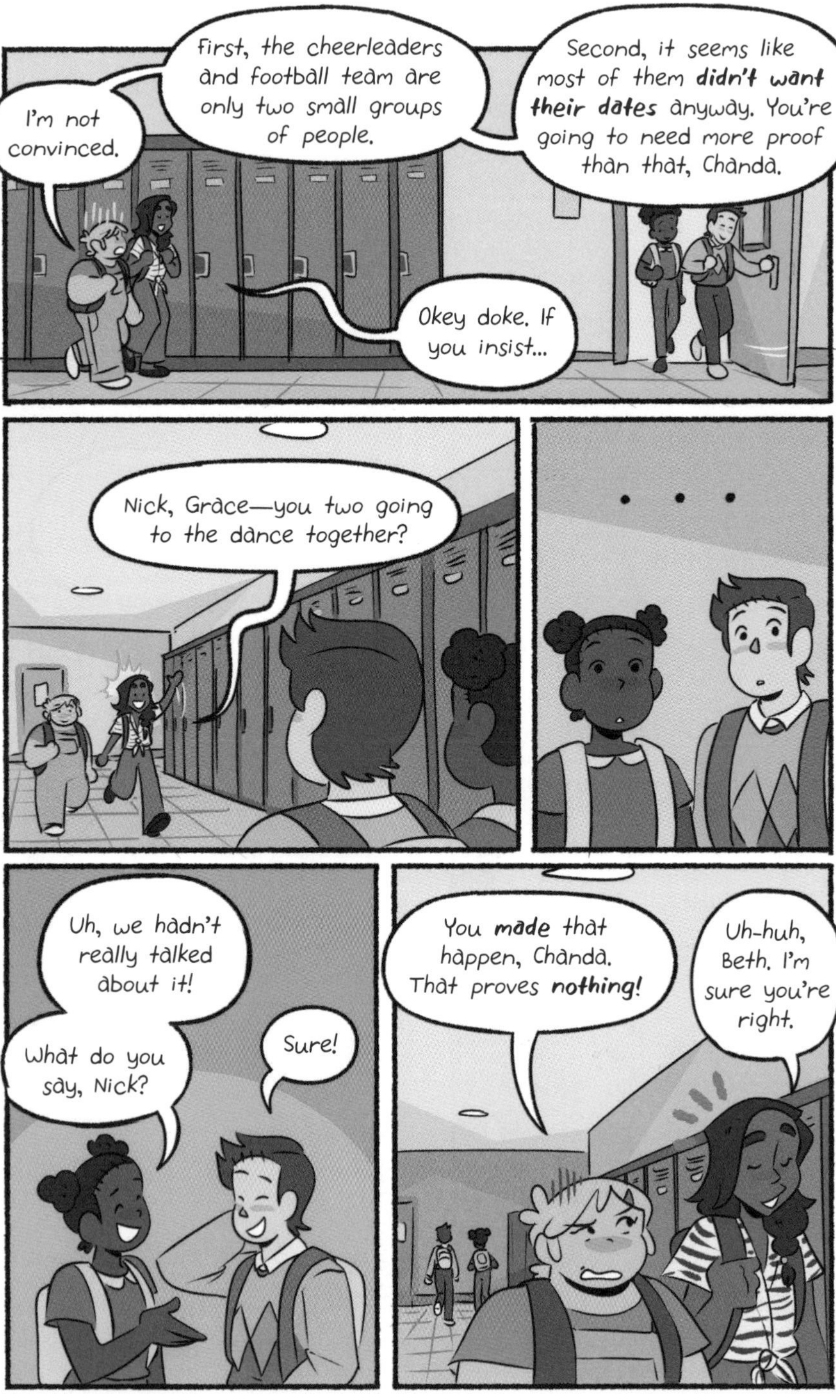
I'm not convinced.
First, the cheerleaders and football team are only two small groups of people.
Second, it seems like most of them **didn't want their dates** anyway. You're going to need more proof than that, Chanda.
Okey doke. If you insist...
Nick, Grace—you two going to the dance together?
• • •
Uh, we hadn't really talked about it!
What do you say, Nick?
Sure!
You **made** that happen, Chanda. That proves **nothing!**
Uh-huh, Beth. I'm sure you're right.

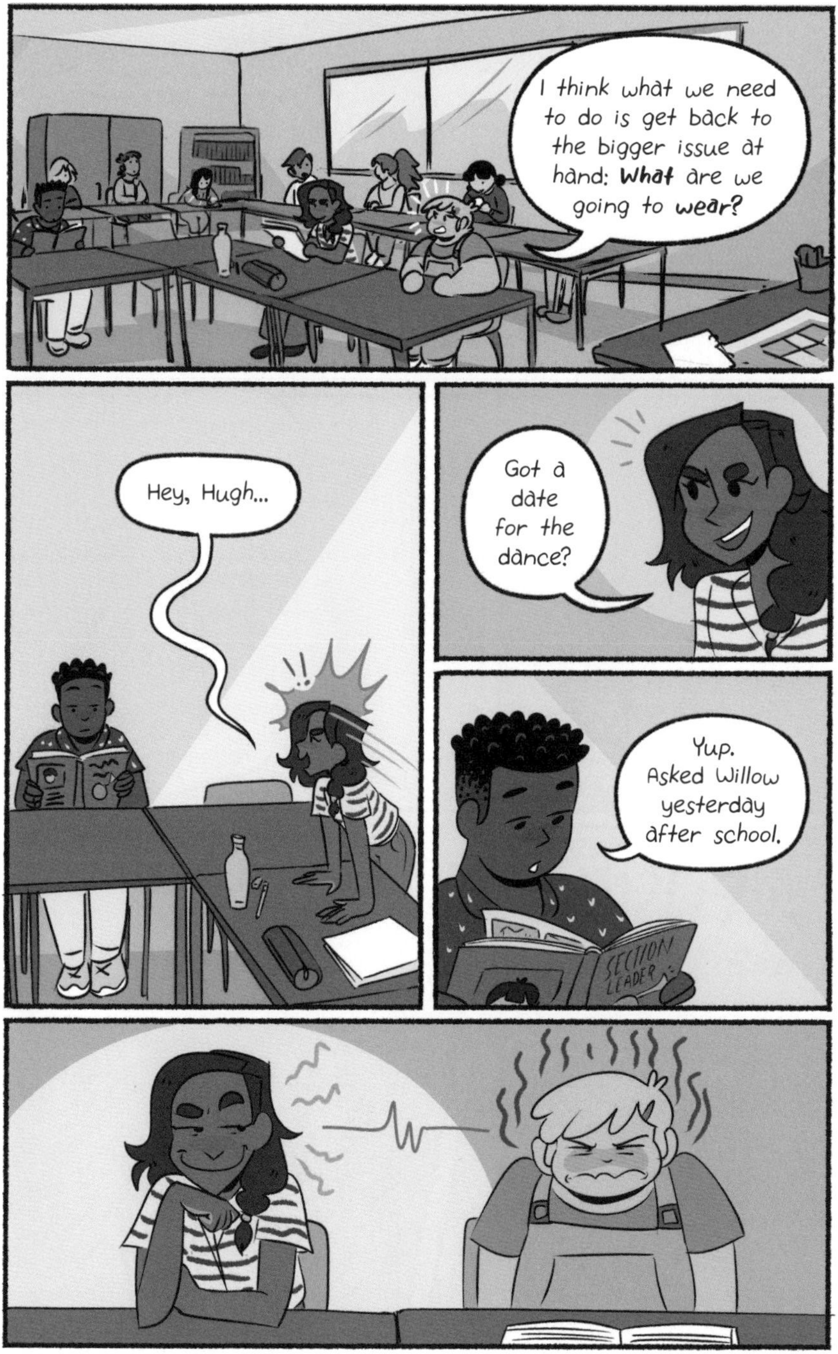
I think what we need to do is get back to the bigger issue at hand: **What** are we going to **wear?**
Hey, Hugh...
Got a date for the dance?
Yup. Asked Willow yesterday after school.
SECTION LEADER

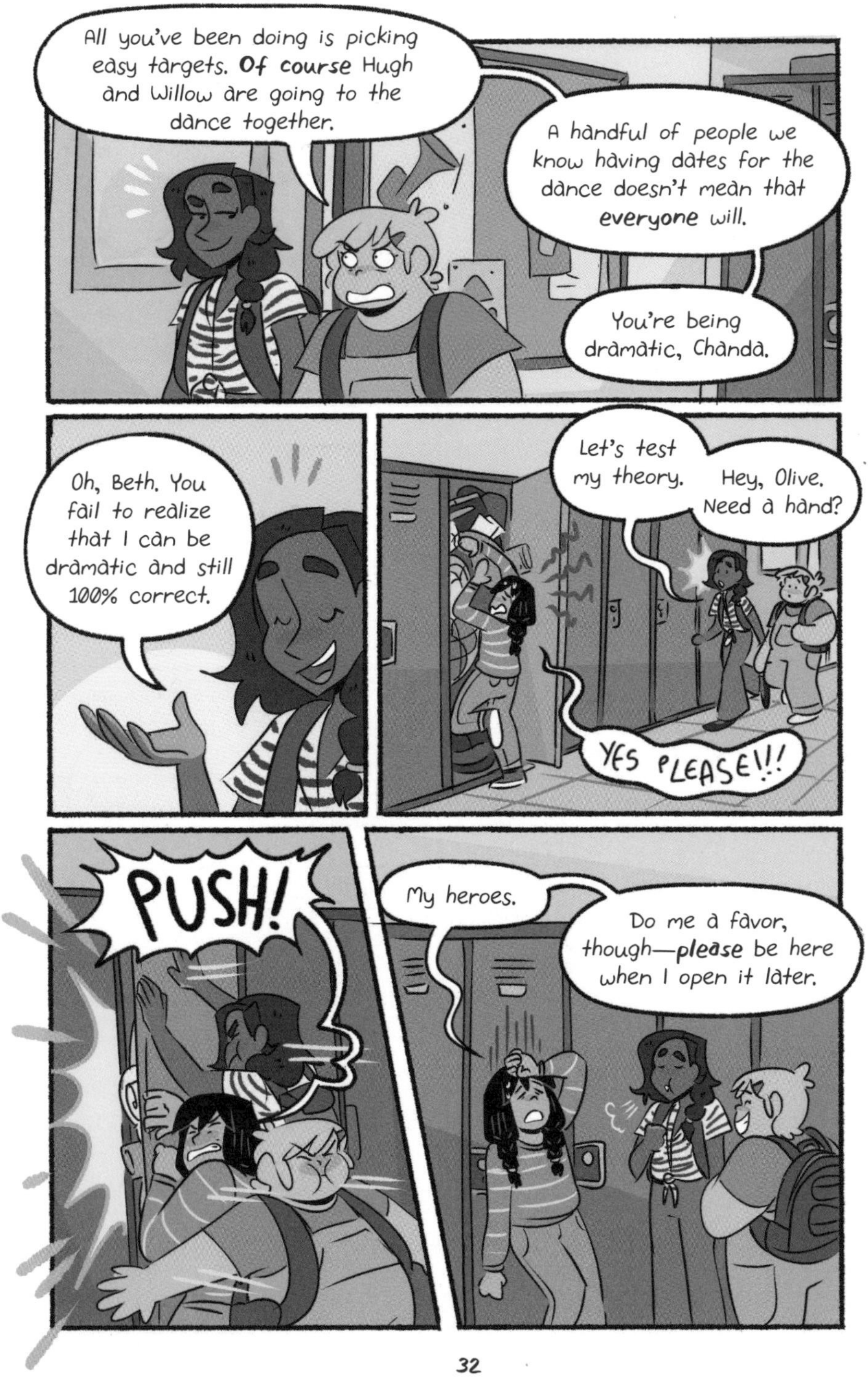
All you've been doing is picking easy targets. **Of course** Hugh and Willow are going to the dance together.
A handful of people we know having dates for the dance doesn't mean that **everyone** will.
You're being dramatic, Chanda.
Oh, Beth. You fail to realize that I can be dramatic and still 100% correct.
Let's test my theory.
Hey, Olive. Need a hand?
YES PLEASE!!!
PUSH!
My heroes.
Do me a favor, though—**please** be here when I open it later.

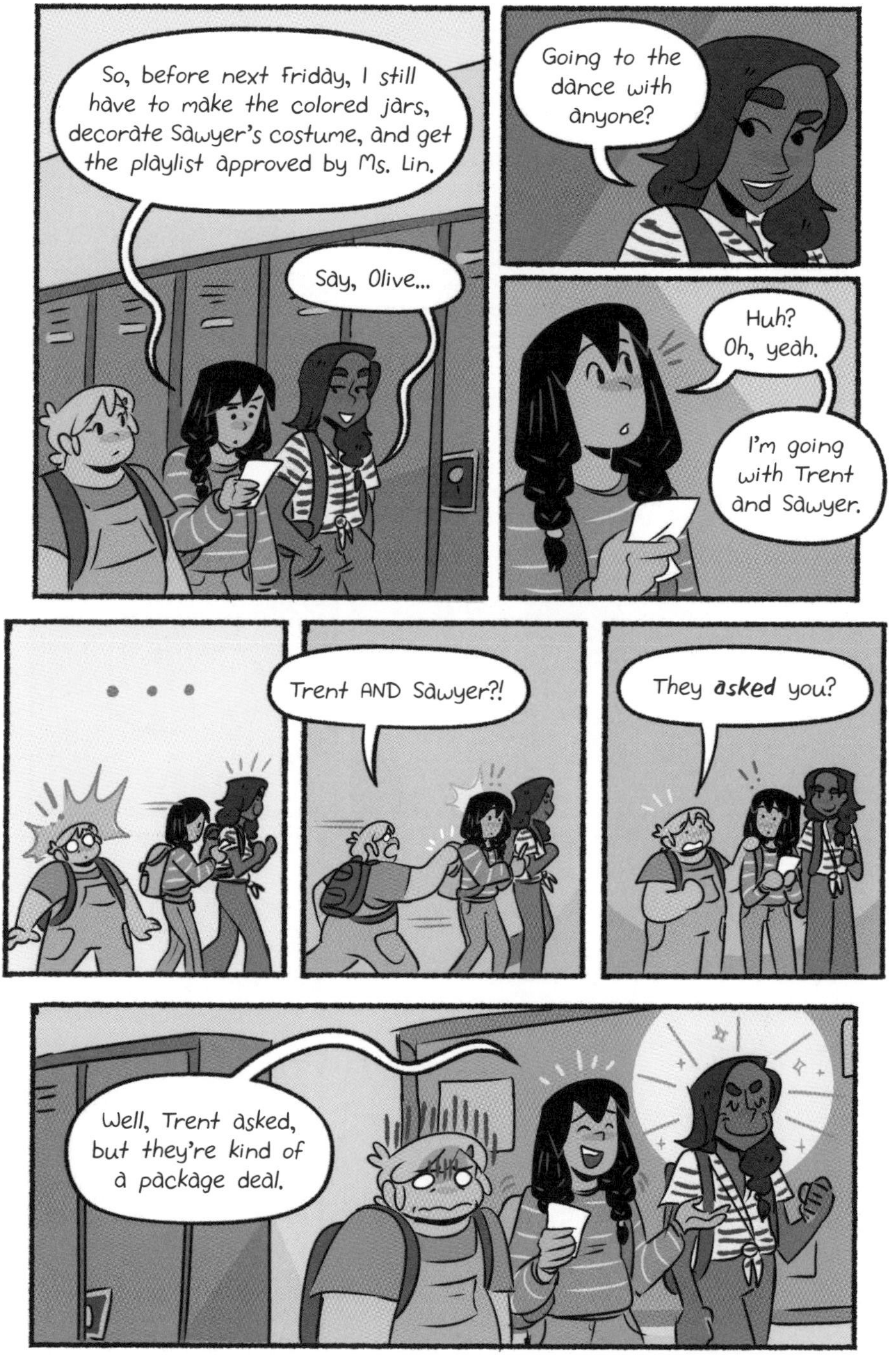
So, before next Friday, I still have to make the colored jars, decorate Sawyer's costume, and get the playlist approved by Ms. Lin.
Say, Olive...
Going to the dance with anyone?
Huh? Oh, yeah.
I'm going with Trent and Sawyer.
Trent AND Sawyer?!
They **asked** you?
Well, Trent asked, but they're kind of a package deal.

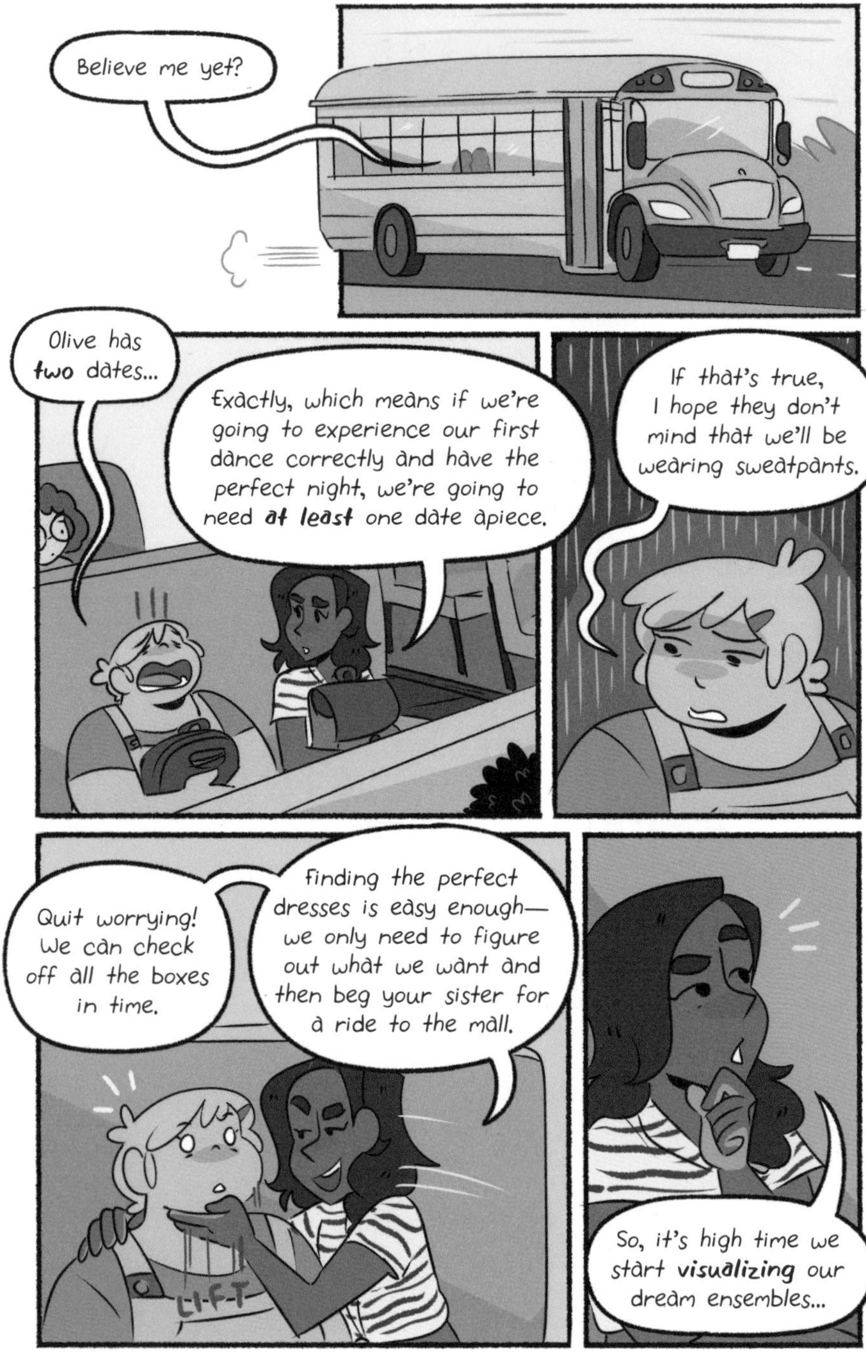

Believe me yet?
Olive has **two** dates...
Exactly, which means if we're going to experience our first dance correctly and have the perfect night, we're going to need **at least** one date apiece.
If that's true, I hope they don't mind that we'll be wearing sweatpants.
Quit worrying! We can check off all the boxes in time.
Finding the perfect dresses is easy enough— we only need to figure out what we want and then beg your sister for a ride to the mall.
L-I-F-T
So, it's high time we start **visualizing** our dream ensembles...

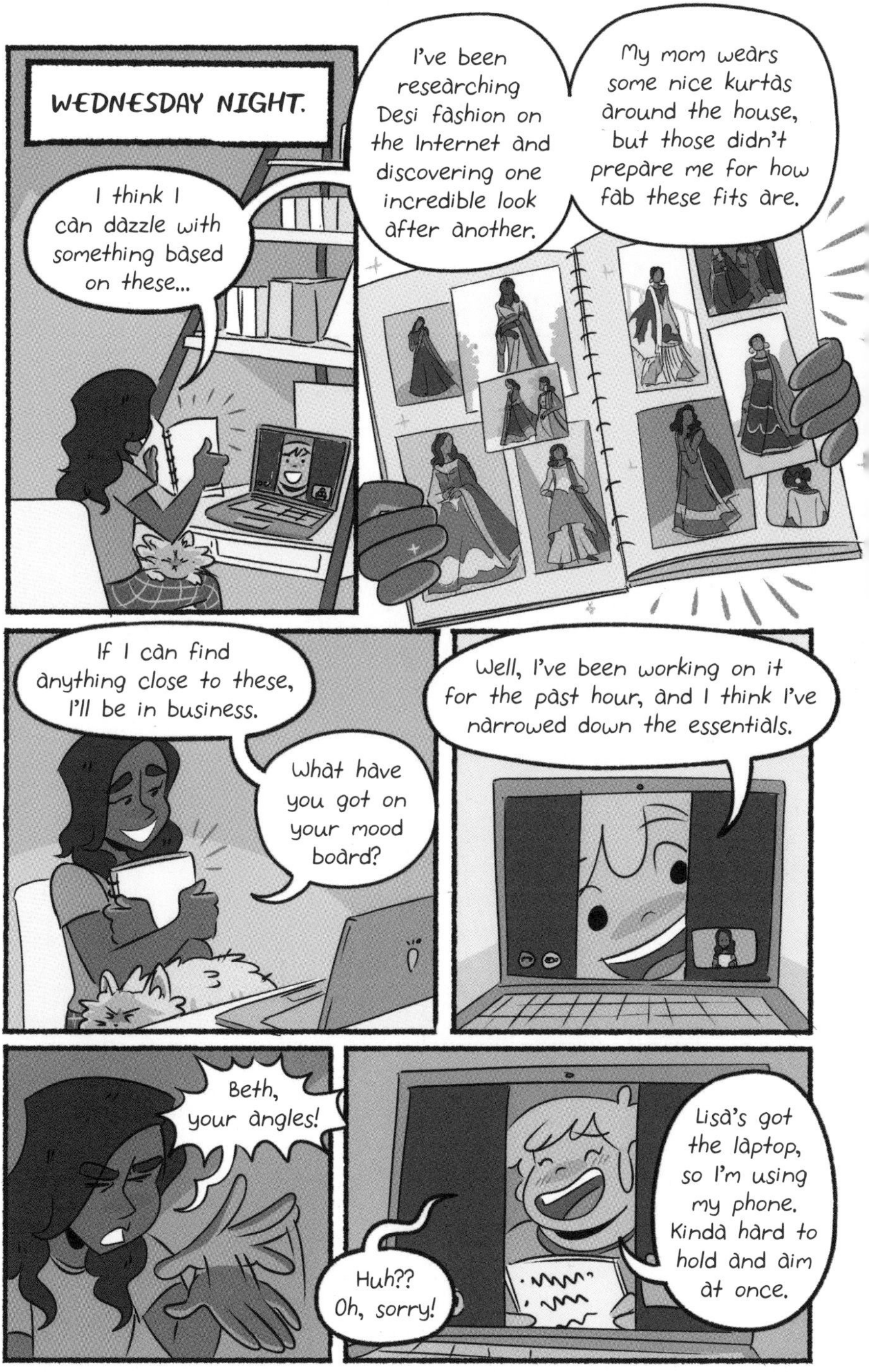
WEDNESDAY NIGHT.
I think I can dazzle with something based on these...
I've been researching Desi fashion on the Internet and discovering one incredible look after another.
My mom wears some nice kurtas around the house, but those didn't prepare me for how fab these fits are.
If I can find anything close to these, I'll be in business.
What have you got on your mood board?
Well, I've been working on it for the past hour, and I think I've narrowed down the essentials.
Beth, your angles!
Huh?? Oh, sorry!
Lisa's got the laptop, so I'm using my phone. Kinda hard to hold and aim at once.

How's this?

- SPARKLES?
- RETRO??
- FITS!
COMFORTABLY!

Well, uh, it's a place to start.

I know it's not much.

I guess I don't want to get any ideas that are too specific.

I can still remember the last time I went dress shopping...

It's okay. I'm sure something will jump out at you when we tear through the mall.

And with the money saved up from all the pet care we've been doing, we can shop the **front racks** at Eleganzà for once. Bless those puppies and kitties.

Yeah, I'm sure you're right...

Okay, that's settled.

Onto securing our lucky suitors...

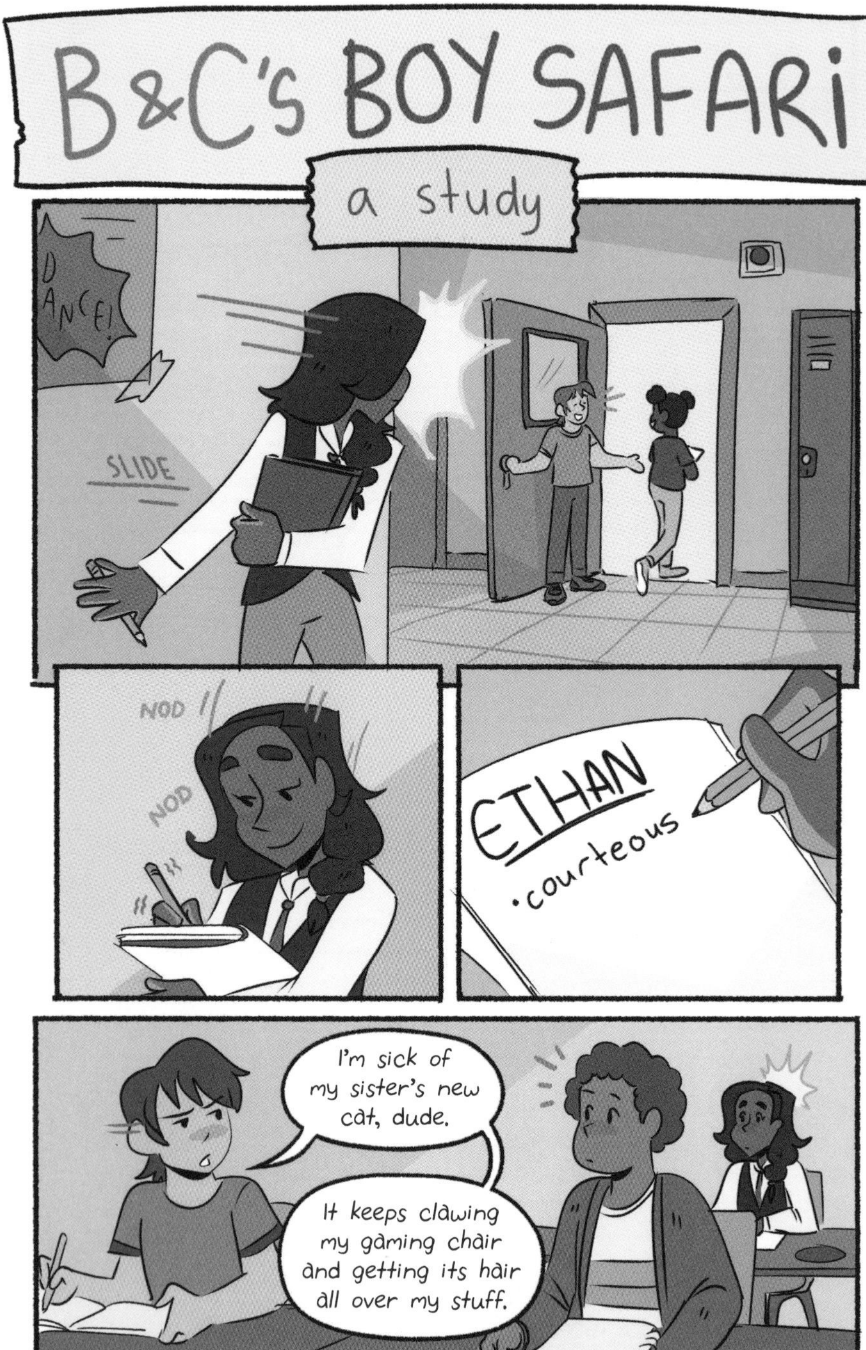
B&C's BOY SAFARI
a study
DANCE!
SLIDE
NOD
NOD
ETHAN
·courteous
I'm sick of my sister's new cat, dude.
It keeps clawing my gaming chair and getting its hair all over my stuff.

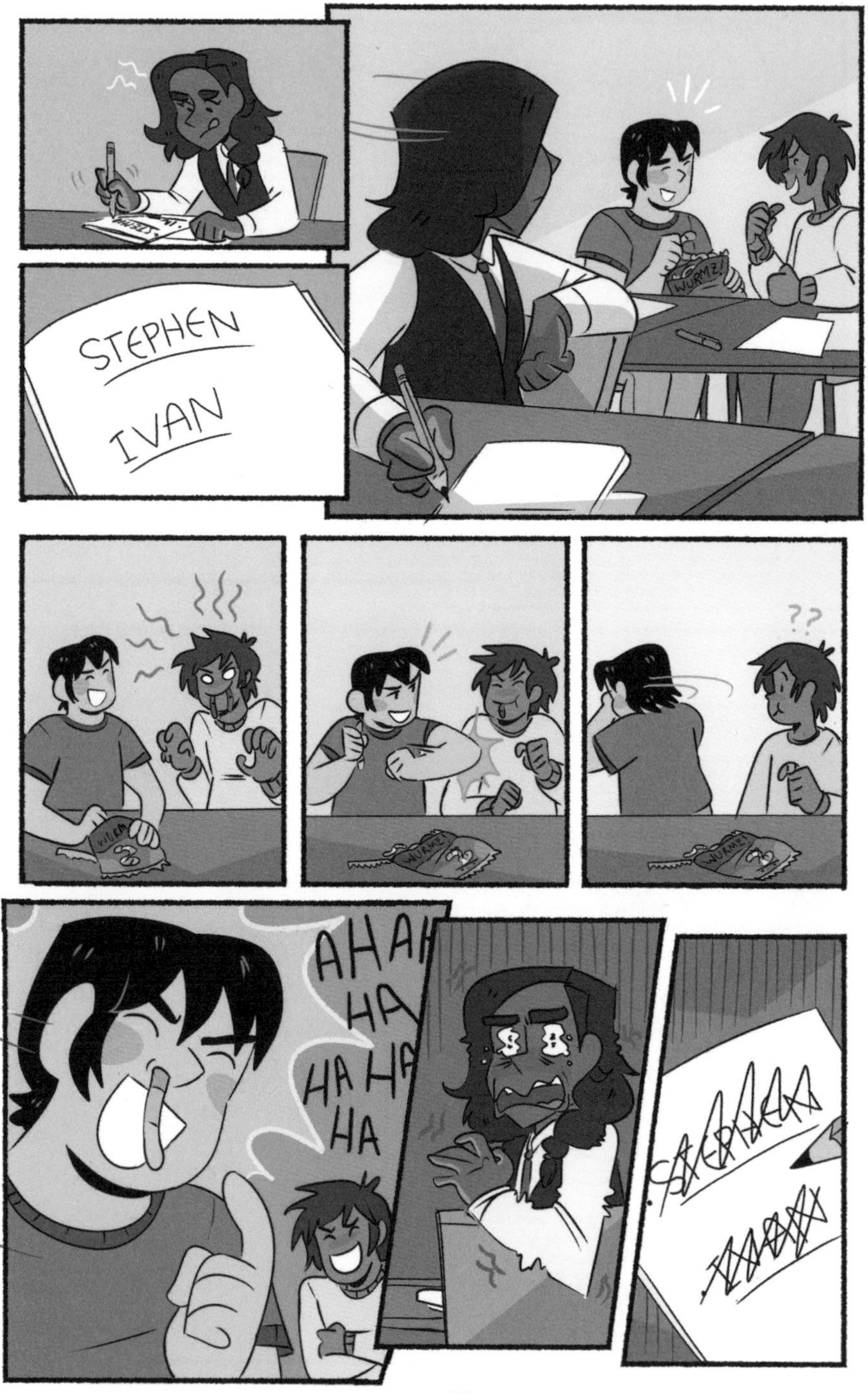
STEPHEN
IVAN
WURMZ!
??
AHAH
HA
HA HA
HA

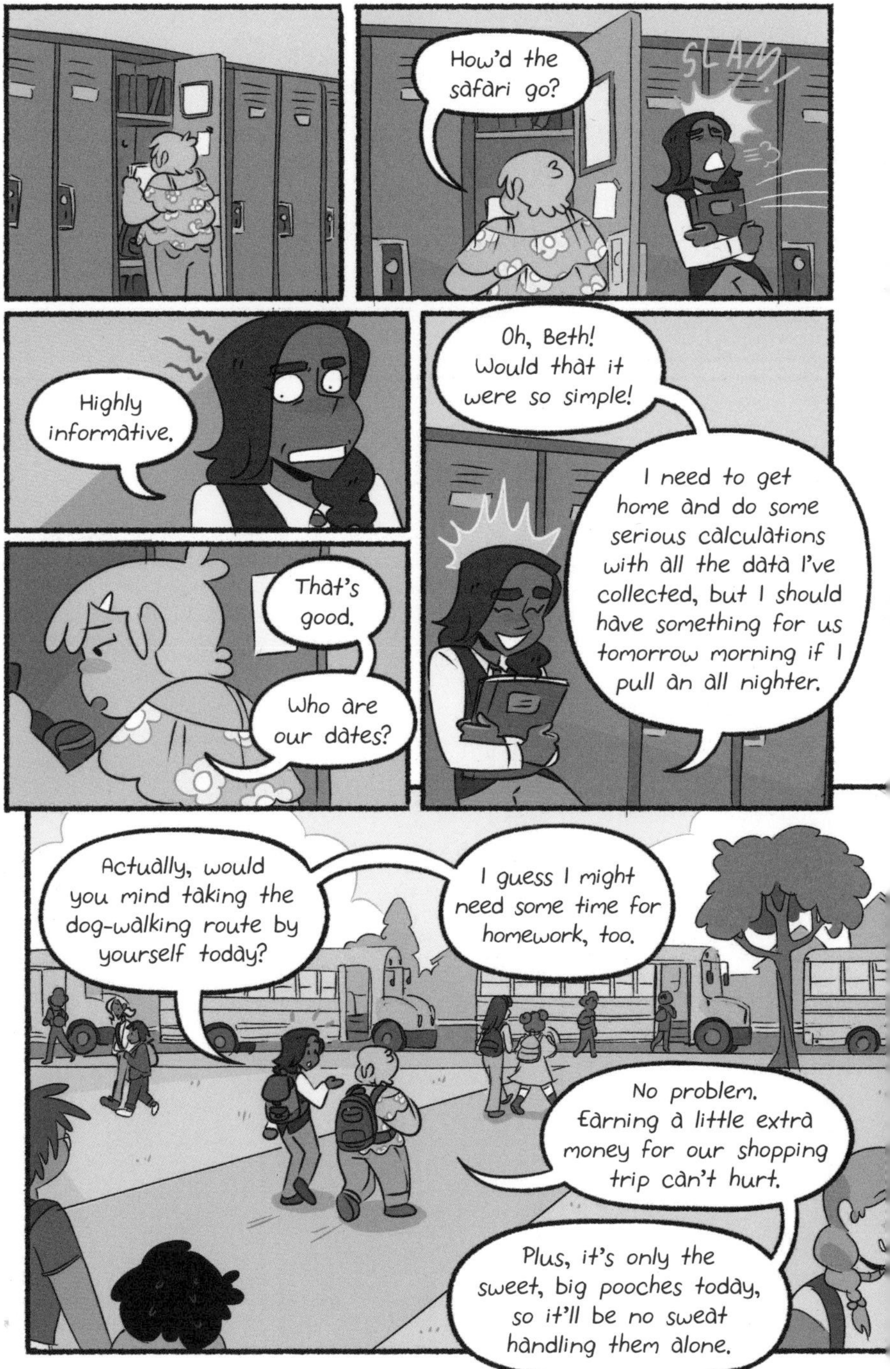
How'd the safari go?
SLAM!
Highly informative.
Oh, Beth! Would that it were so simple!
I need to get home and do some serious calculations with all the data I've collected, but I should have something for us tomorrow morning if I pull an all nighter.
That's good.
Who are our dates?
Actually, would you mind taking the dog-walking route by yourself today?
I guess I might need some time for homework, too.
No problem. Earning a little extra money for our shopping trip can't hurt.
Plus, it's only the sweet, big pooches today, so it'll be no sweat handling them alone.

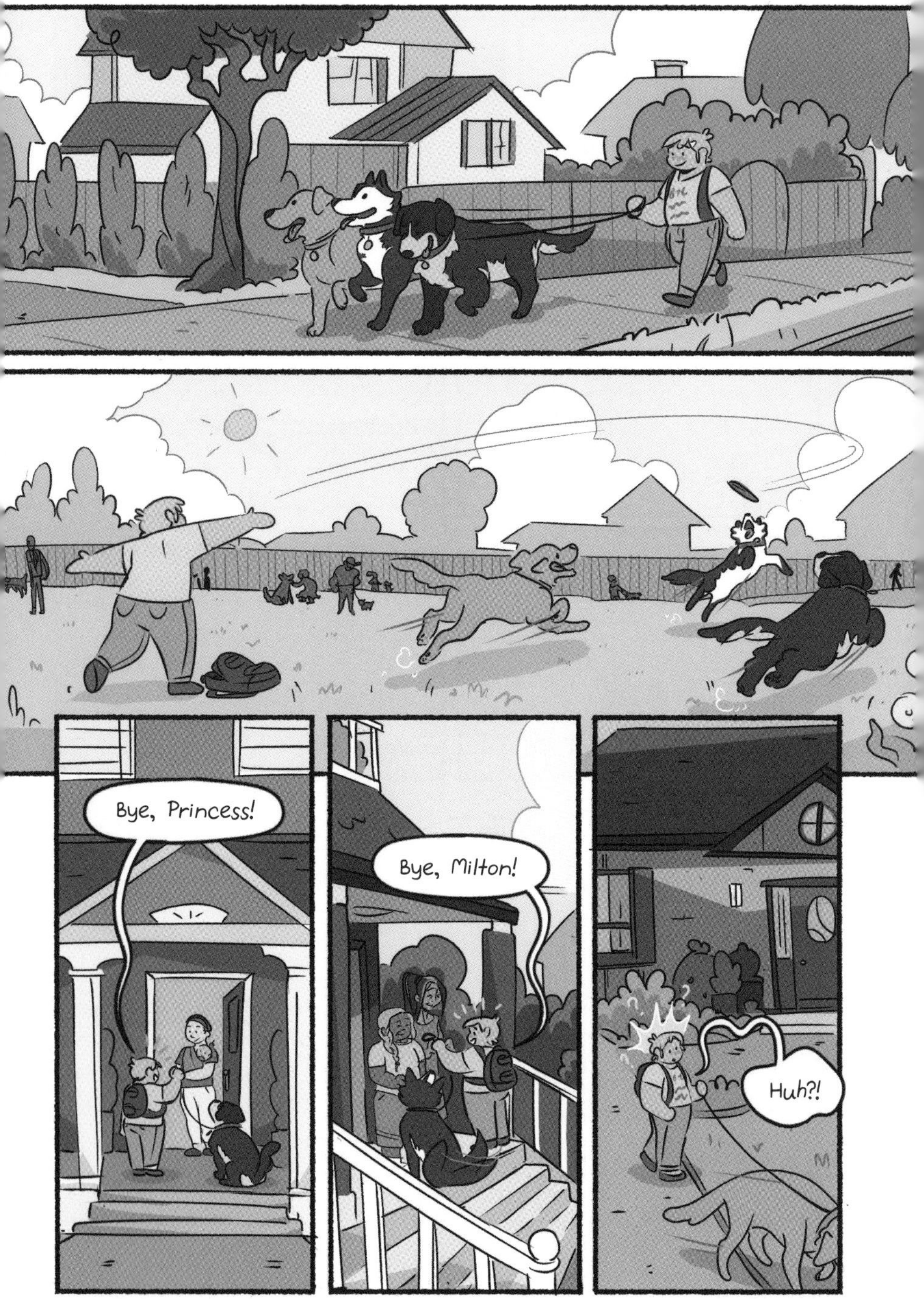
Bye, Princess!
Bye, Milton!
Huh?!

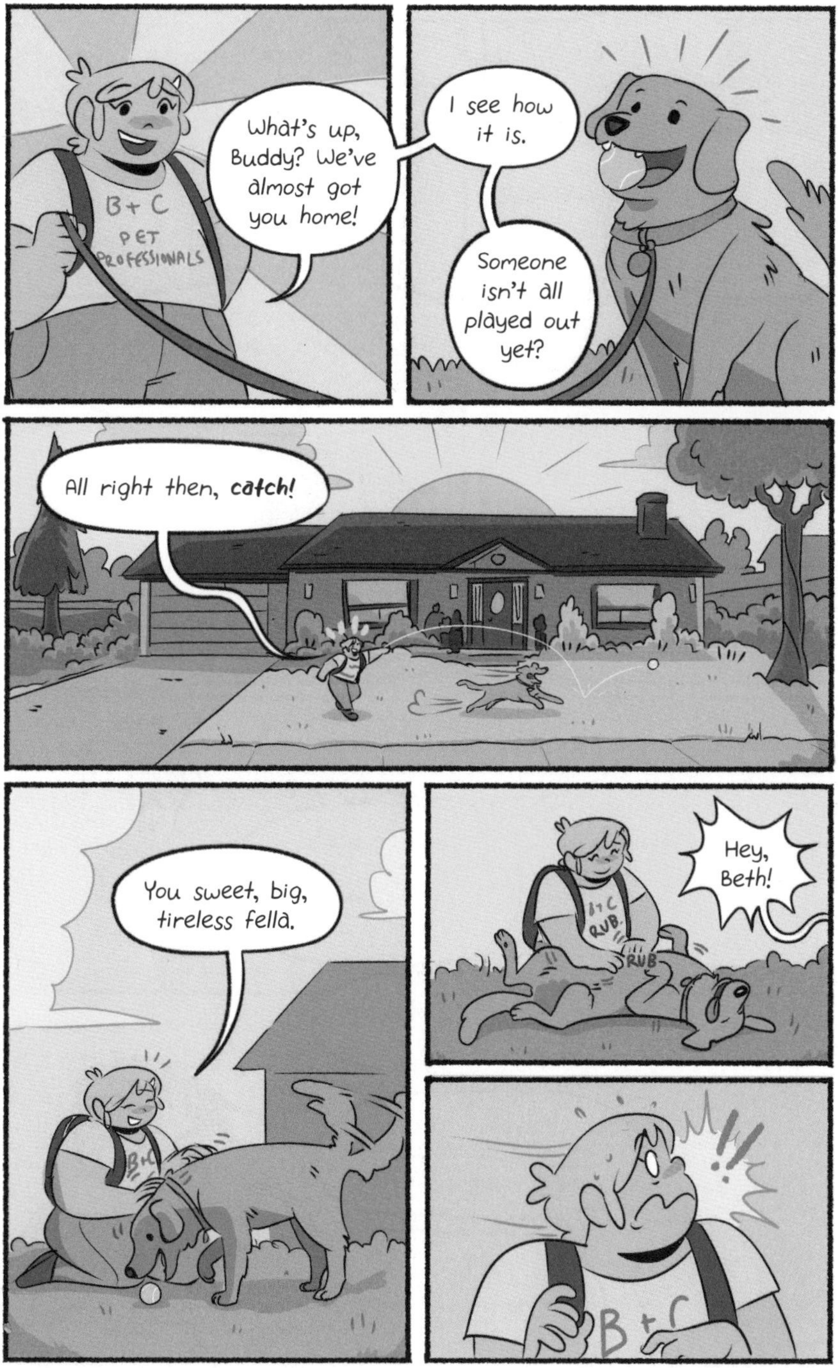
B + C PET PROFESSIONALS
What's up, Buddy? We've almost got you home!
I see how it is.
Someone isn't all played out yet?
All right then, **catch!**
You sweet, big, tireless fella.
B+C
Hey, Beth!
B+C
RUB
RUB
!!
B + C

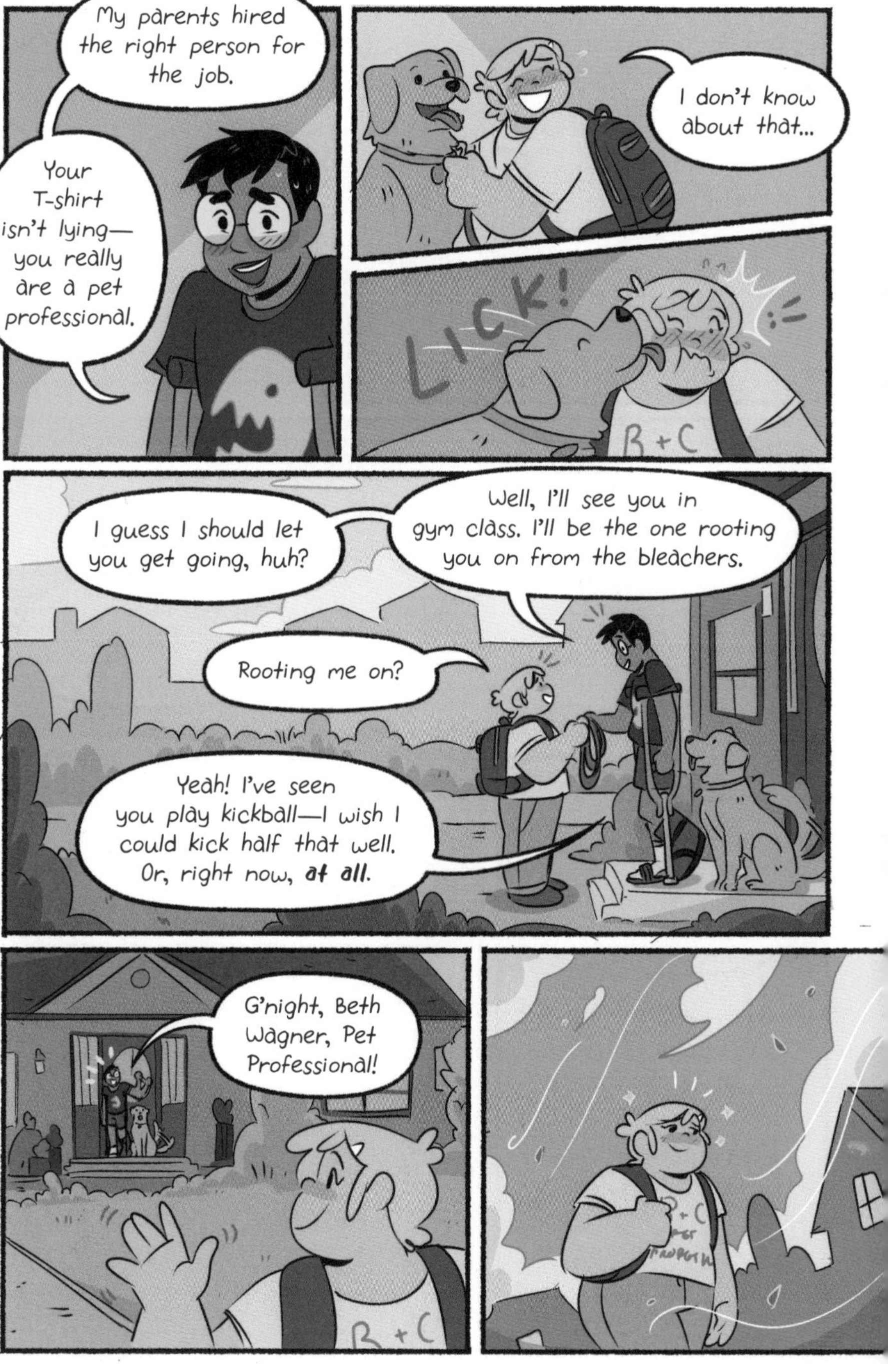
My parents hired the right person for the job.
Your T-shirt isn't lying—you really are a pet professional.
I don't know about that...
LICK!
B + C
I guess I should let you get going, huh?
Well, I'll see you in gym class. I'll be the one rooting you on from the bleachers.
Rooting me on?
Yeah! I've seen you play kickball—I wish I could kick half that well. Or, right now, **at all**.
G'night, Beth Wagner, Pet Professional!
B + C

46

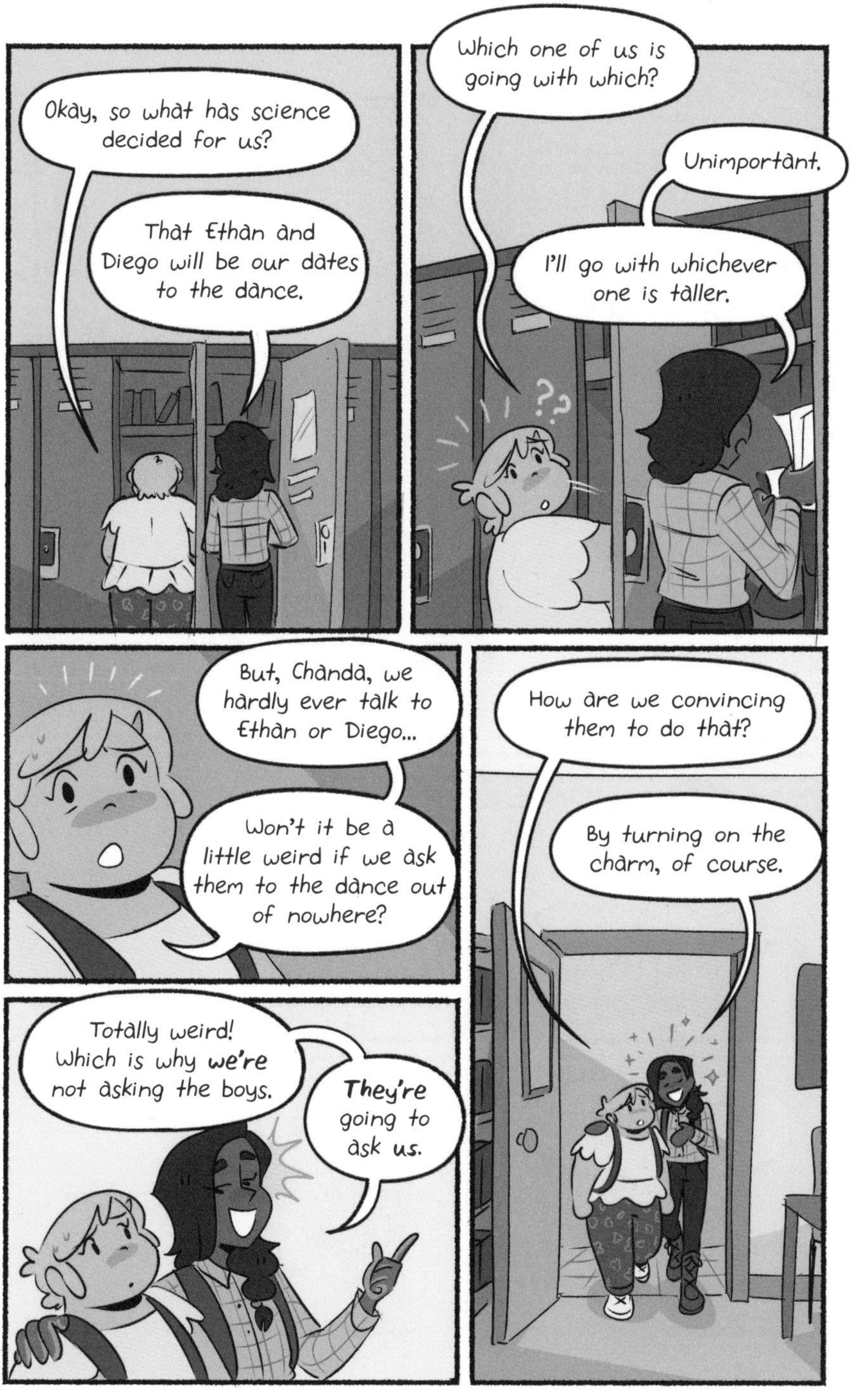
Okay, so what has science decided for us?
That Ethan and Diego will be our dates to the dance.
Which one of us is going with which?
??
Unimportant.
I'll go with whichever one is taller.
But, Chanda, we hardly ever talk to Ethan or Diego...
Won't it be a little weird if we ask them to the dance out of nowhere?
How are we convincing them to do that?
By turning on the charm, of course.
Totally weird! Which is why **we're** not asking the boys.
They're going to ask **us**.

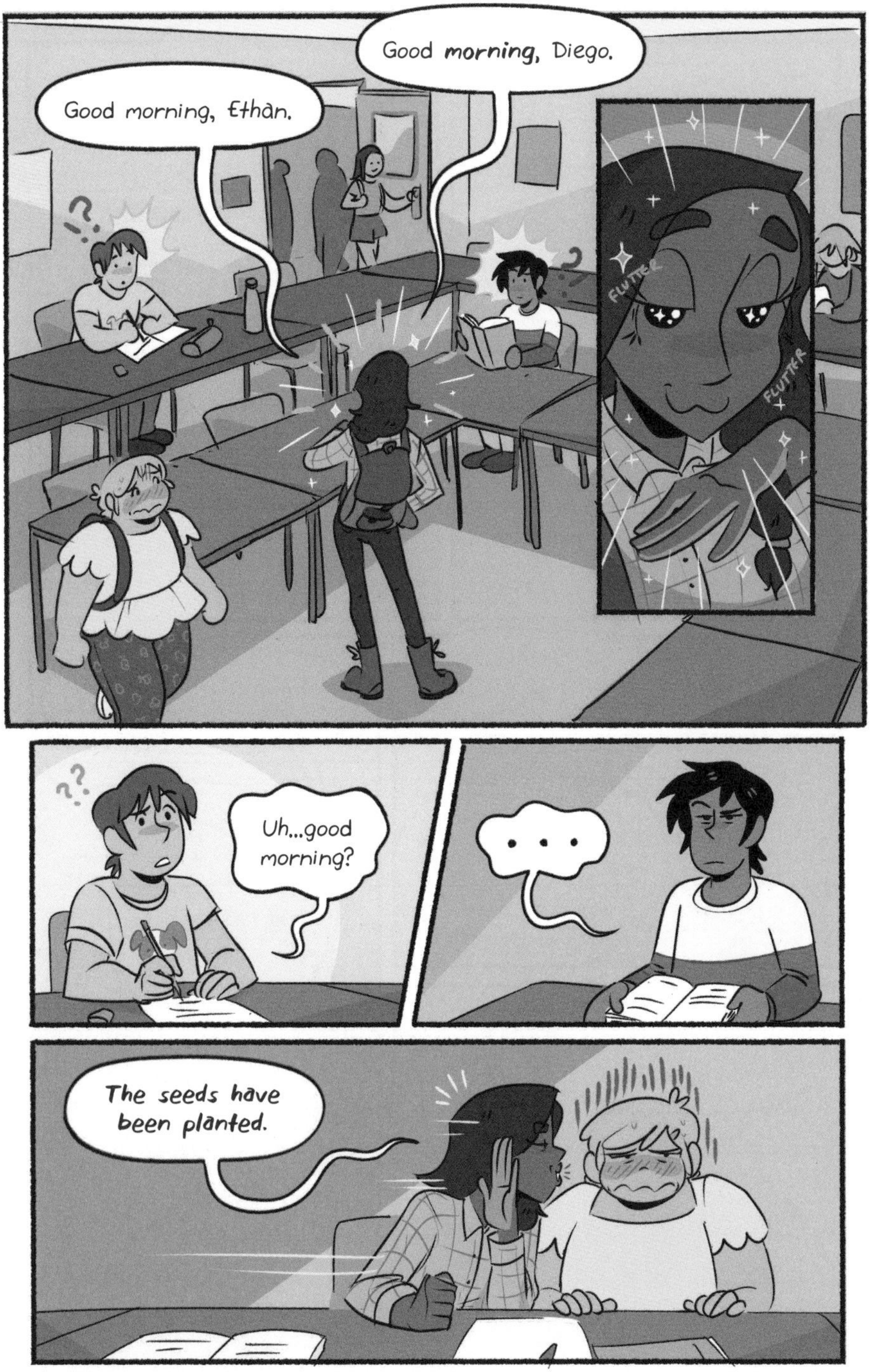
Good morning, Ethan.
Good morning, Diego.
FLUTTER
FLUTTER
Uh...good morning?
. . .
The seeds have been planted.

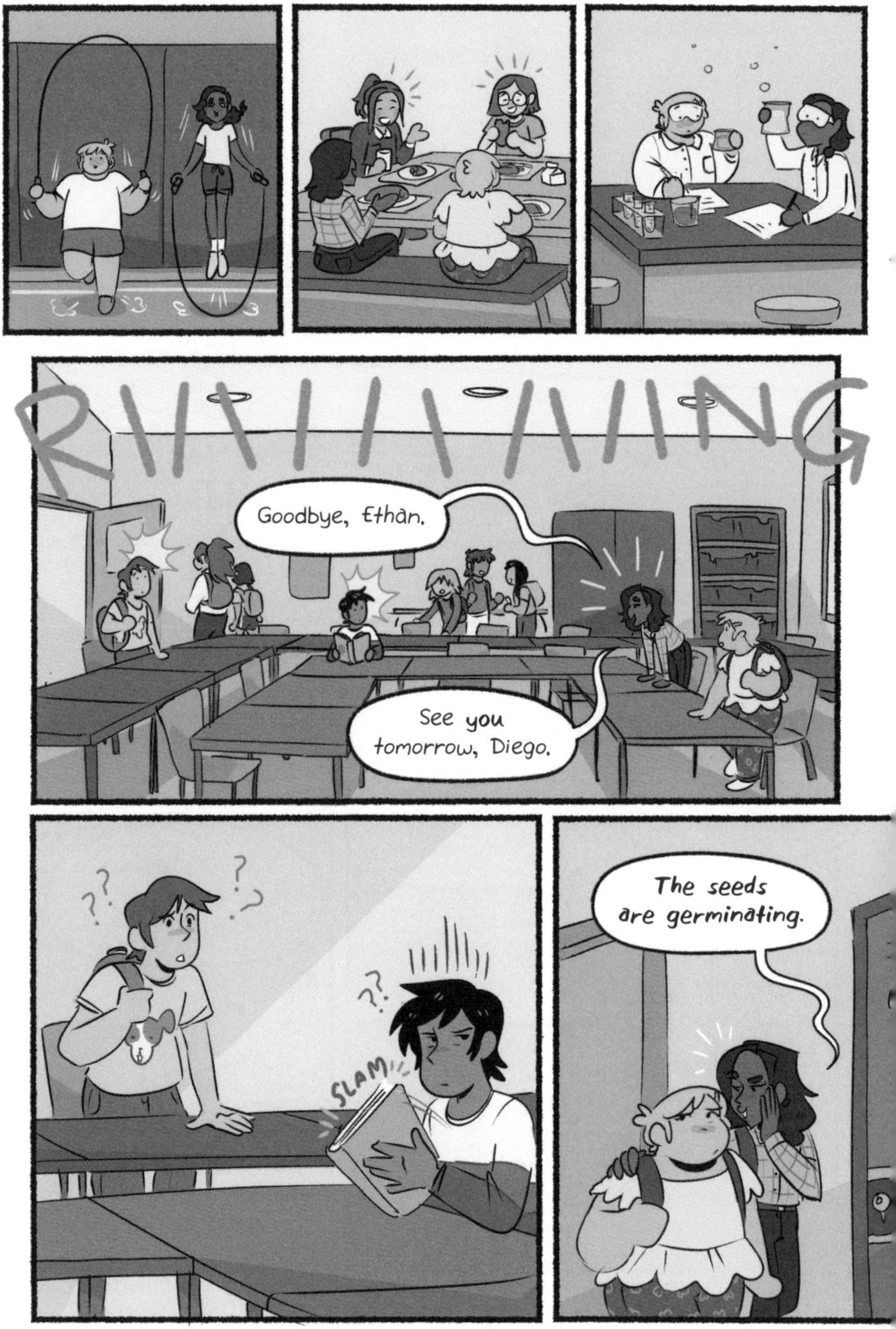
RIIIIIIIIING
Goodbye, Ethan.
See you tomorrow, Diego.
SLAM
The seeds are germinating.

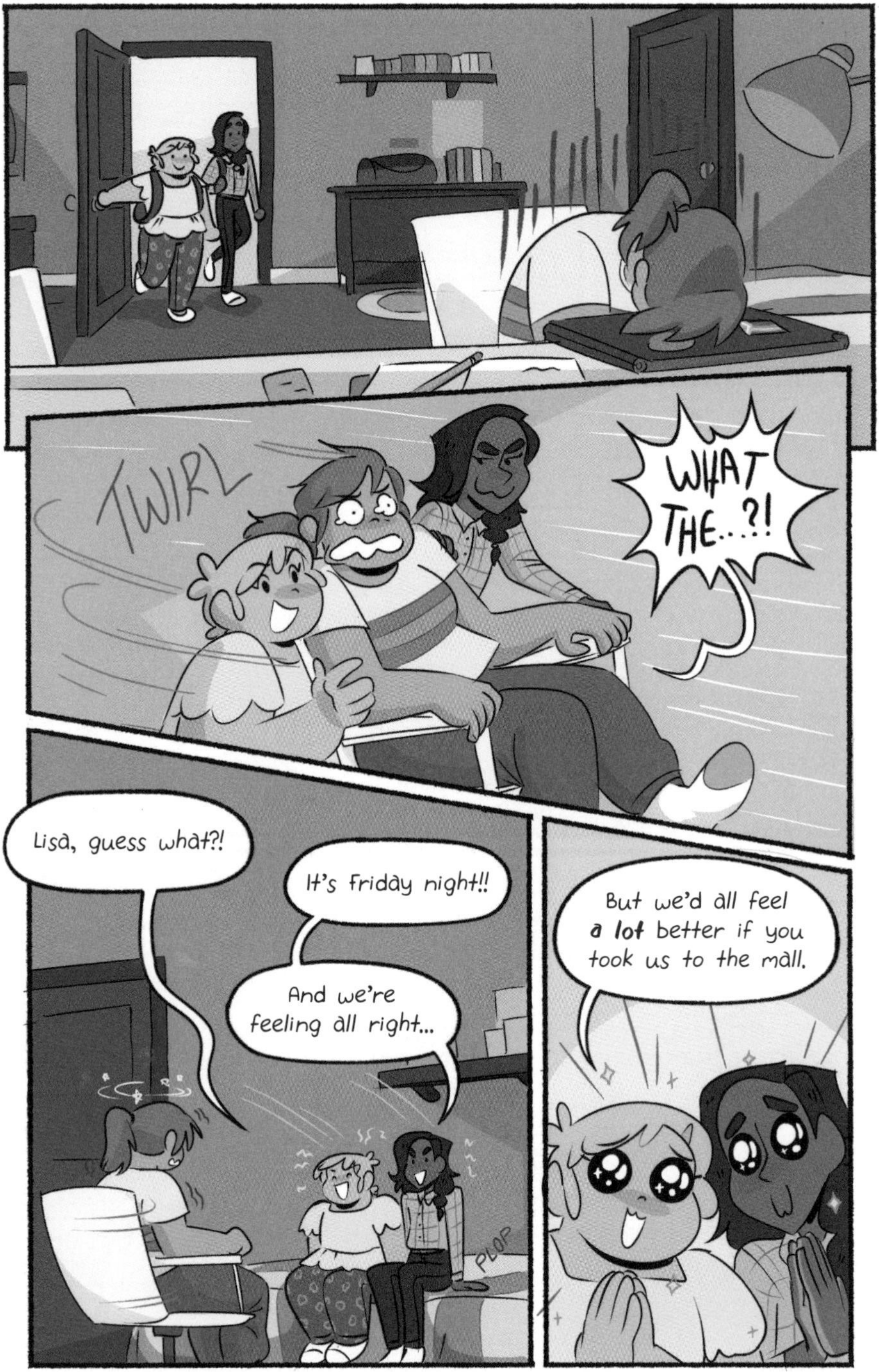
TWIRL
WHAT THE...?!
Lisa, guess what?!
It's friday night!!
And we're feeling all right...
PLOP
But we'd all feel **a lot** better if you took us to the mall.

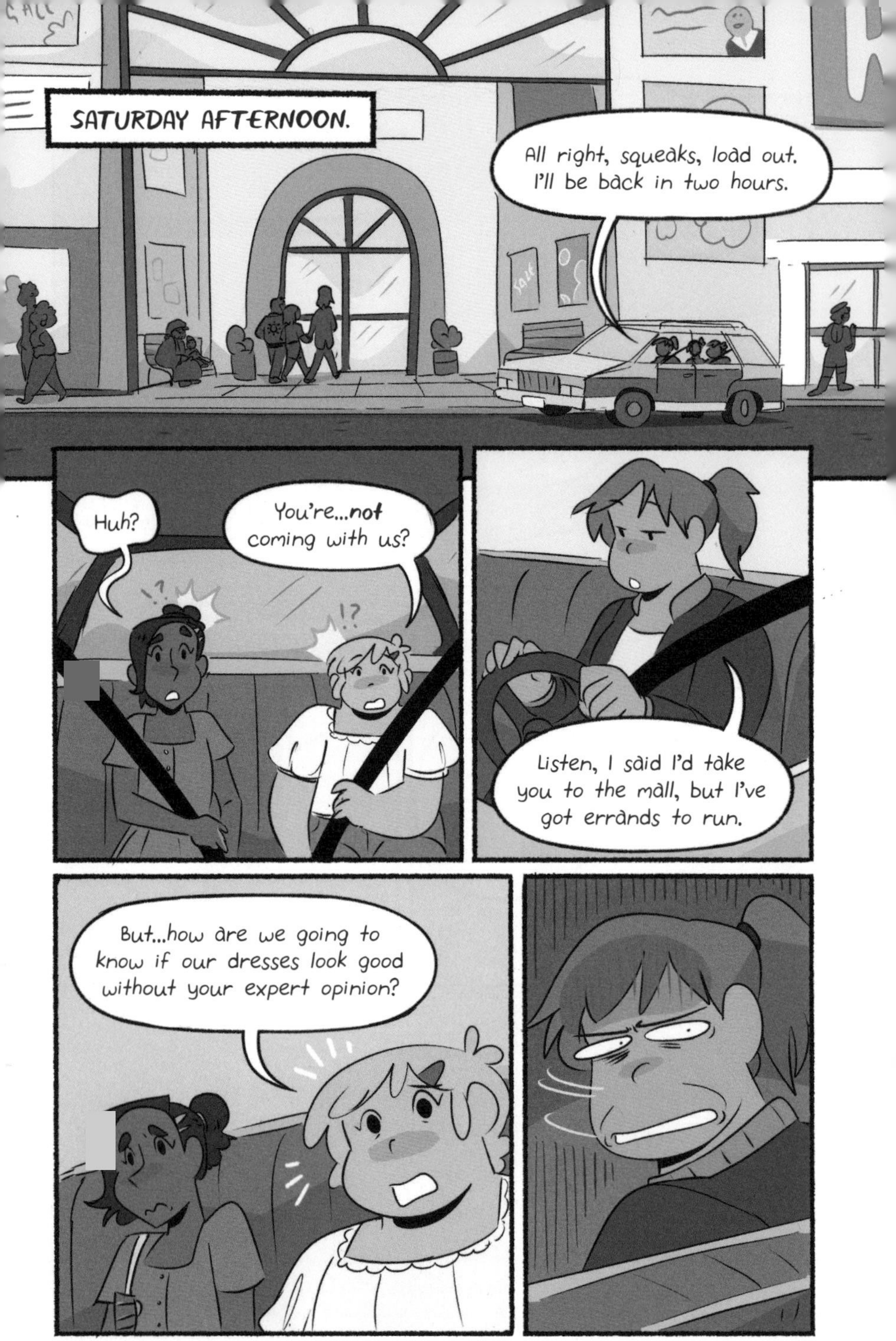
SATURDAY AFTERNOON.
All right, squeaks, load out. I'll be back in two hours.
Huh?
You're...**not** coming with us?
!?
!?
Listen, I said I'd take you to the mall, but I've got errands to run.
But...how are we going to know if our dresses look good without your expert opinion?

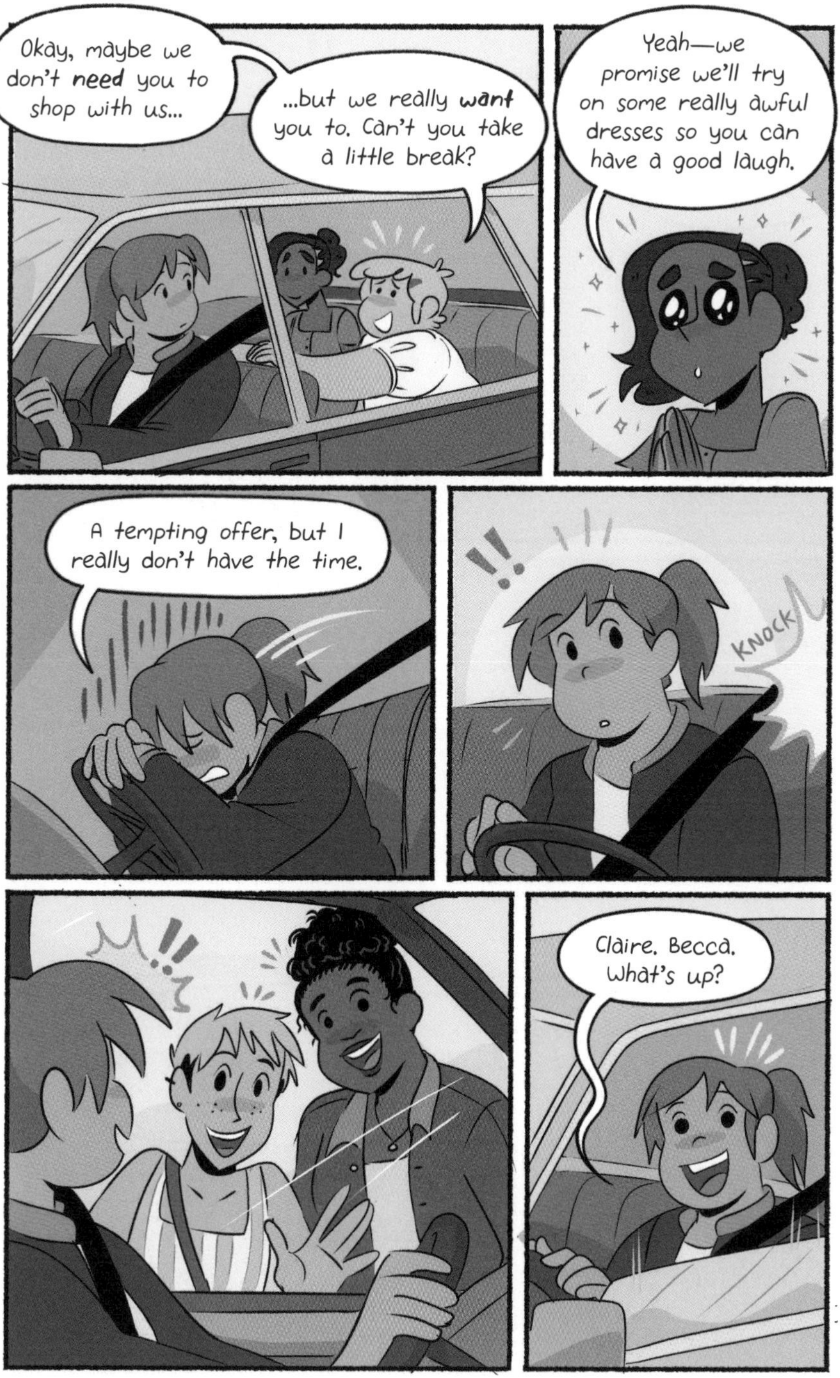

Okay, maybe we don't **need** you to shop with us...
...but we really **want** you to. Can't you take a little break?
Yeah—we promise we'll try on some really awful dresses so you can have a good laugh.
A tempting offer, but I really don't have the time.
!!
KNOCK
!!
Claire. Becca. What's up?

55

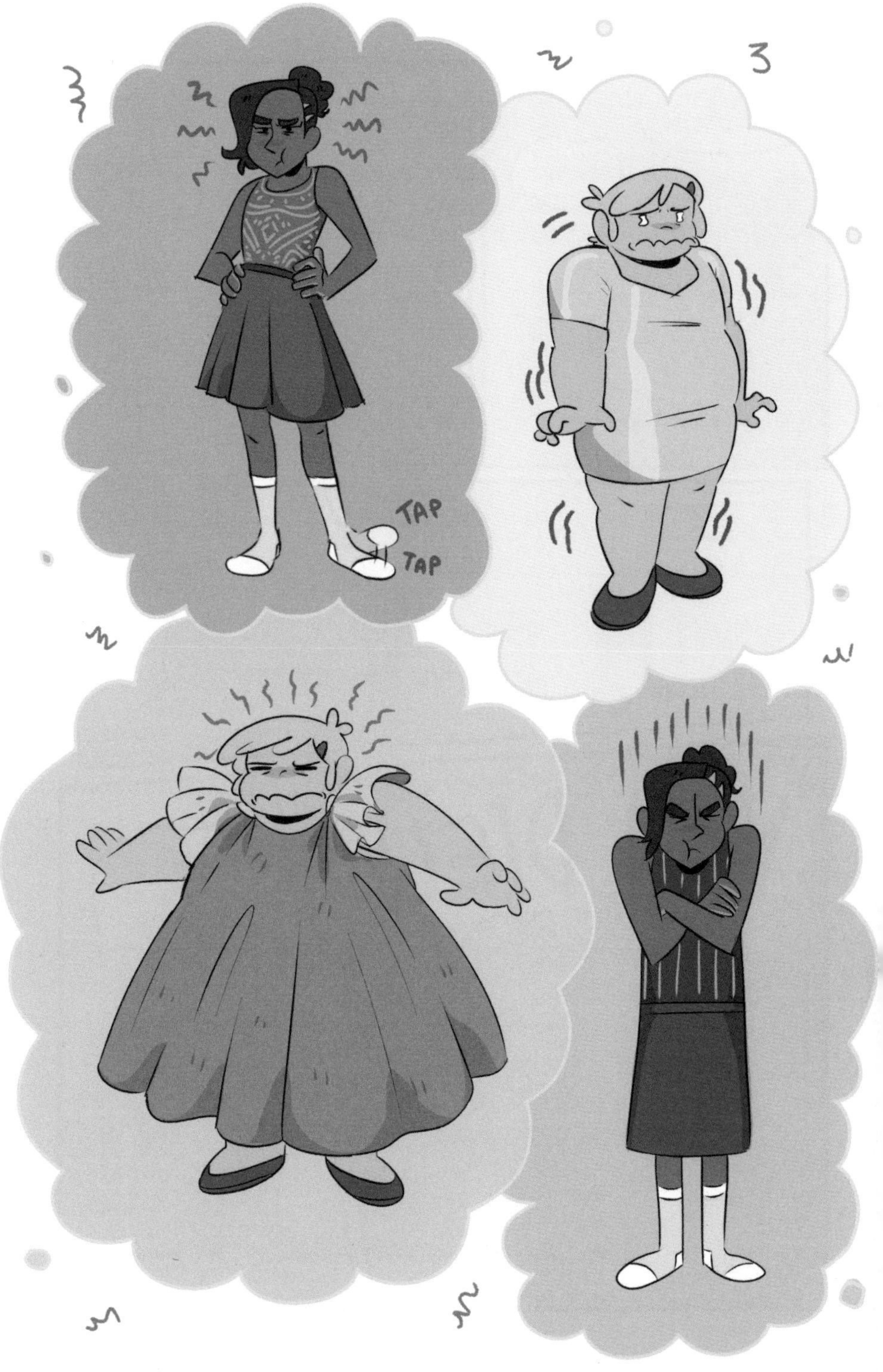
TAP
TAP

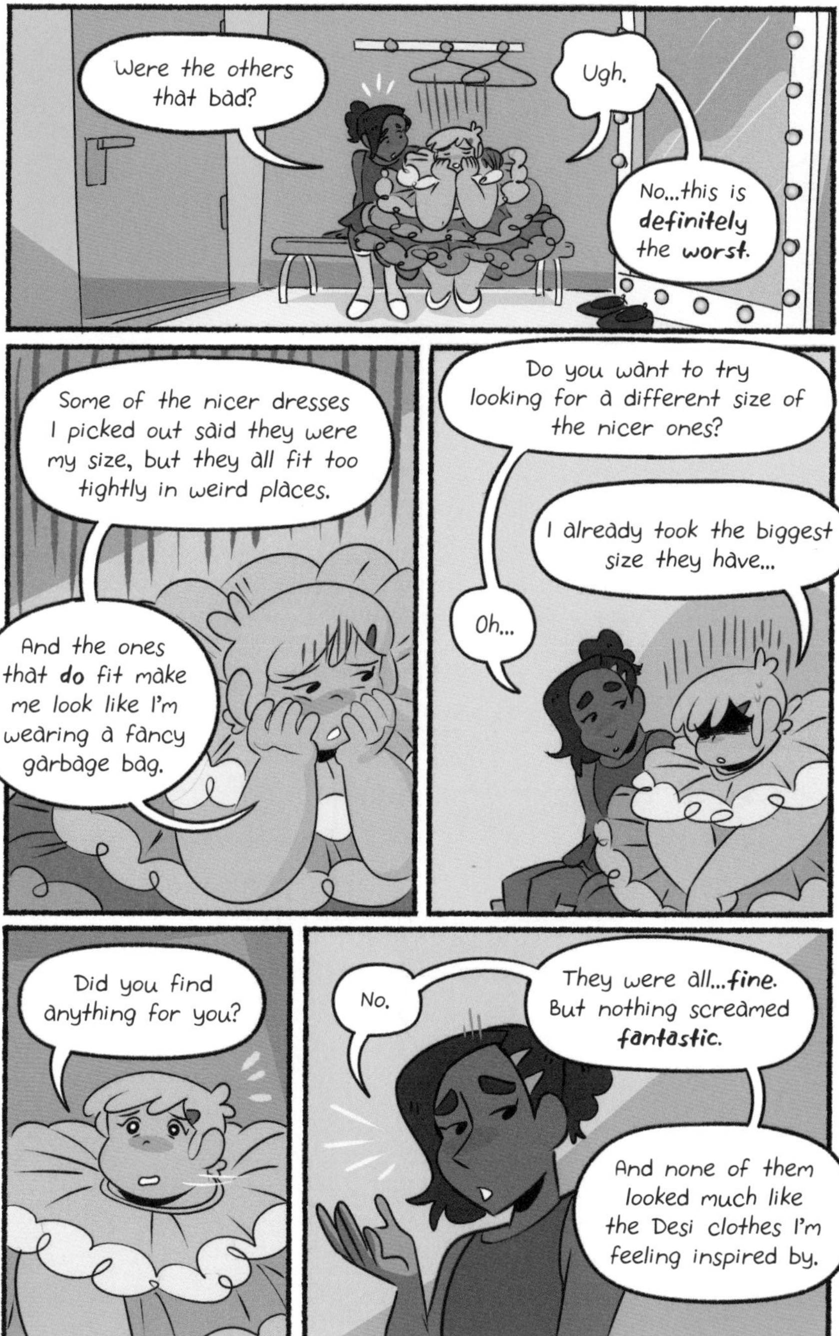
Were the others that bad?
Ugh.
No...this is **definitely** the **worst**.
Some of the nicer dresses I picked out said they were my size, but they all fit too tightly in weird places.
And the ones that **do** fit make me look like I'm wearing a fancy garbage bag.
Do you want to try looking for a different size of the nicer ones?
I already took the biggest size they have...
Oh...
Did you find anything for you?
No.
They were all...**fine**. But nothing screamed **fantastic**.
And none of them looked much like the Desi clothes I'm feeling inspired by.

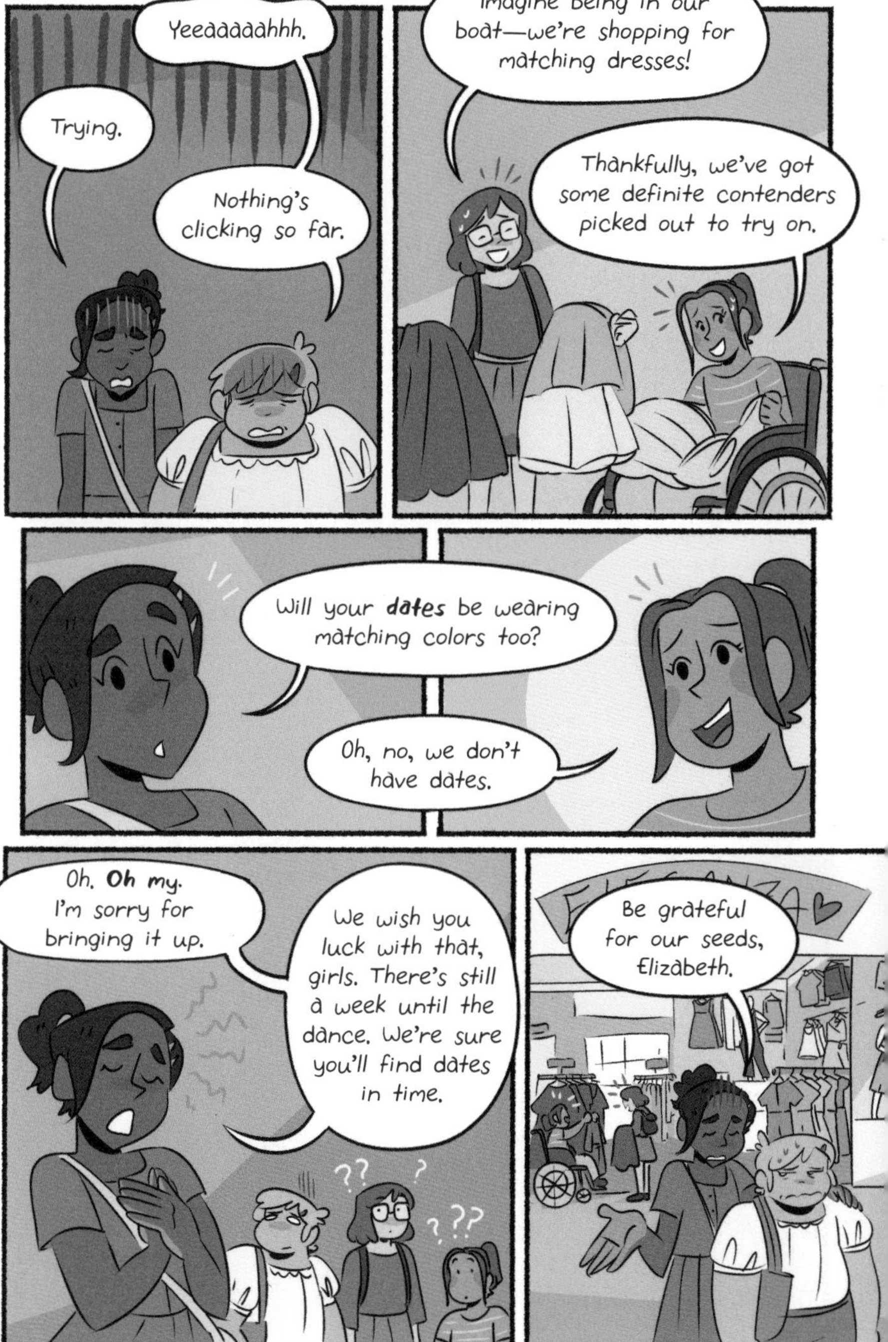
Yeeaaaaahhh.
Trying.
Nothing's clicking so far.
Imagine being in our boat—we're shopping for matching dresses!
Thankfully, we've got some definite contenders picked out to try on.
Will your **dates** be wearing matching colors too?
Oh, no, we don't have dates.
Oh. **Oh my.** I'm sorry for bringing it up.
We wish you luck with that, girls. There's still a week until the dance. We're sure you'll find dates in time.
??
?
??
?
Be grateful for our seeds, Elizabeth.

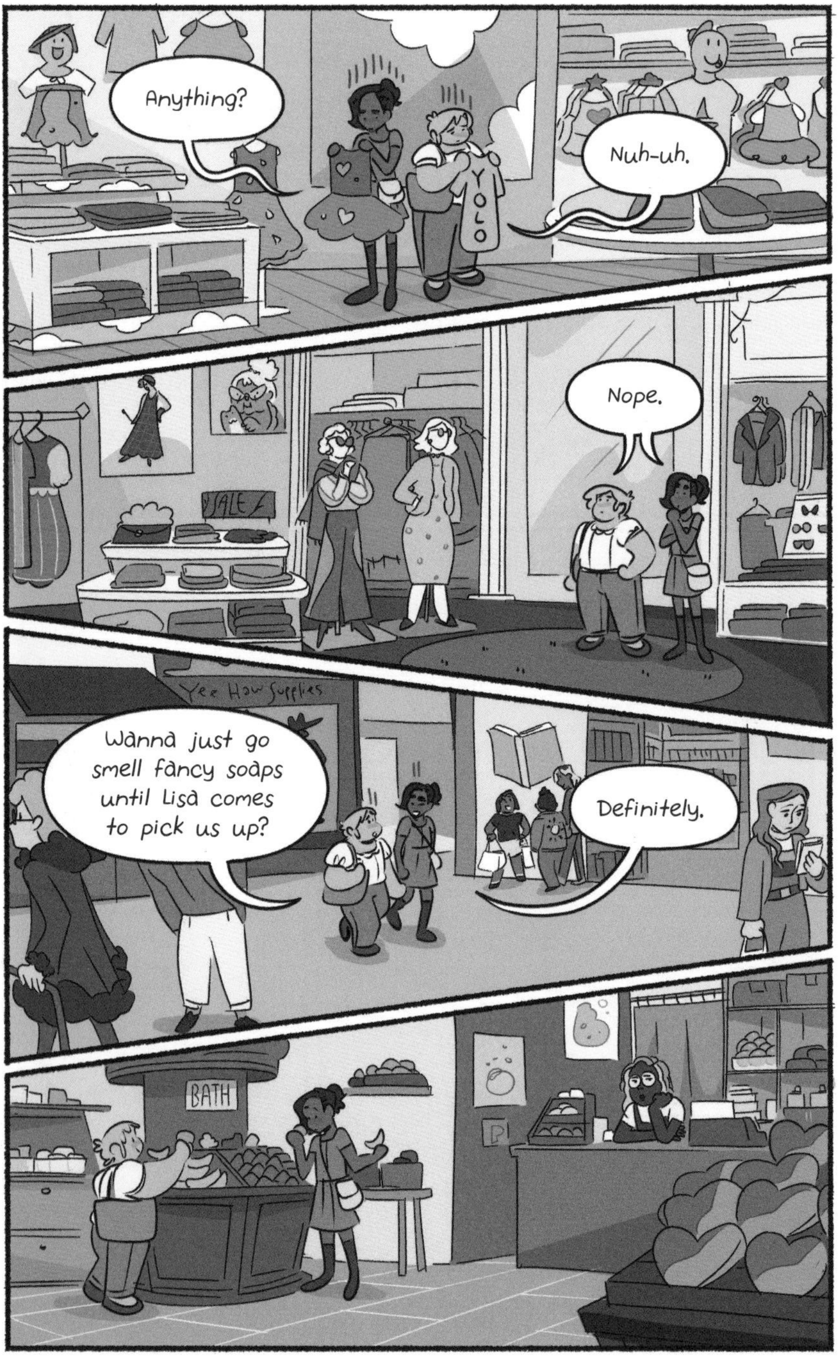
Anything?
YOLO
Nuh-uh.
Nope.
SALE
Yee Haw Supplies
Wanna just go smell fancy soaps until Lisa comes to pick us up?
Definitely.
BATH

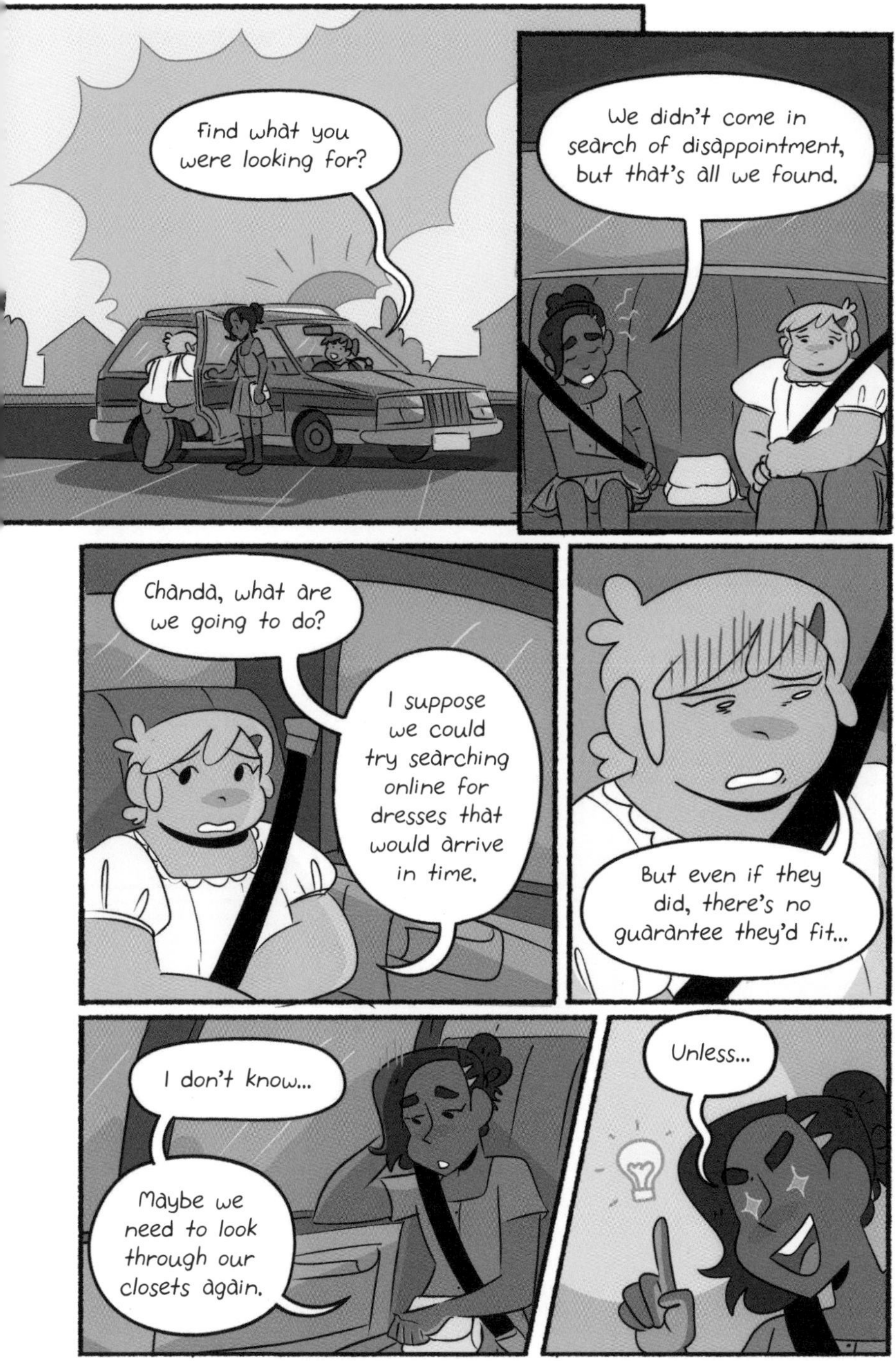
Find what you were looking for?
We didn't come in search of disappointment, but that's all we found.
Chanda, what are we going to do?
I suppose we could try searching online for dresses that would arrive in time.
But even if they did, there's no guarantee they'd fit...
I don't know...
Maybe we need to look through our closets again.
Unless...

65

69

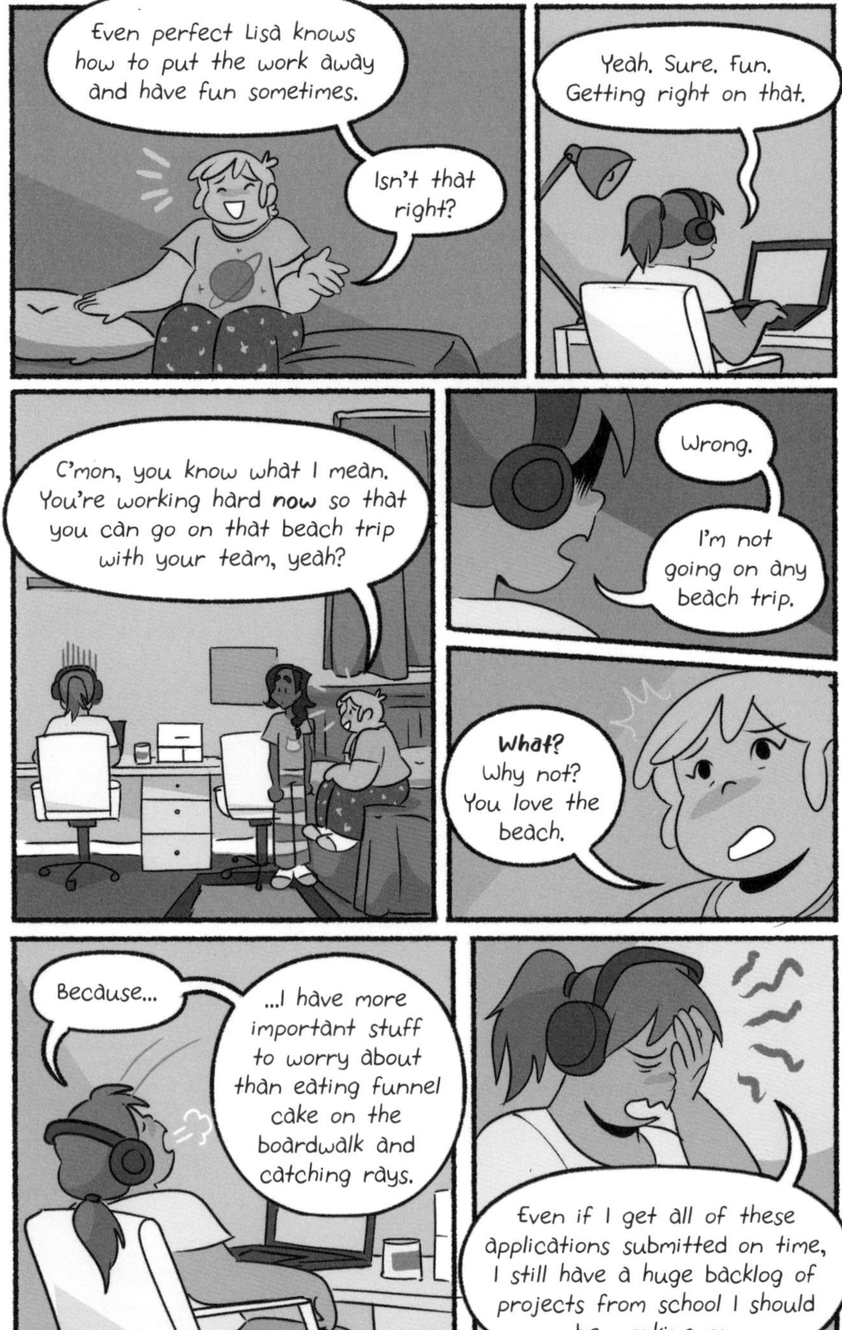
Even perfect Lisa knows how to put the work away and have fun sometimes.
Isn't that right?
Yeah. Sure. Fun. Getting right on that.
C'mon, you know what I mean. You're working hard **now** so that you can go on that beach trip with your team, yeah?
Wrong.
I'm not going on any beach trip.
What? Why not? You love the beach.
Because...
...I have more important stuff to worry about than eating funnel cake on the boardwalk and catching rays.
Even if I get all of these applications submitted on time, I still have a huge backlog of projects from school I should be working on.

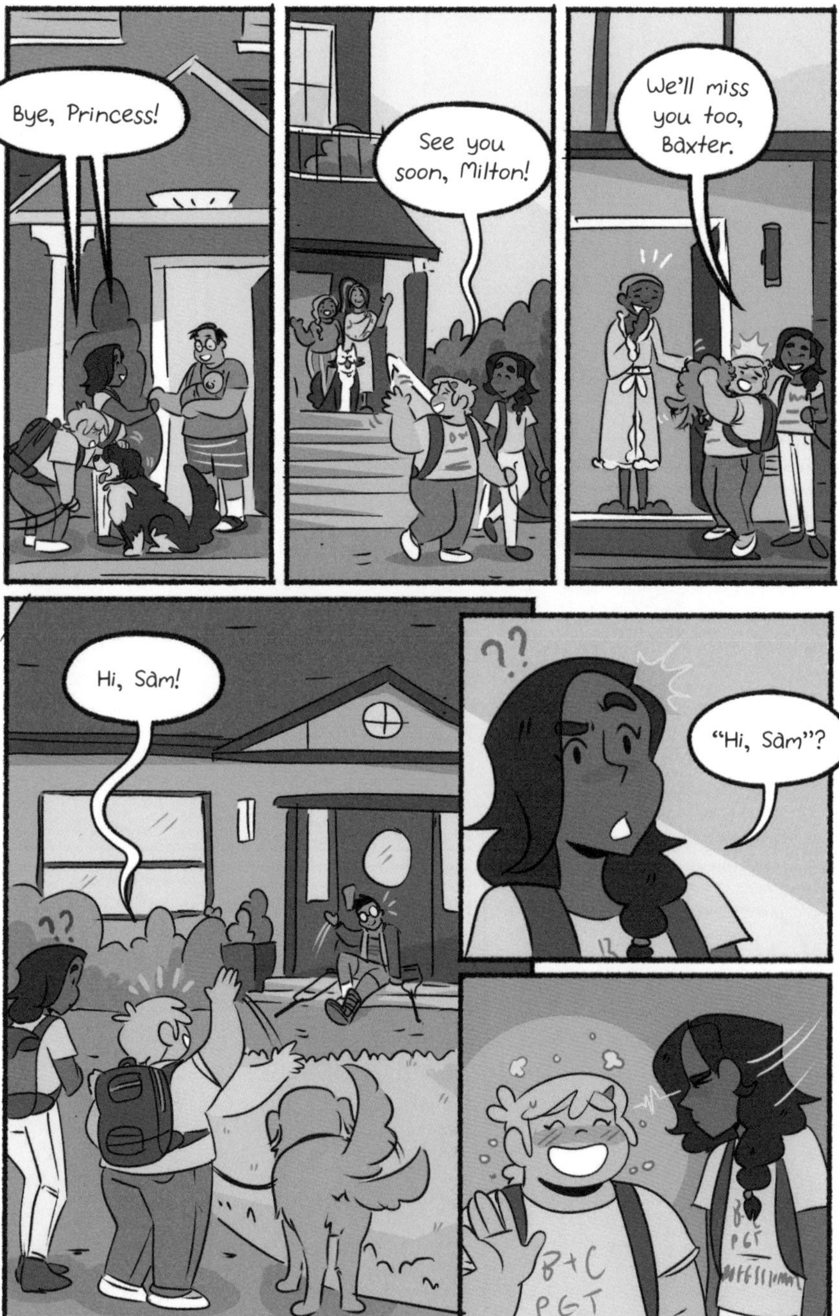
Bye, Princess!
See you soon, Milton!
We'll miss you too, Baxter.
Hi, Sam!
"Hi, Sam"?

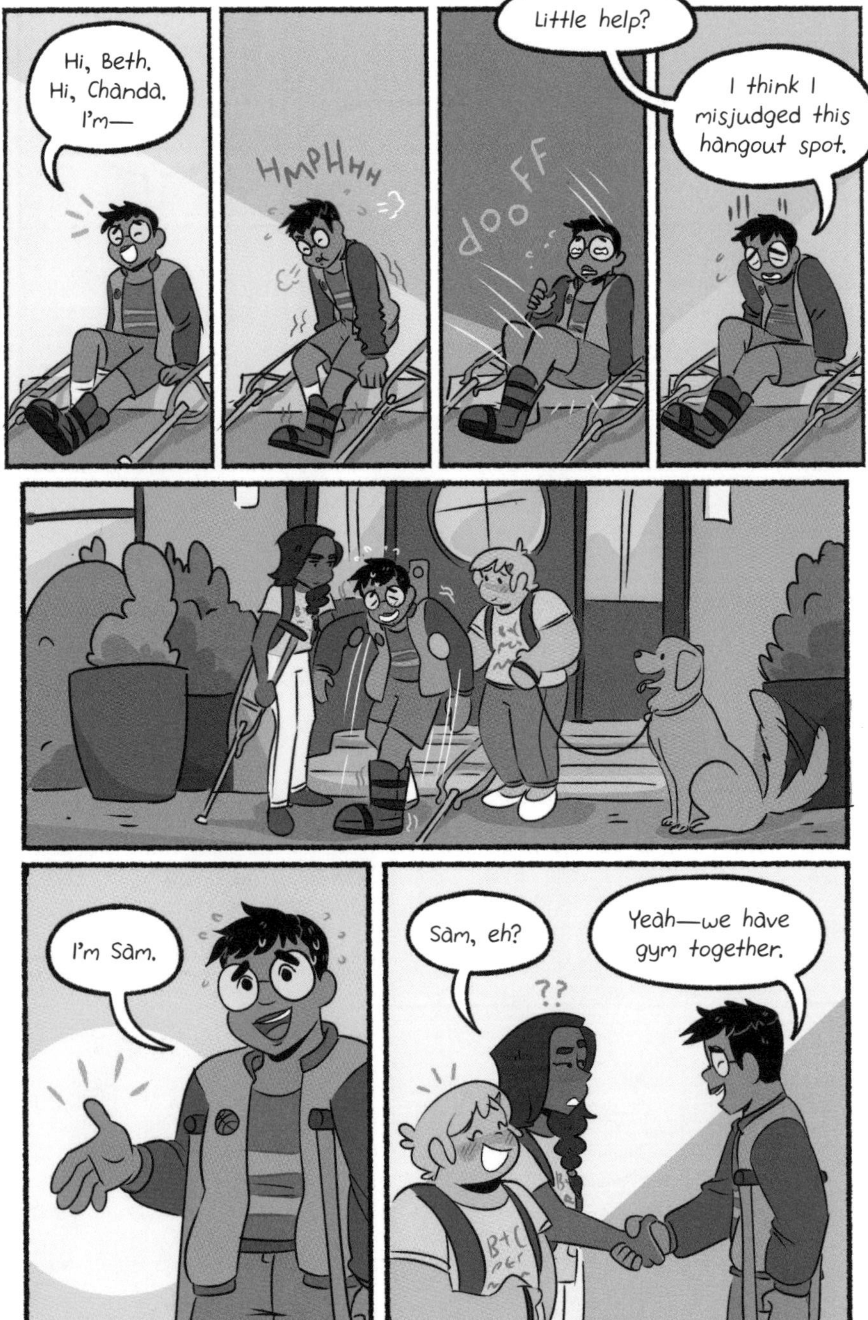
Hi, Beth. Hi, Chanda. I'm—
HMPHHH
Little help?
dooFF
I think I misjudged this hangout spot.
I'm Sam.
Sam, eh?
Yeah—we have gym together.
??

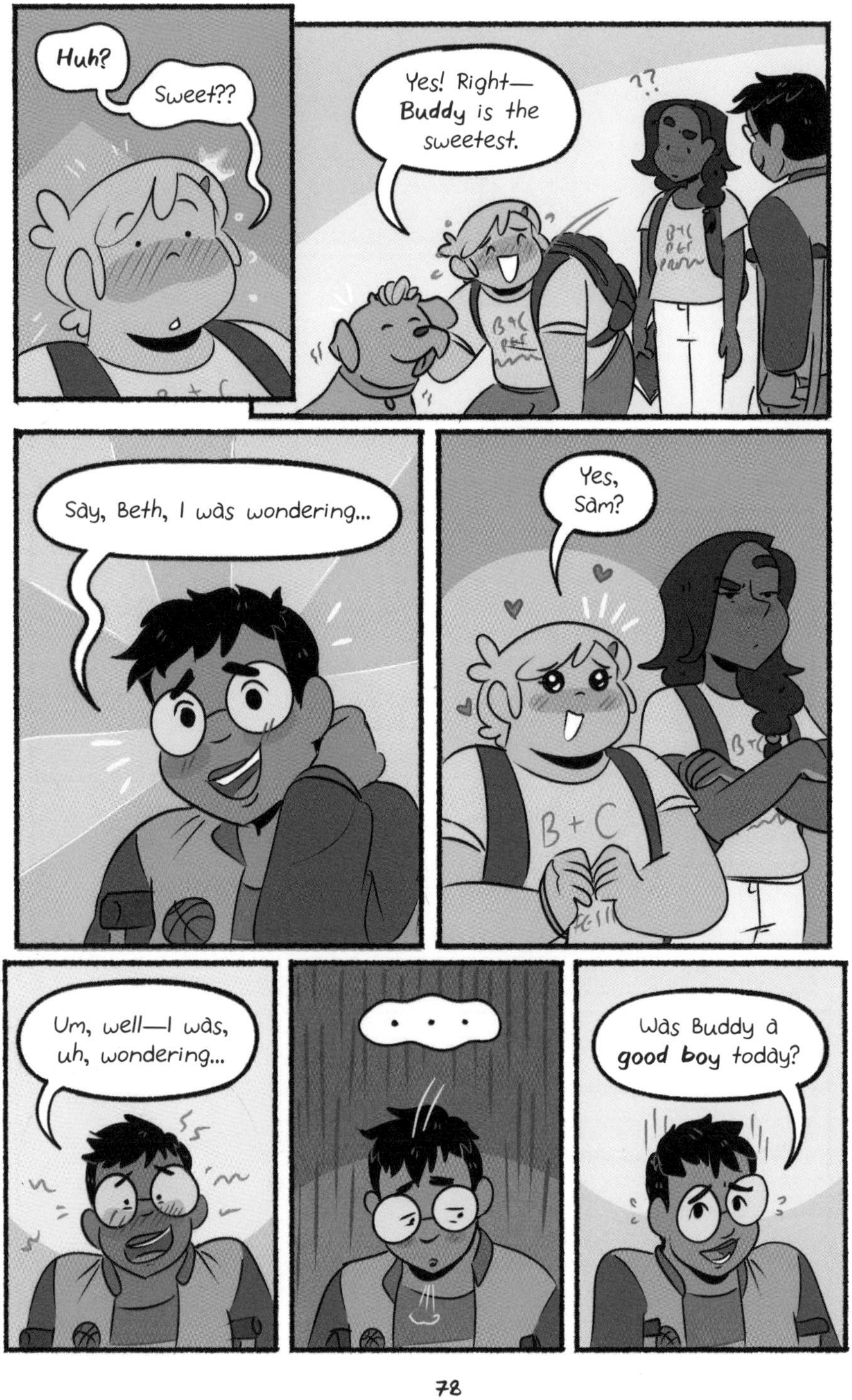
Huh?
Sweet??
Yes! Right—
Buddy is the sweetest.
Say, Beth, I was wondering...
Yes, Sam?
Um, well—I was, uh, wondering...
. . .
Was Buddy a **good boy** today?

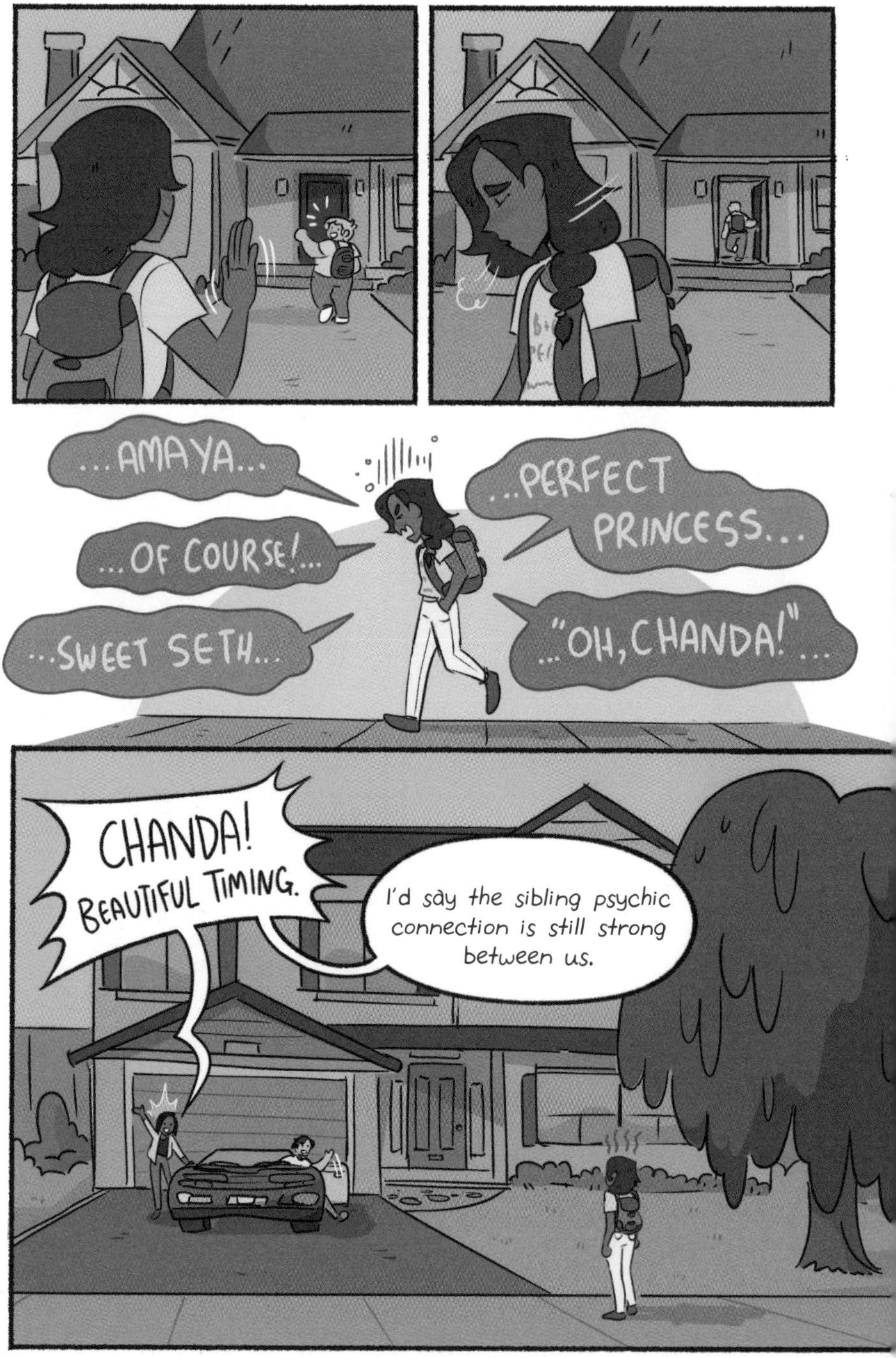
...AMAYA...
...OF COURSE!...
...SWEET SETH...
...PERFECT PRINCESS...
..."OH, CHANDA!"...
CHANDA! BEAUTIFUL TIMING.
I'd say the sibling psychic connection is still strong between us.

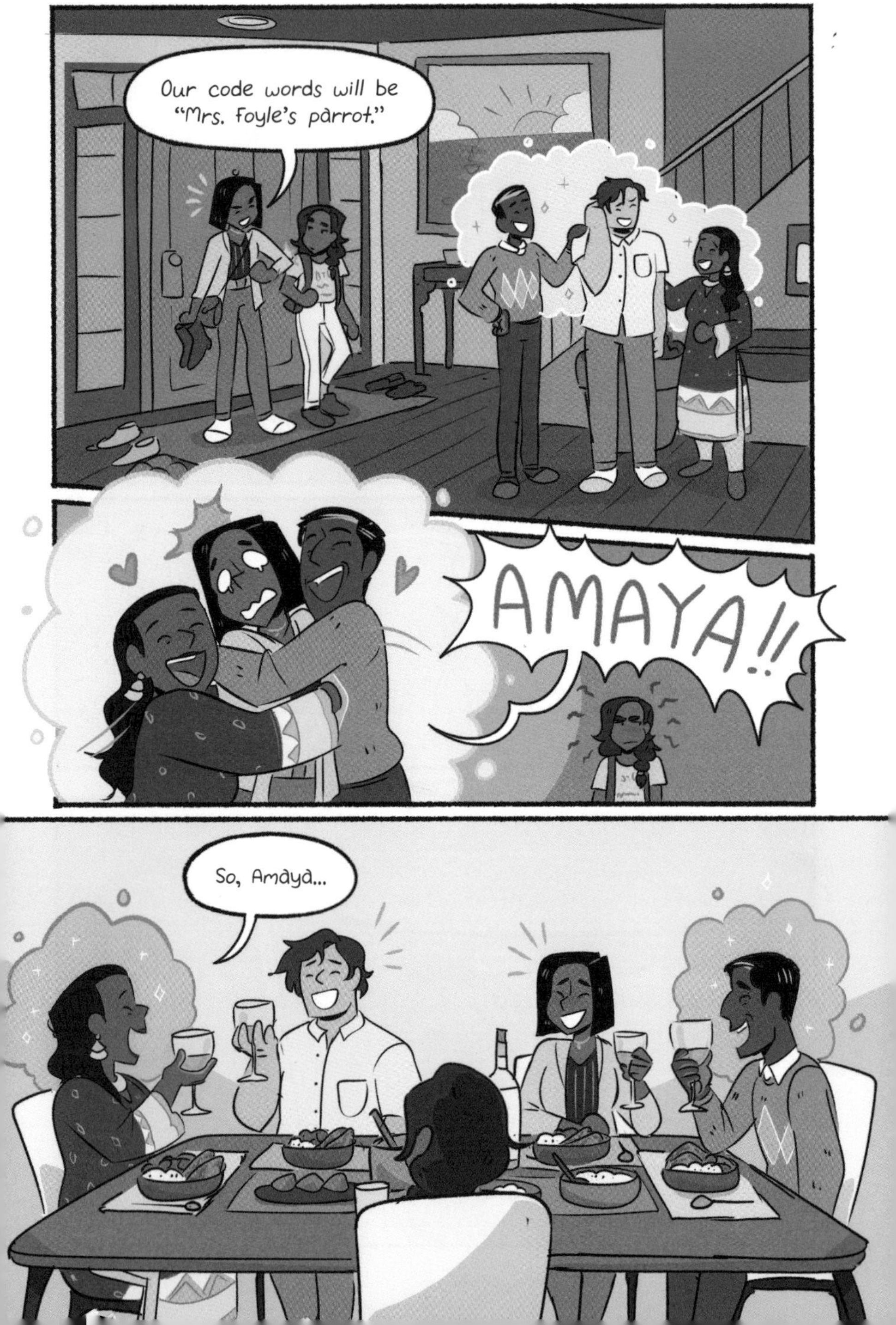
Our code words will be "Mrs. Foyle's parrot."
AMAYA!!
So, Amaya...

Good night, sis.

MRROW?

Yeah, Countess, I know...

CLICK

SIGH.

What makes Amaya so evil is that she's the **perfect** sister, too.

I wish she and her perfectly perfect fiancé would hurry up with their perfectly perfect wedding and find their perfectly perfect house so we could all forget about them and their perfectly perfect life.

PURRRRR

Wouldn't that be **perfect**?

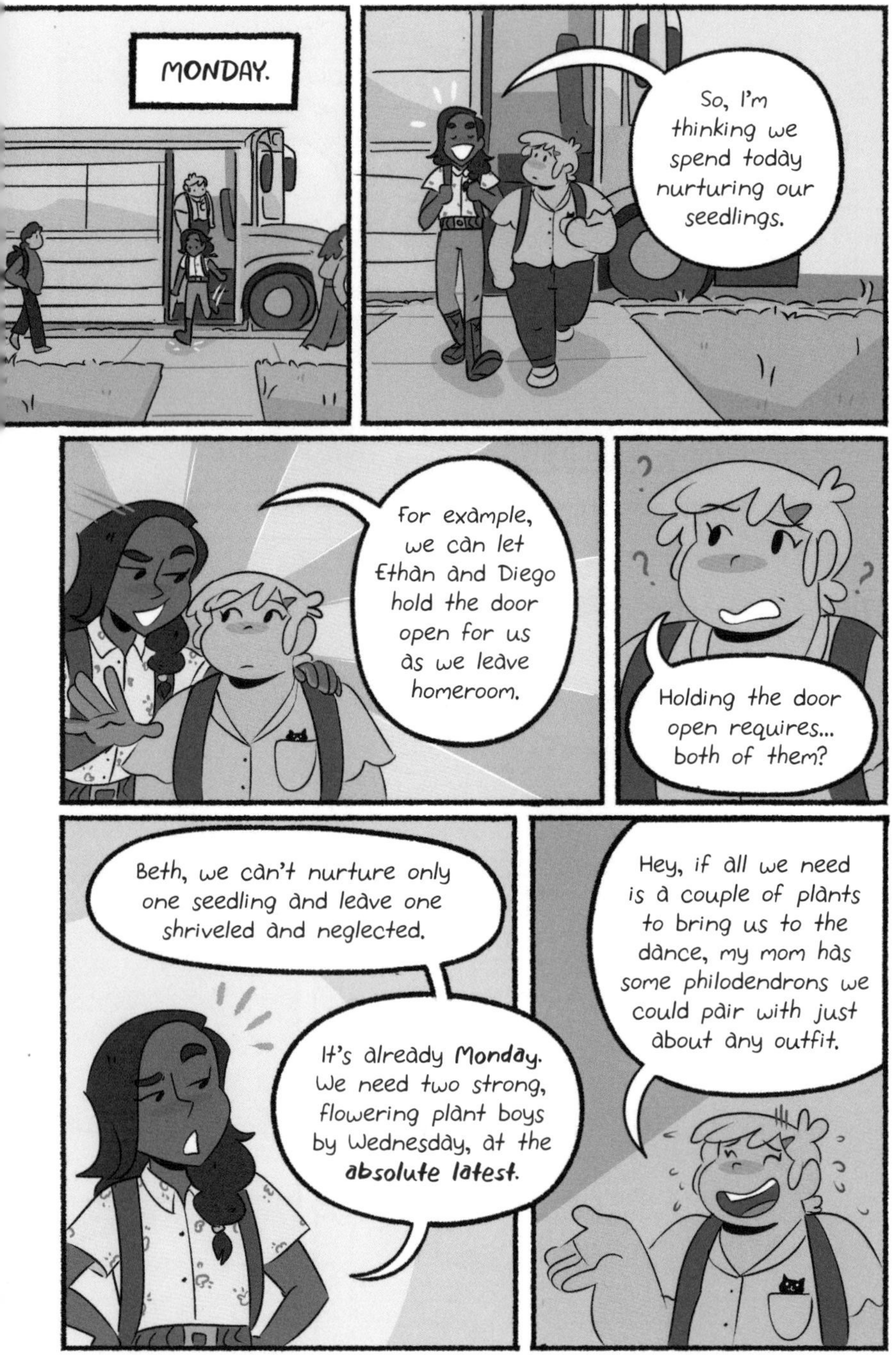
MONDAY.
So, I'm thinking we spend today nurturing our seedlings.
For example, we can let Ethan and Diego hold the door open for us as we leave homeroom.
Holding the door open requires... both of them?
Beth, we can't nurture only one seedling and leave one shriveled and neglected.
It's already **Monday**. We need two strong, flowering plant boys by Wednesday, at the **absolute latest**.
Hey, if all we need is a couple of plants to bring us to the dance, my mom has some philodendrons we could pair with just about any outfit.

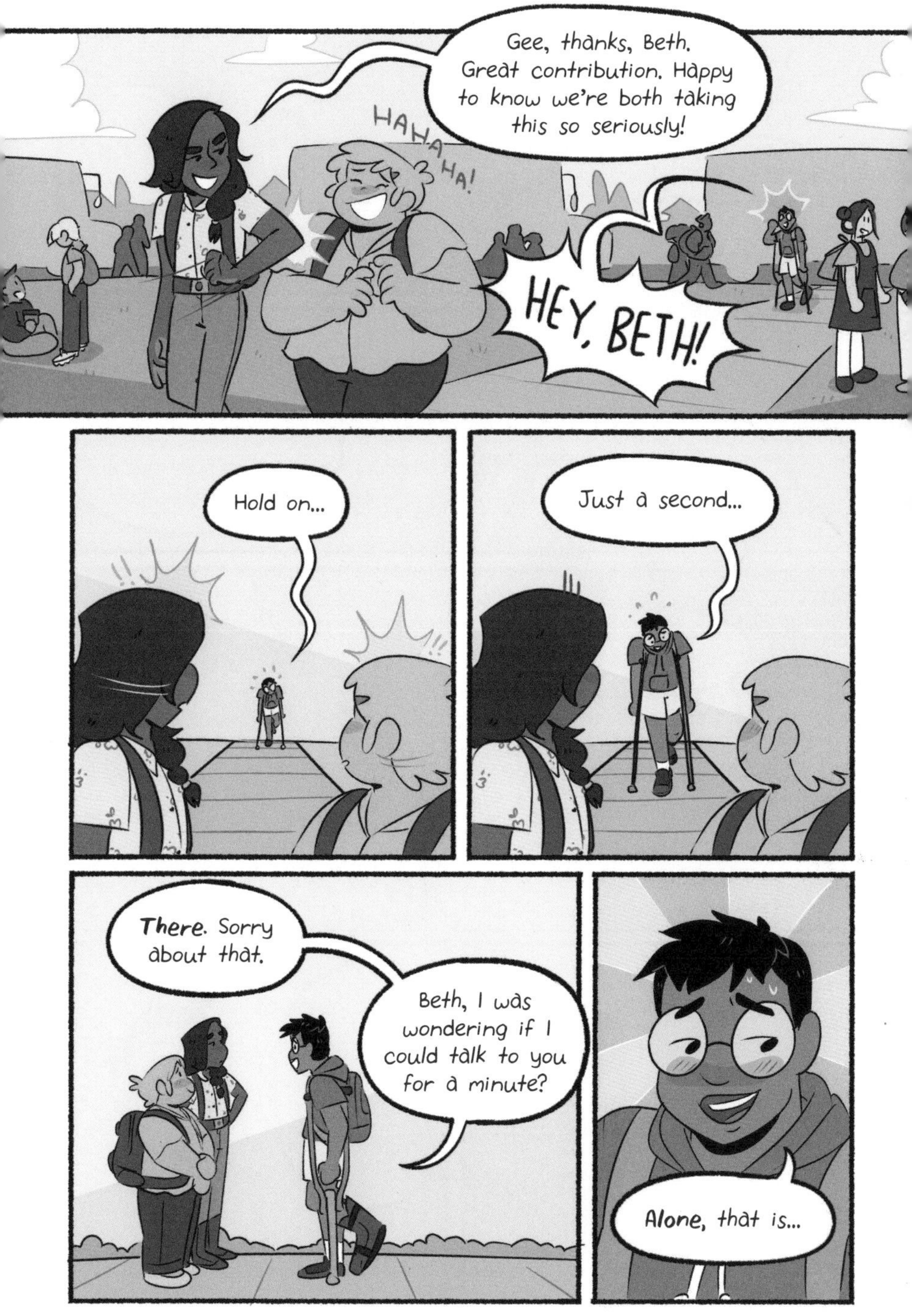
Gee, thanks, Beth. Great contribution. Happy to know we're both taking this so seriously!
HAHAHA HA!
HEY, BETH!
Hold on...
Just a second...
There. Sorry about that.
Beth, I was wondering if I could talk to you for a minute?
Alone, that is...

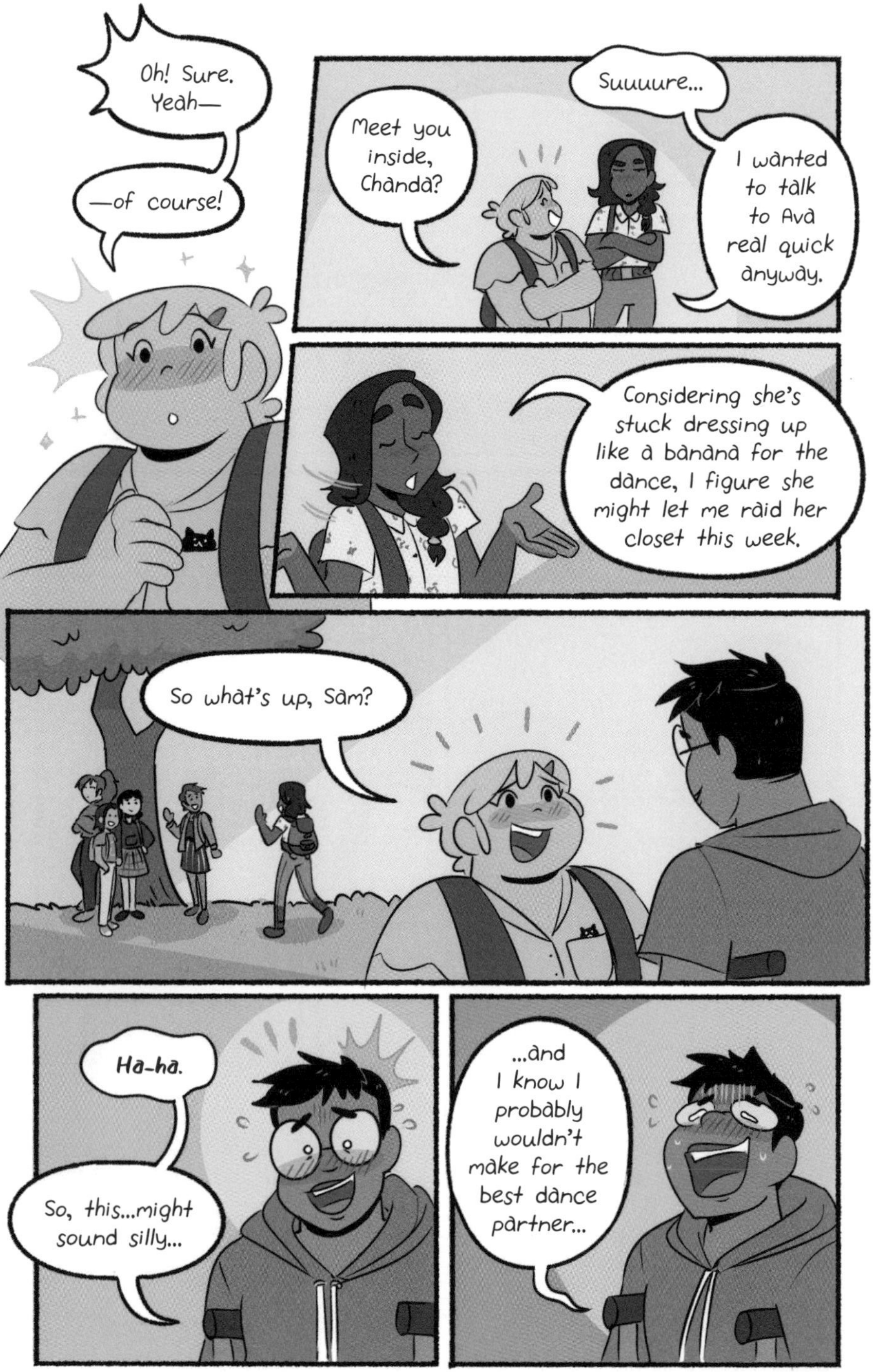
Oh! Sure. Yeah—
—of course!
Meet you inside, Chanda?
Suuuure...
I wanted to talk to Ava real quick anyway.
Considering she's stuck dressing up like a banana for the dance, I figure she might let me raid her closet this week.
So what's up, Sam?
Ha-ha.
So, this...might sound silly...
...and I know I probably wouldn't make for the best dance partner...

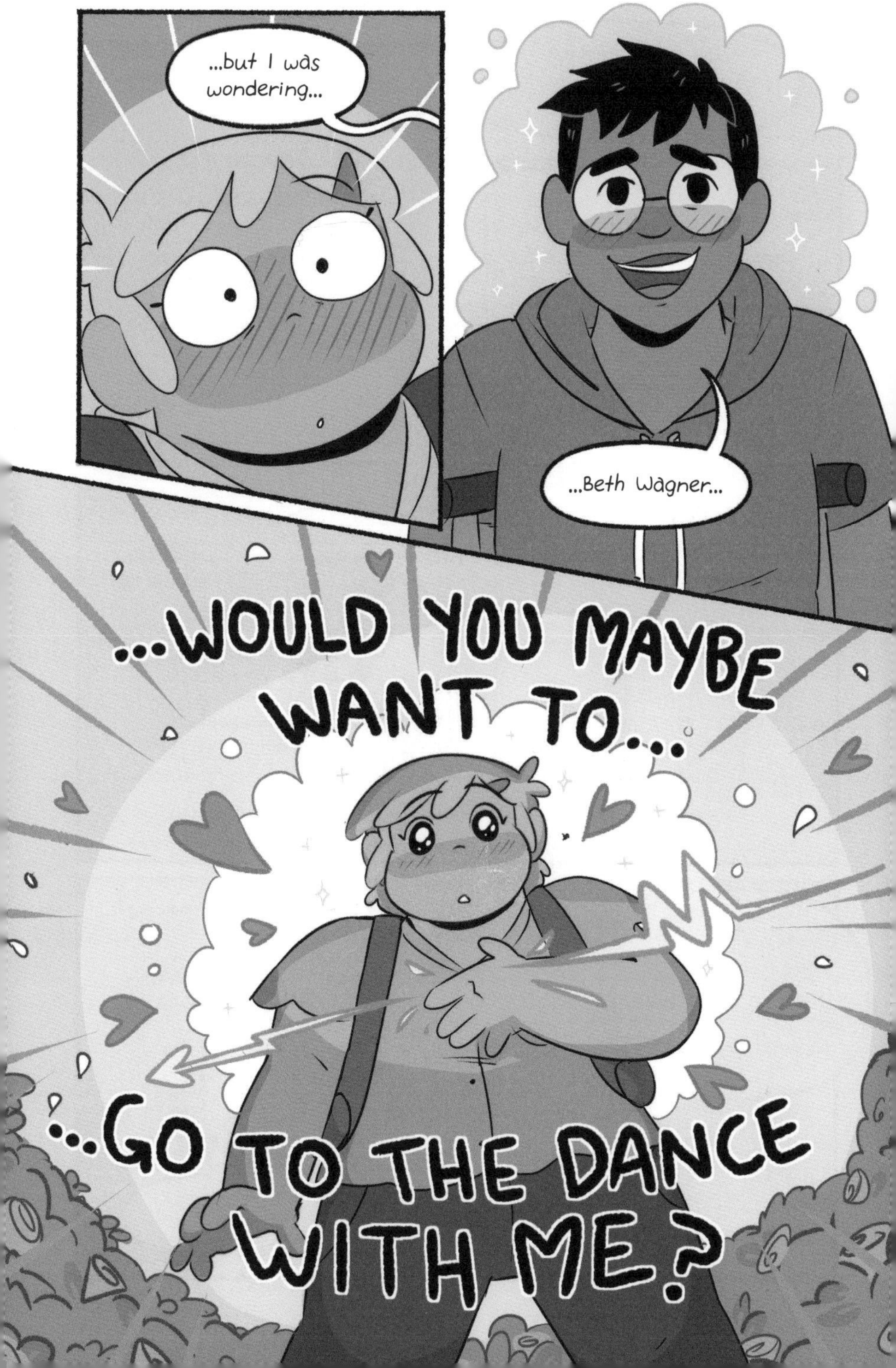
...but I was wondering...
...Beth Wagner...
...WOULD YOU MAYBE WANT TO...
...GO TO THE DANCE WITH ME?

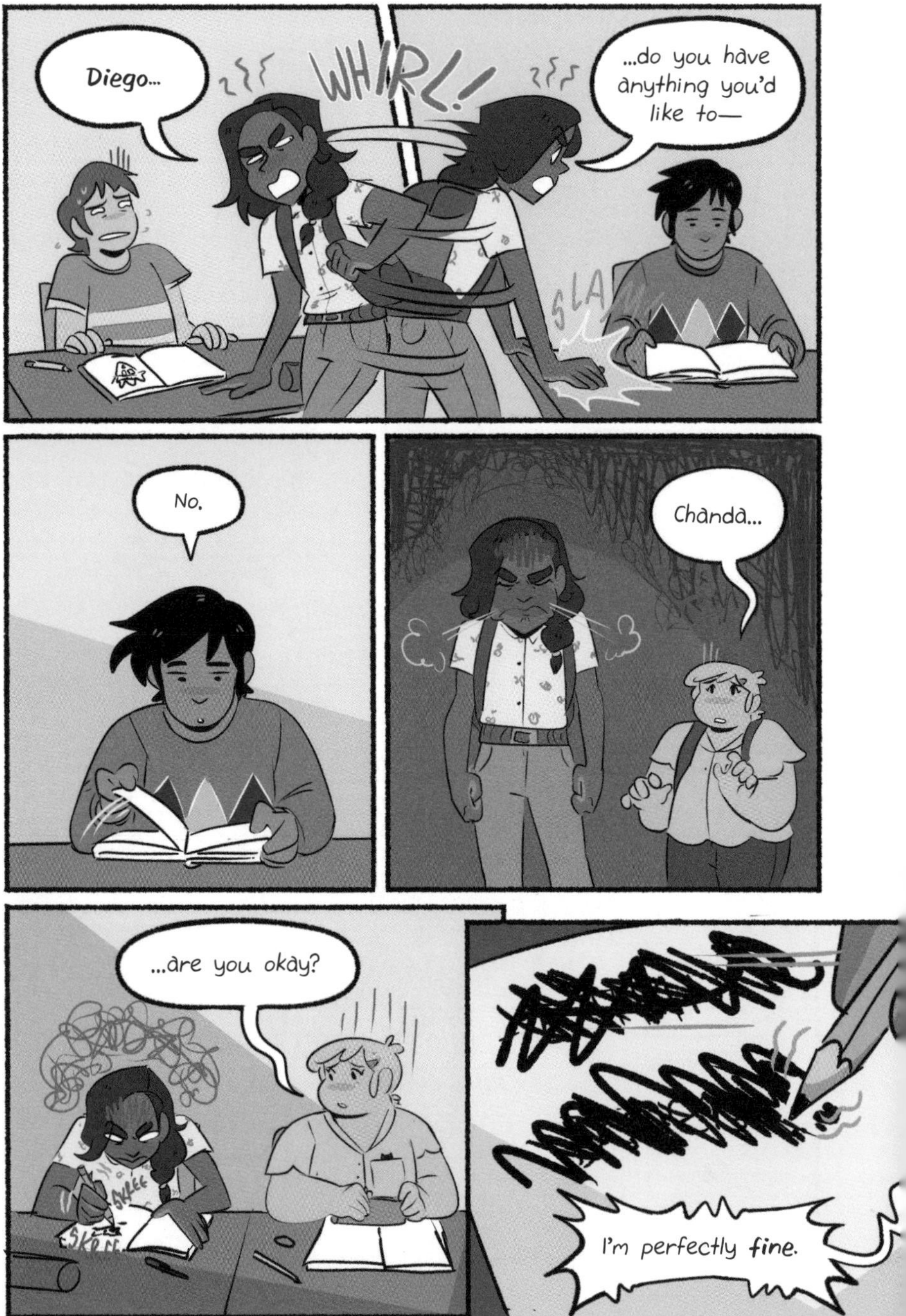
Diego...
WHIRL!
...do you have anything you'd like to—
SLAM
No.
Chanda...
...are you okay?
I'm perfectly fine.

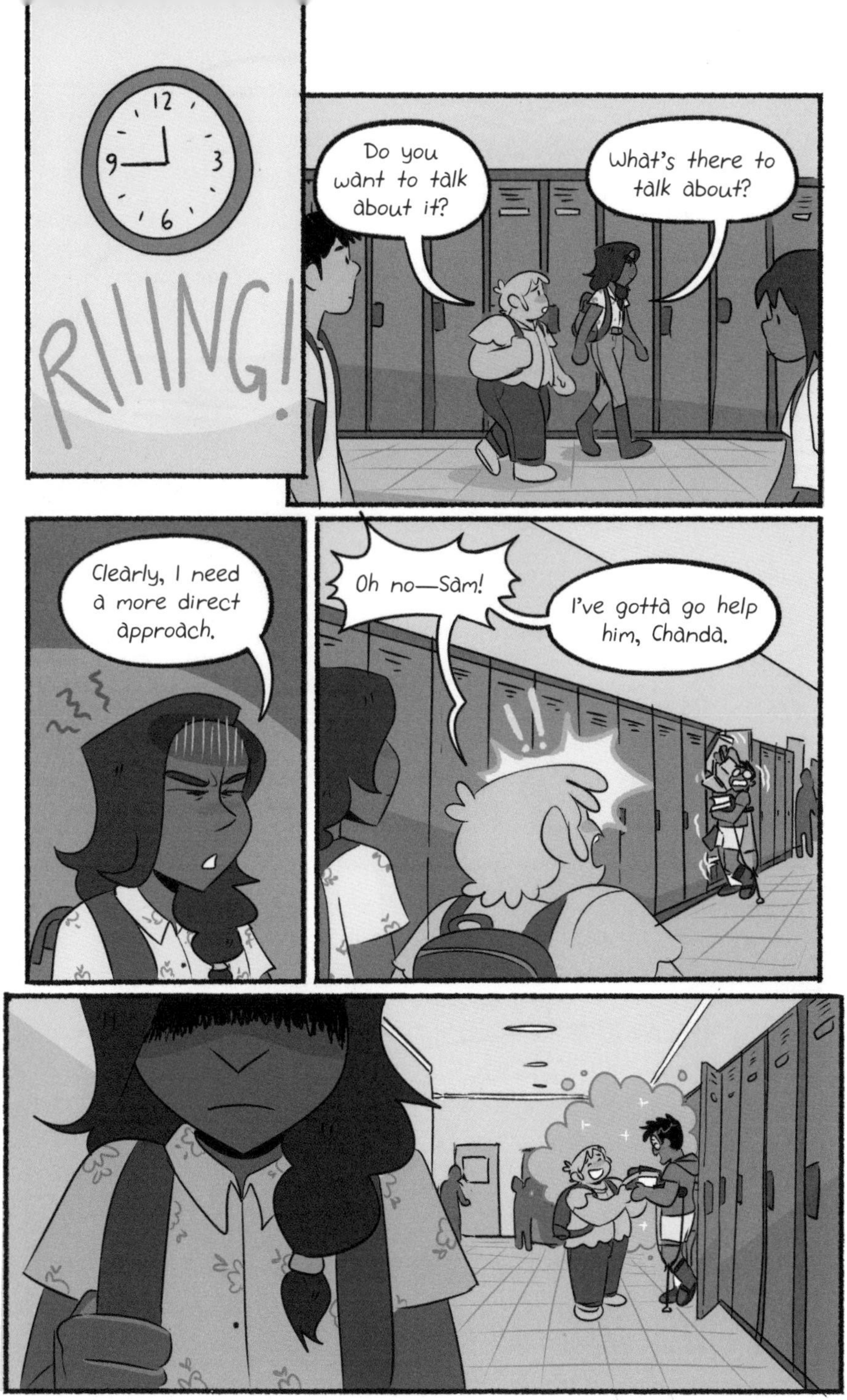
RIIING!
Do you want to talk about it?
What's there to talk about?
Clearly, I need a more direct approach.
Oh no—Sam!
I've gotta go help him, Chanda.

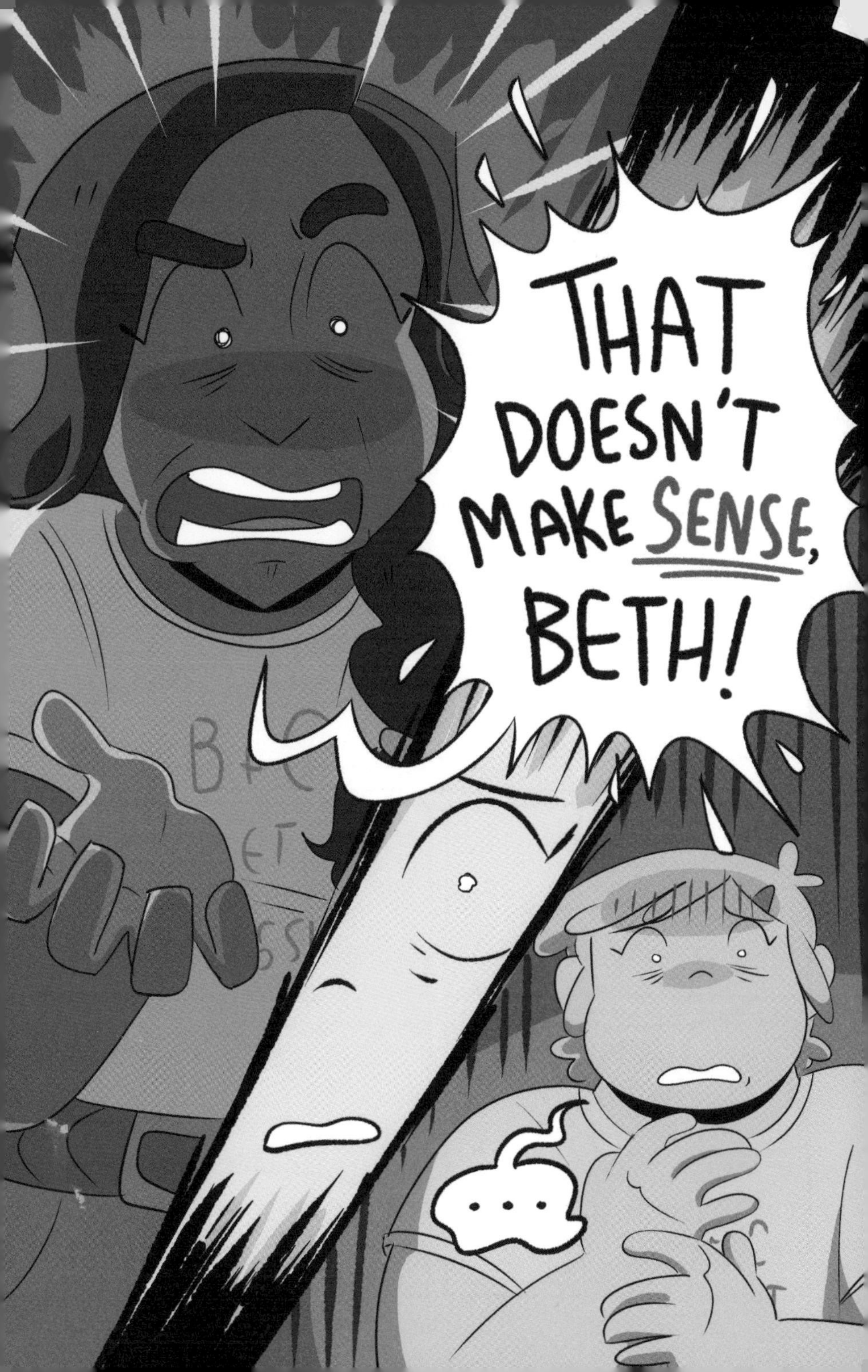
THAT DOESN'T MAKE SENSE, BETH!
...

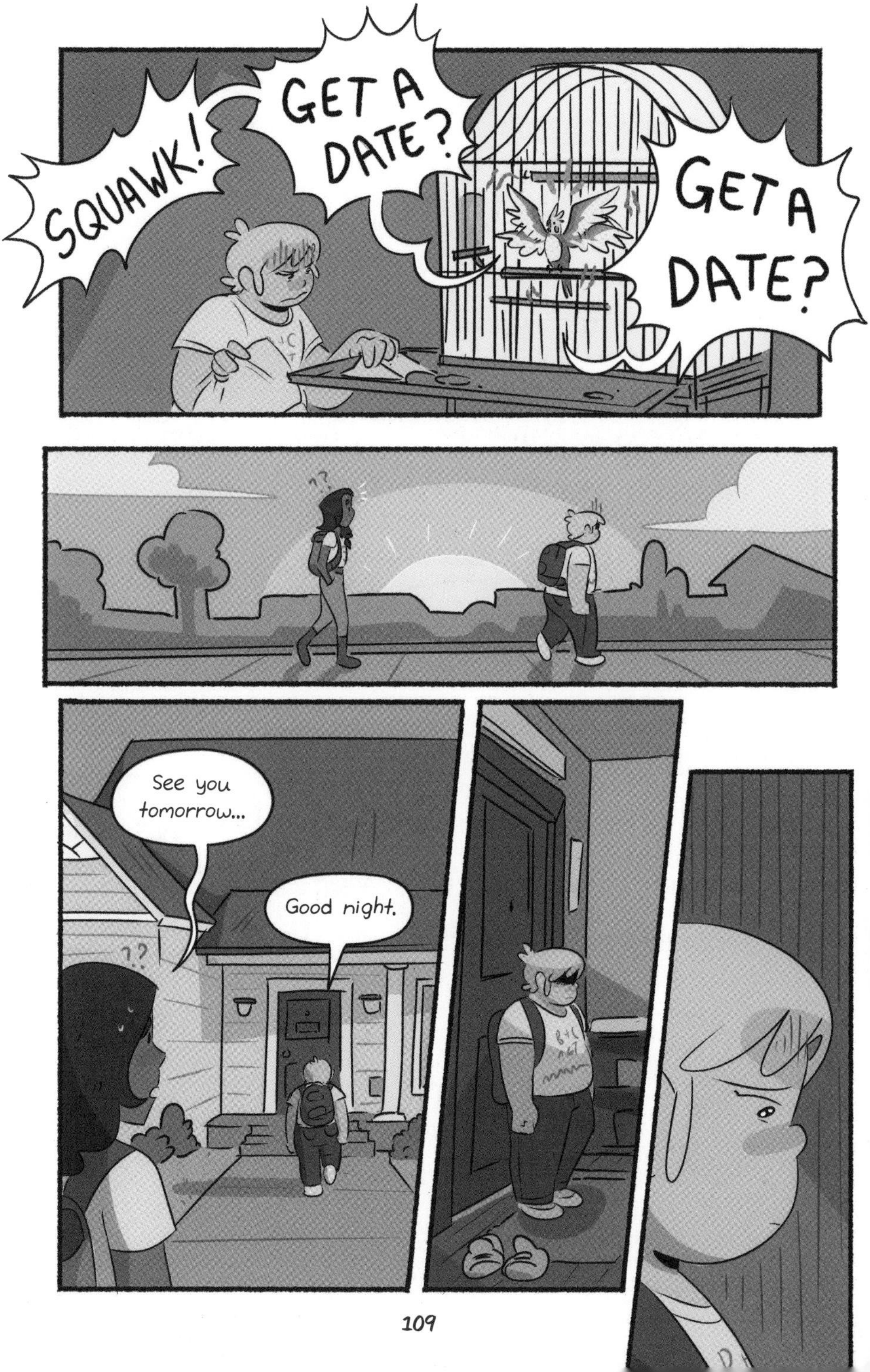

SQUAWK!
GET A DATE?
GET A DATE?
See you tomorrow...
Good night.

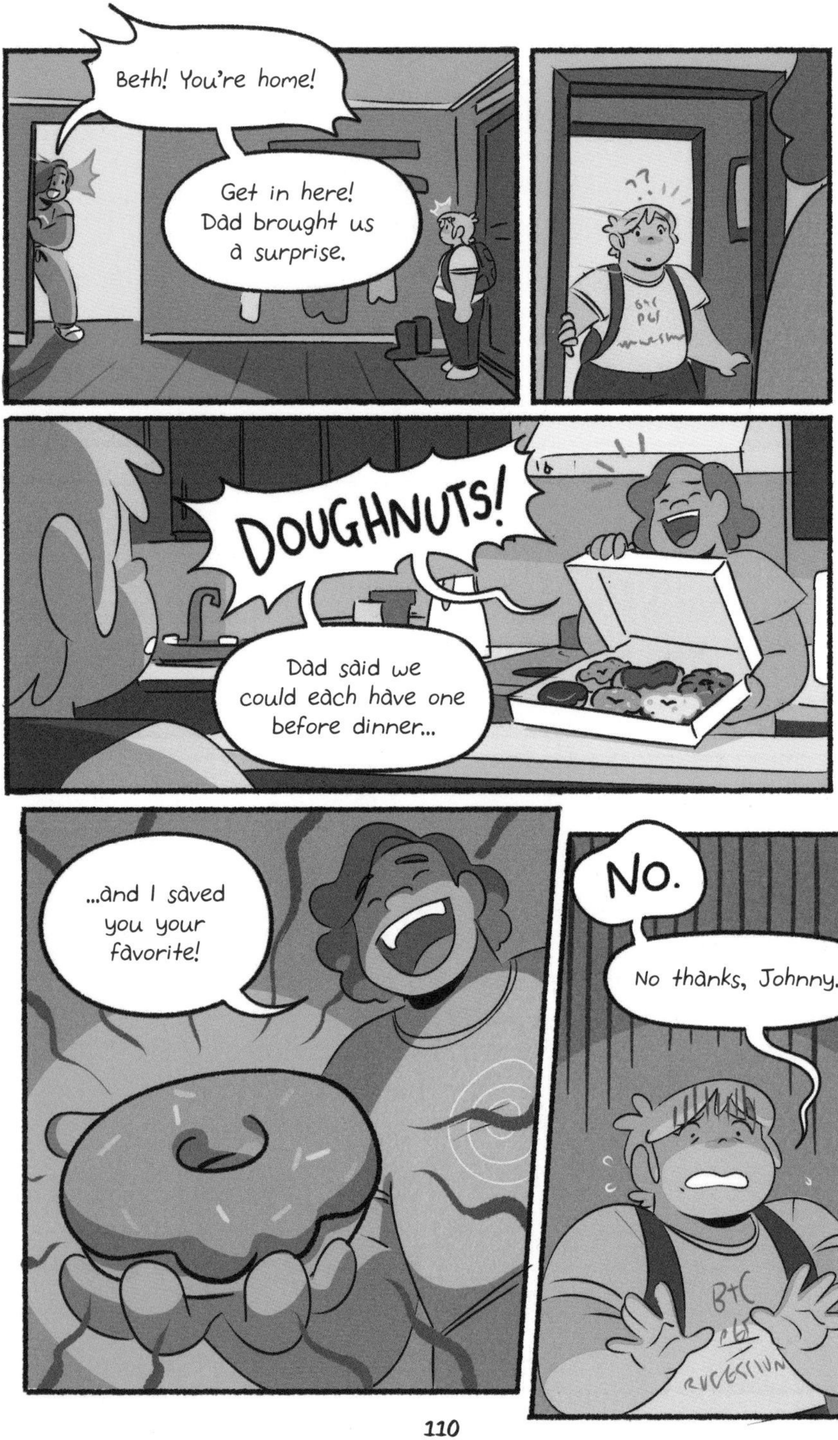
Beth! You're home!
Get in here! Dad brought us a surprise.
DOUGHNUTS!
Dad said we could each have one before dinner...
...and I saved you your favorite!
NO.
No thanks, Johnny.

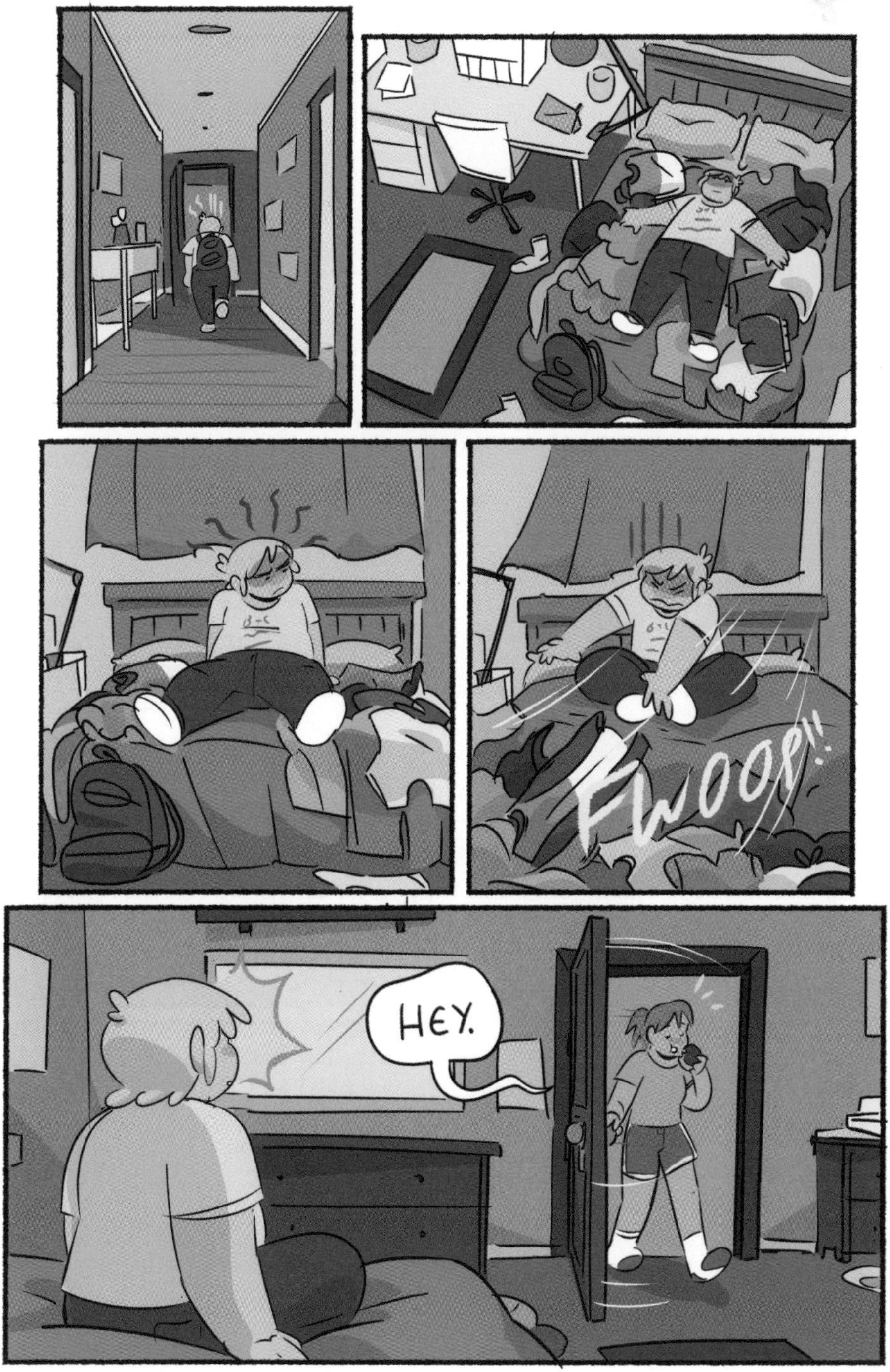
FWOOP!!
HEY.

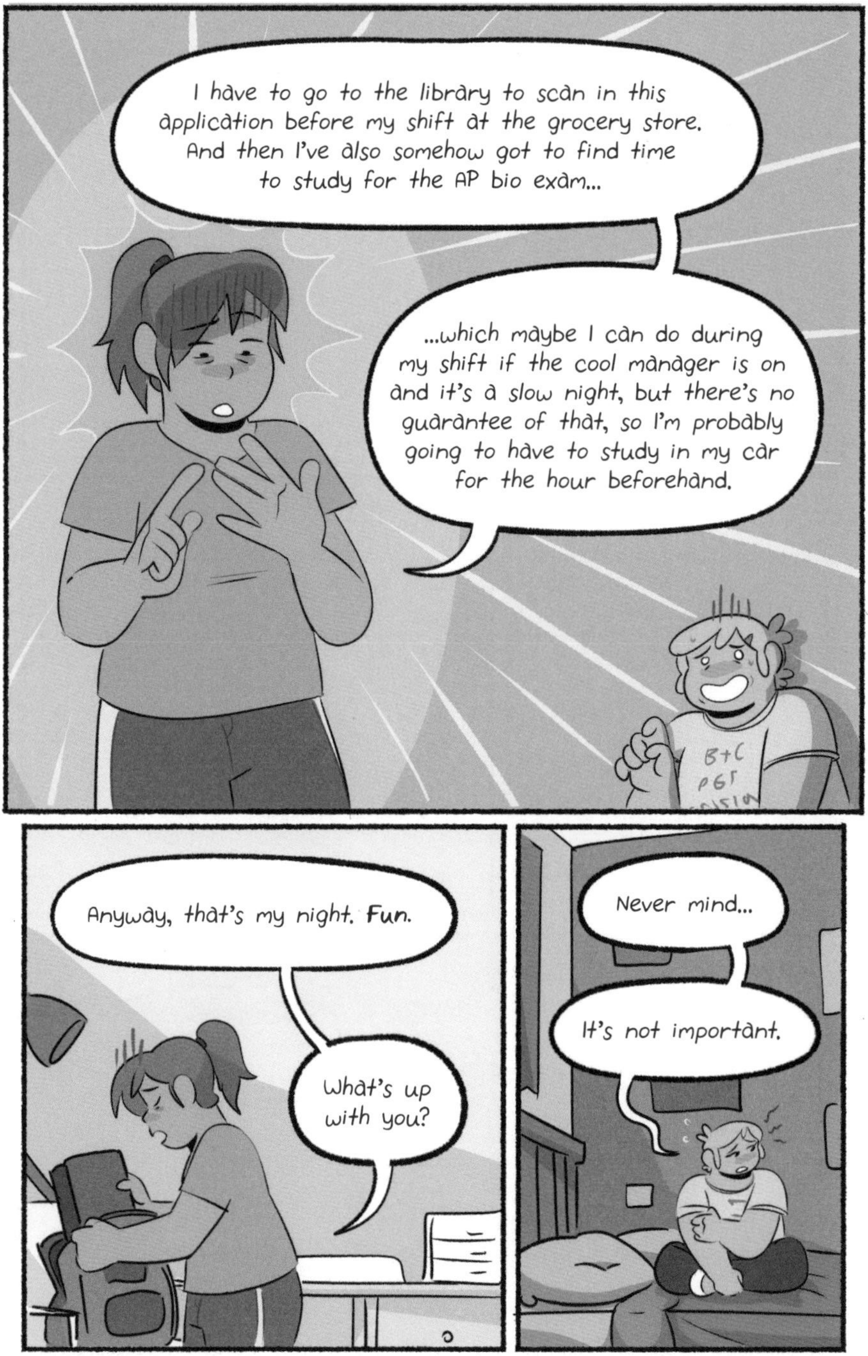
I have to go to the library to scan in this application before my shift at the grocery store. And then I've also somehow got to find time to study for the AP bio exam...
...which maybe I can do during my shift if the cool manager is on and it's a slow night, but there's no guarantee of that, so I'm probably going to have to study in my car for the hour beforehand.
Anyway, that's my night. **Fun.**
What's up with you?
Never mind...
It's not important.

I also thought we could make dinner together!

I've been itching to have you and the 'rents try this amazing sweet noodle casserole Seth's grandmother taught me how to cook.

Do we **have** to make dinner together?

I'd be fine eating some cookies and calling it a night.

No way!

Seriously, Grandma Geller's kugel is like eating dessert for dinner. You're gonna love it.

Fill me up a pot of water to boil, will ya?

FSHHH

117

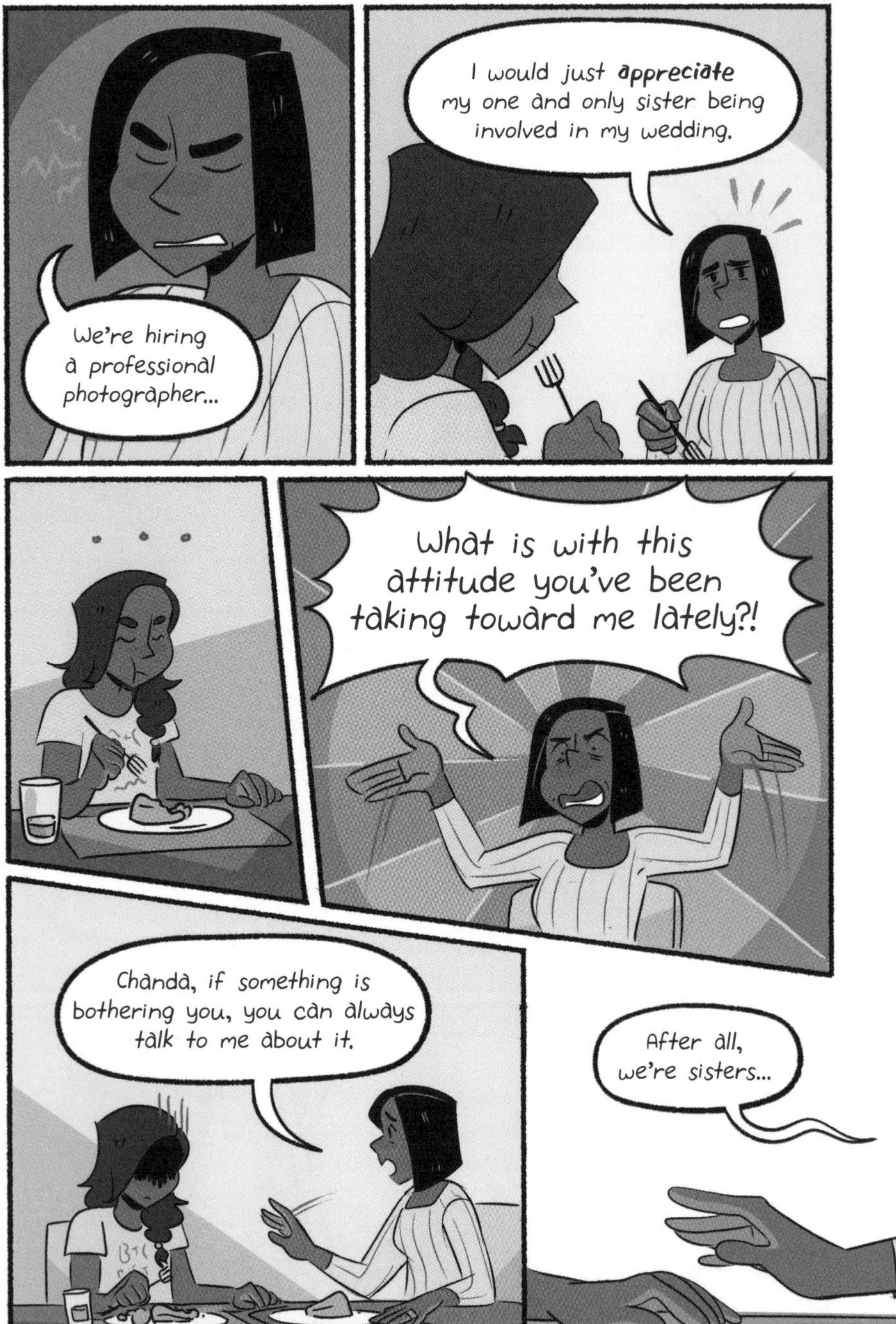
We're hiring a professional photographer...
I would just **appreciate** my one and only sister being involved in my wedding.
What is with this attitude you've been taking toward me lately?!
Chanda, if something is bothering you, you can always talk to me about it.
After all, we're sisters...

121

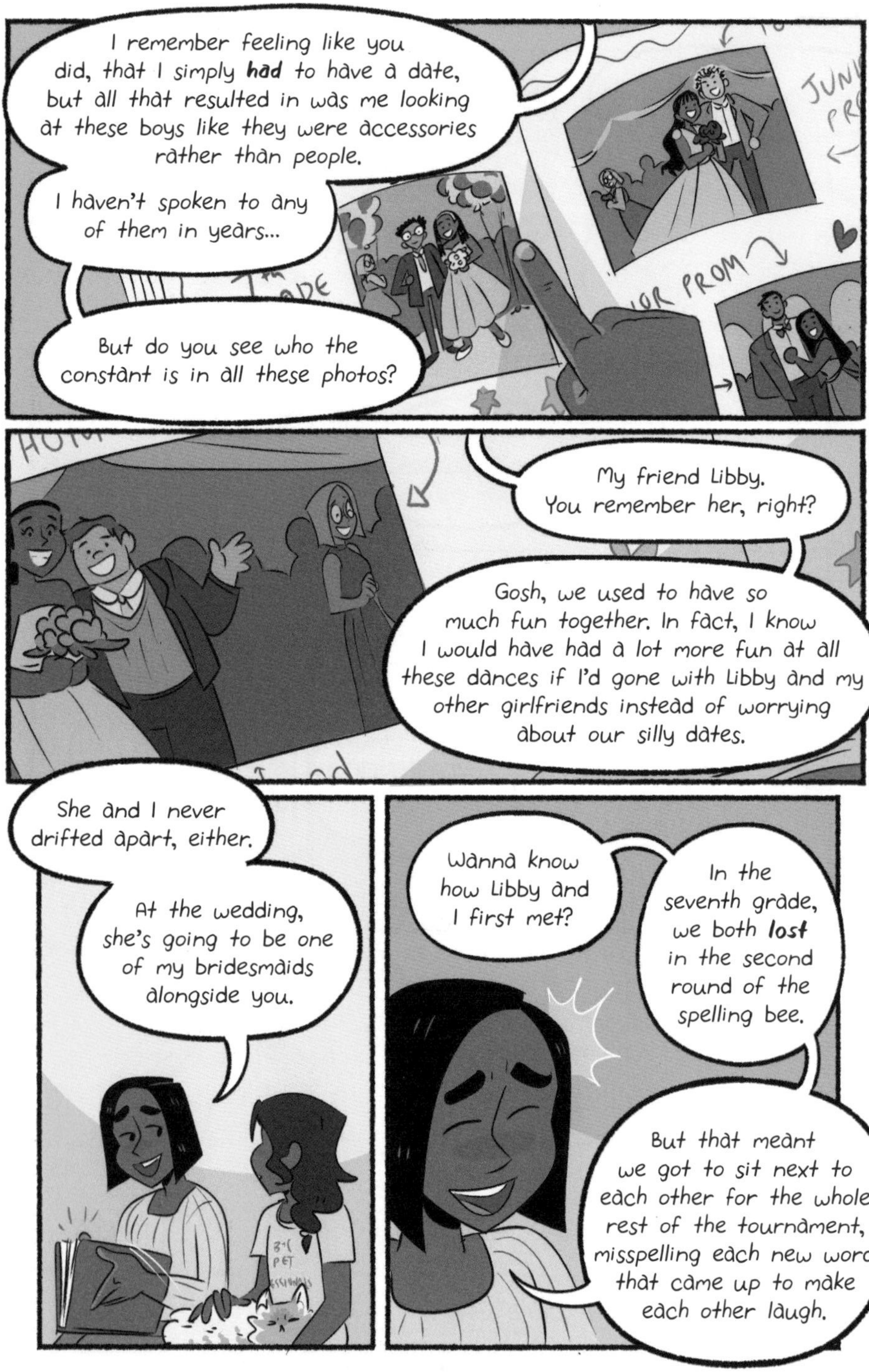
I remember feeling like you did, that I simply **had** to have a date, but all that resulted in was me looking at these boys like they were accessories rather than people.
I haven't spoken to any of them in years...
But do you see who the constant is in all these photos?
OR PROM
My friend Libby. You remember her, right?
Gosh, we used to have so much fun together. In fact, I know I would have had a lot more fun at all these dances if I'd gone with Libby and my other girlfriends instead of worrying about our silly dates.
She and I never drifted apart, either.
At the wedding, she's going to be one of my bridesmaids alongside you.
Wanna know how Libby and I first met?
In the seventh grade, we both **lost** in the second round of the spelling bee.
But that meant we got to sit next to each other for the whole rest of the tournament, misspelling each new word that came up to make each other laugh.

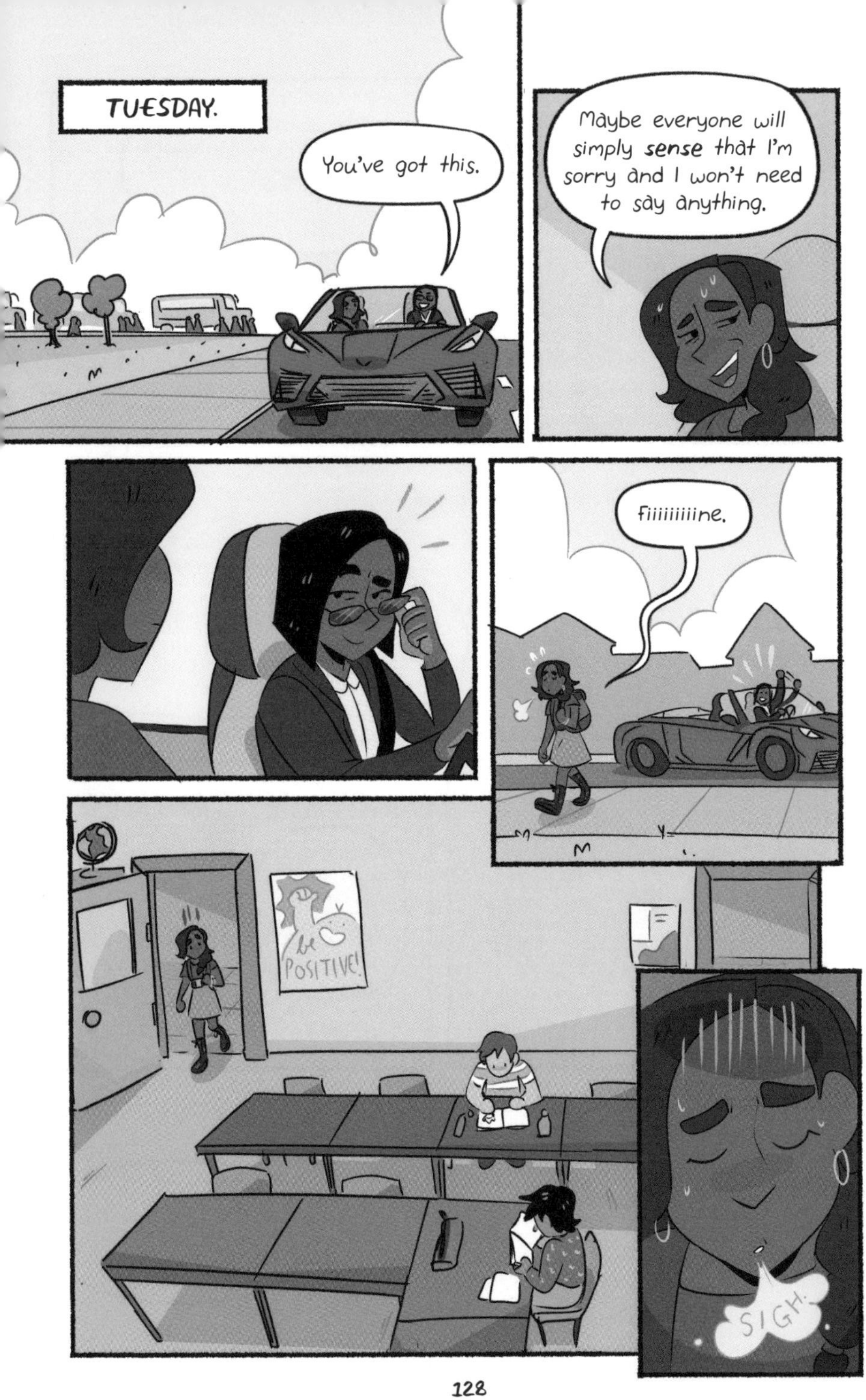
TUESDAY.
You've got this.
Maybe everyone will simply sense that I'm sorry and I won't need to say anything.
Fiiiiiiiiiine.
be POSITIVE!
SIGH.

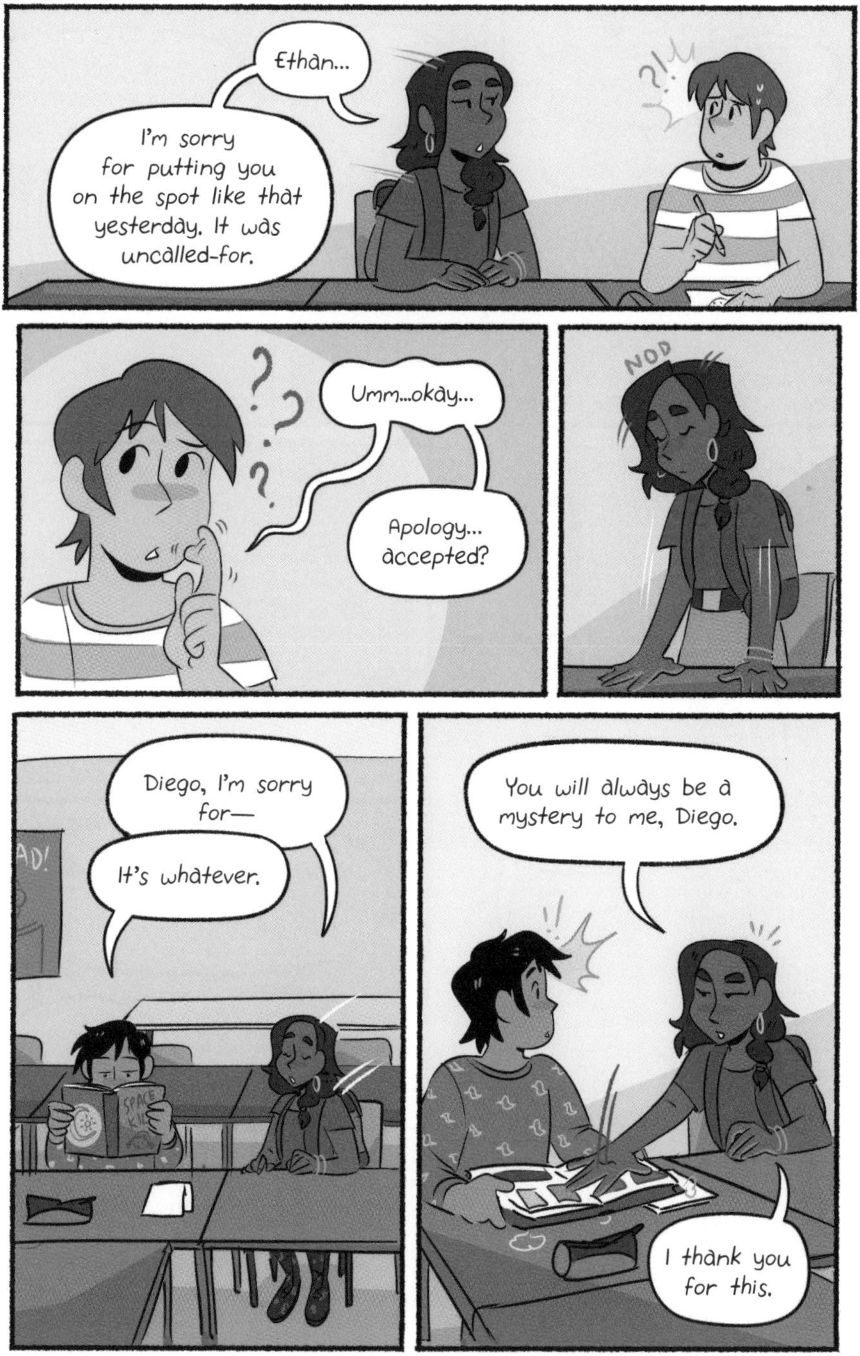
Ethan...
I'm sorry for putting you on the spot like that yesterday. It was uncalled-for.
?!
Umm...okay...
Apology... accepted?
NOD
Diego, I'm sorry for—
It's whatever.
SPACE KI
You will always be a mystery to me, Diego.
I thank you for this.

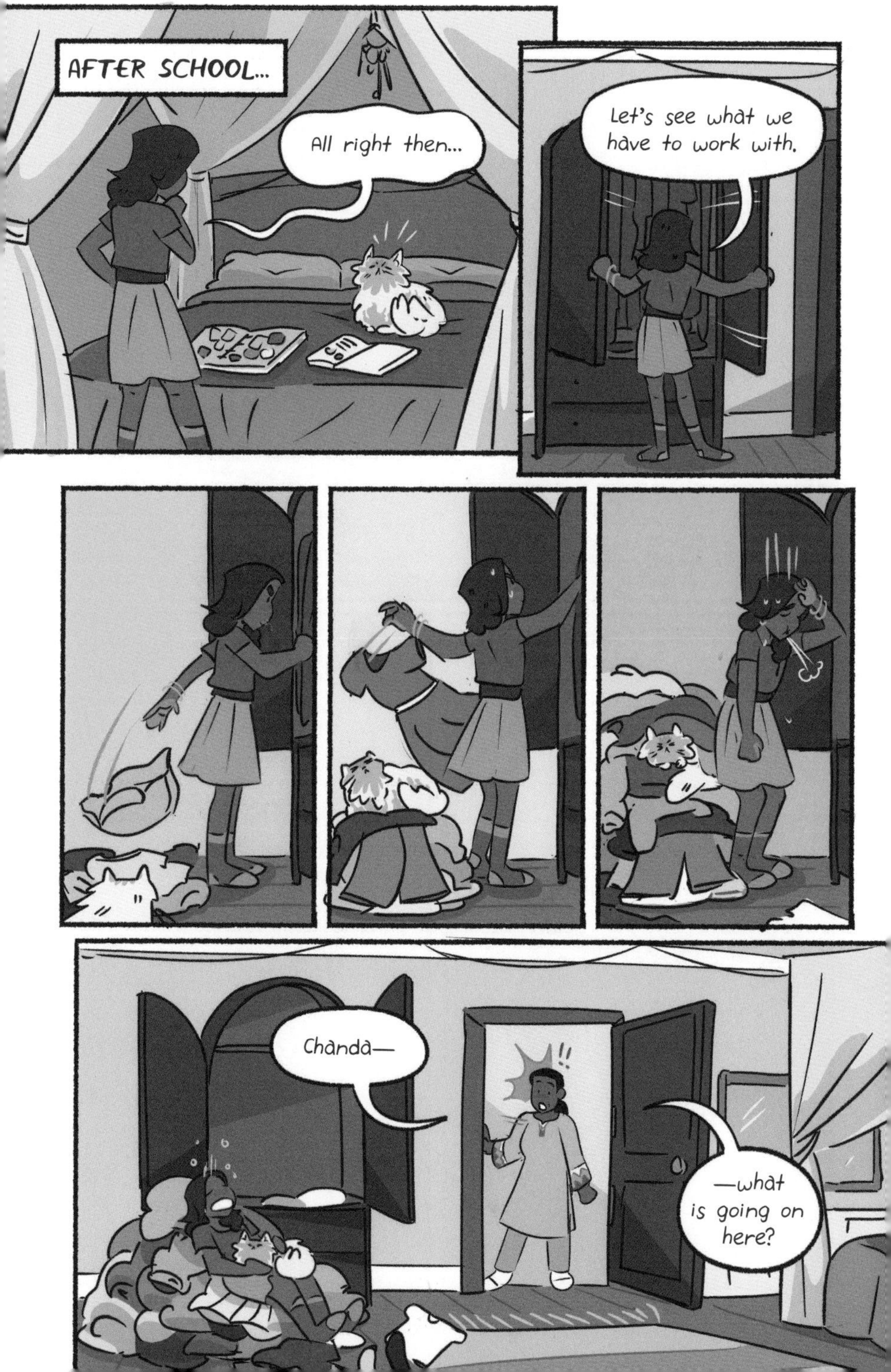
AFTER SCHOOL...
All right then...
Let's see what we have to work with.
Chanda—
—what is going on here?

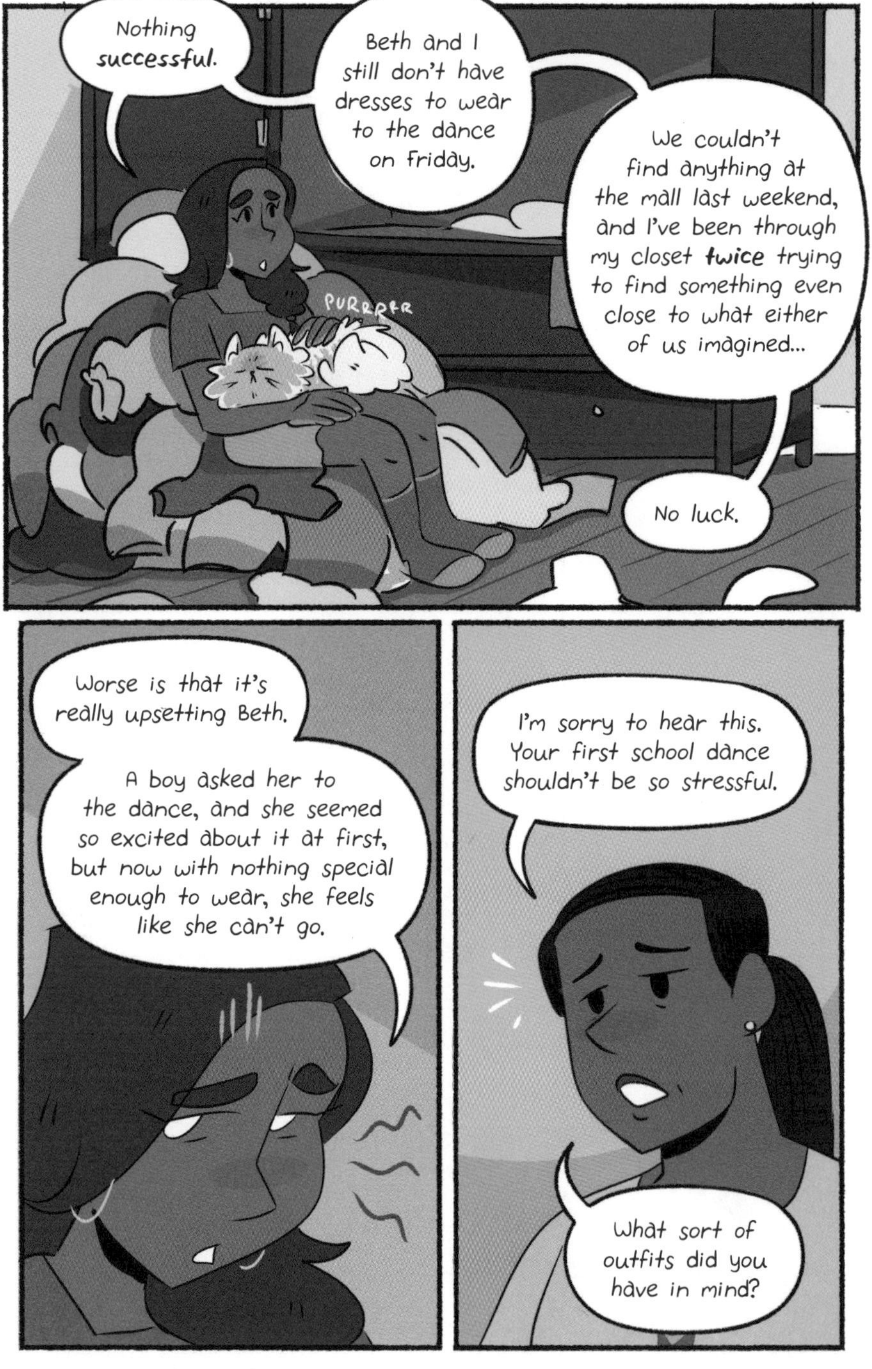
Nothing **successful.**
Beth and I still don't have dresses to wear to the dance on Friday.
We couldn't find anything at the mall last weekend, and I've been through my closet **twice** trying to find something even close to what either of us imagined...
No luck.
PURRRRR
Worse is that it's really upsetting Beth.
A boy asked her to the dance, and she seemed so excited about it at first, but now with nothing special enough to wear, she feels like she can't go.
I'm sorry to hear this. Your first school dance shouldn't be so stressful.
What sort of outfits did you have in mind?

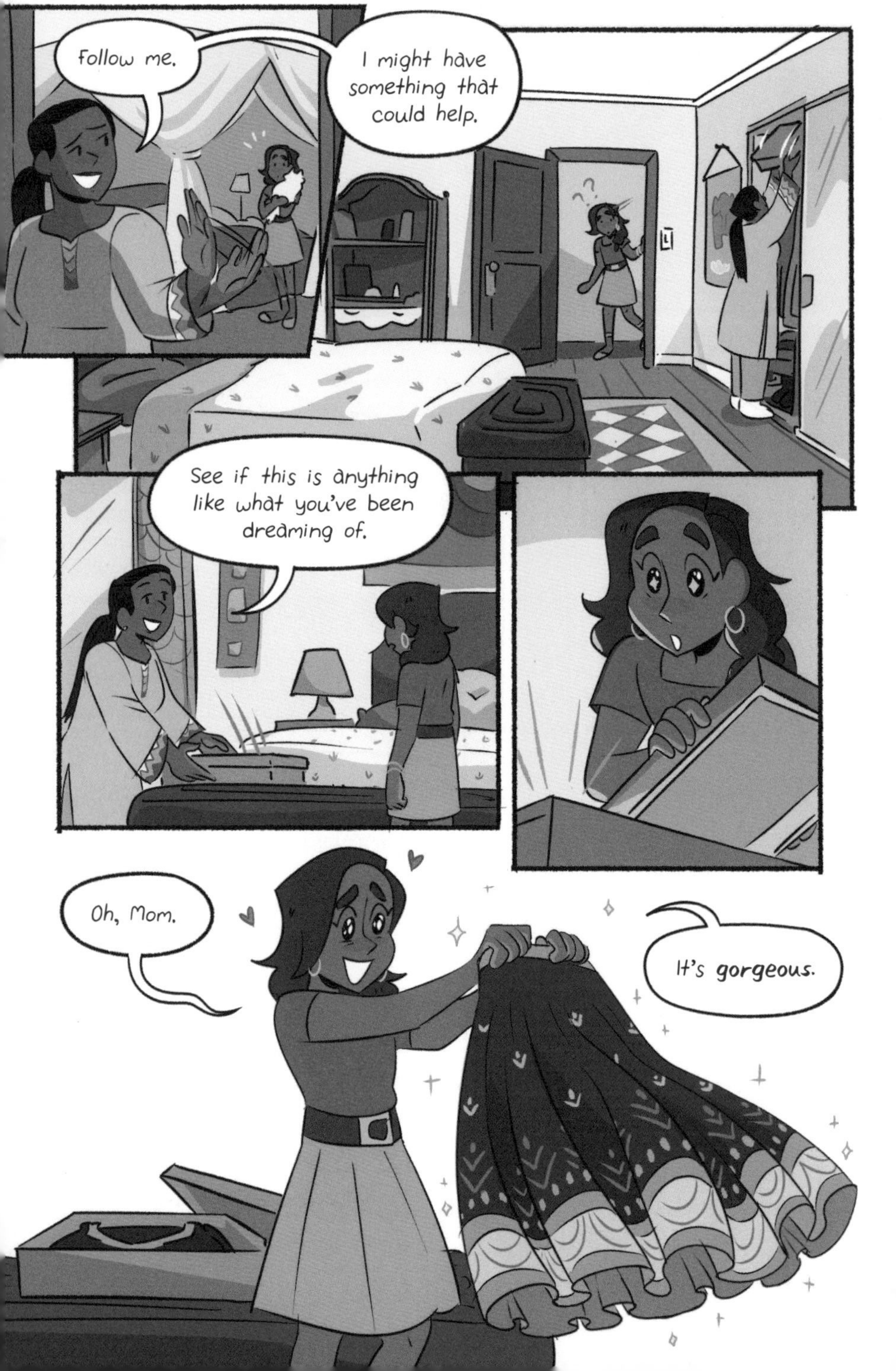
Follow me.
I might have something that could help.
See if this is anything like what you've been dreaming of.
Oh, Mom.
It's **gorgeous**.

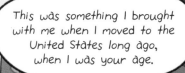

This was something I brought with me when I moved to the United States long ago, when I was your age.

I always loved its color and patterning, but outside of some family weddings, I didn't have many opportunities to wear it.

Everyone I knew, even all the Desi kids, dressed like the teenagers they saw in American movies and TV shows, so it would never have crossed my mind to wear something like this to a school dance.

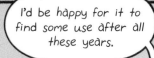

I'd be happy for it to find some use after all these years.

And I'd be proud to see you display your heritage.

You mean... I can wear it to the dance??

Well, you **should** probably try it on first.

139

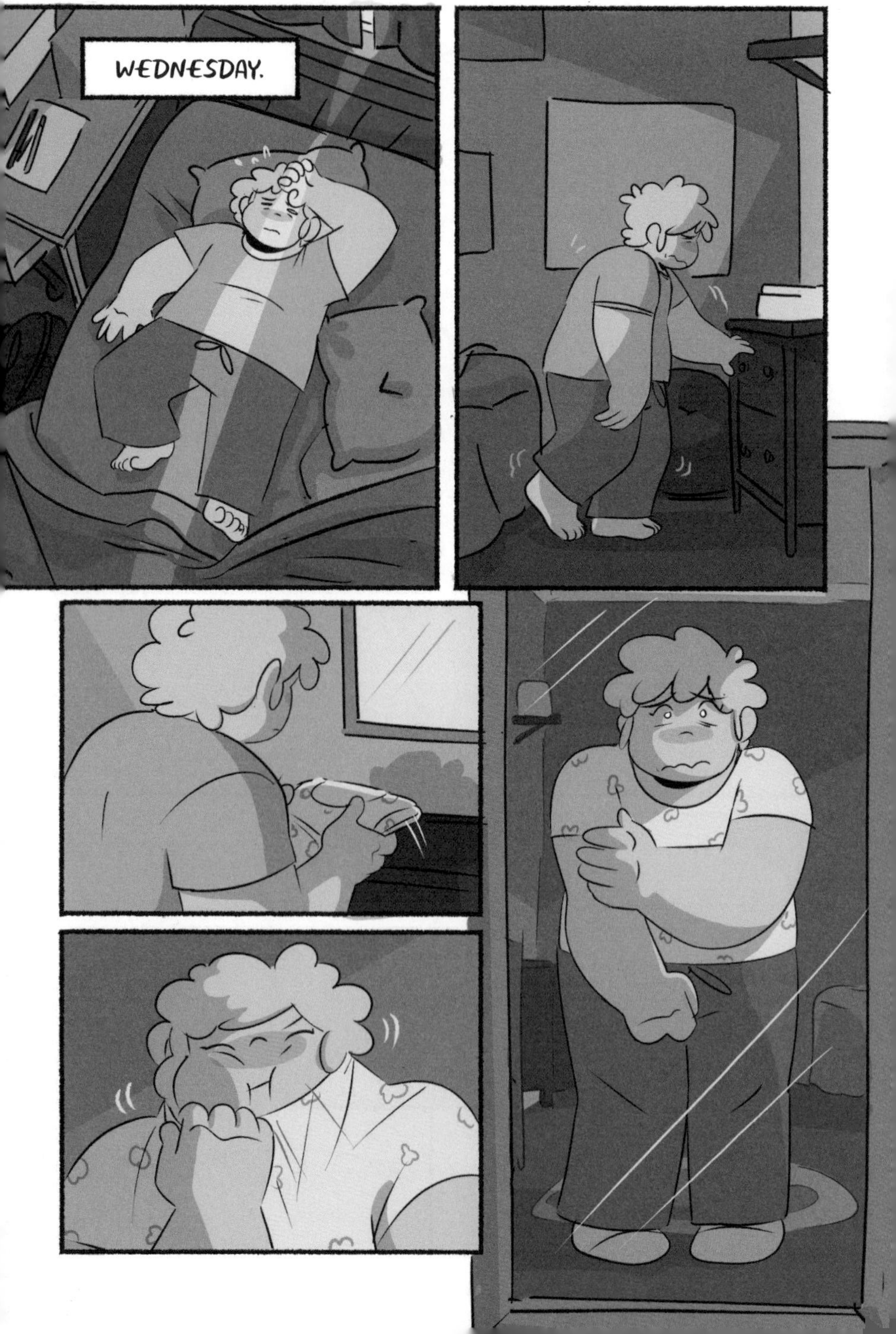
WEDNESDAY.

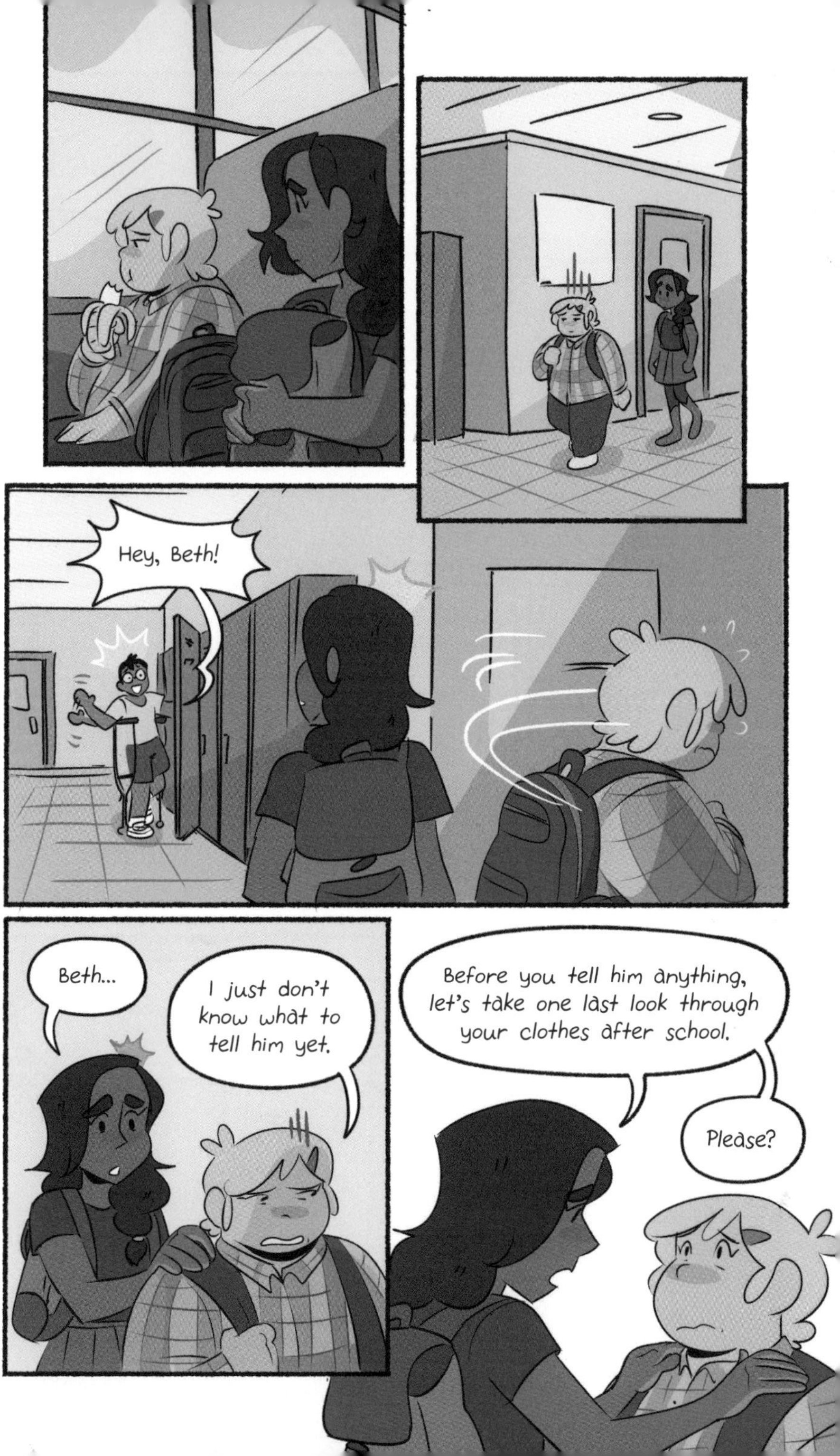

Hey, Beth!
Beth...
I just don't know what to tell him yet.
Before you tell him anything, let's take one last look through your clothes after school.
Please?

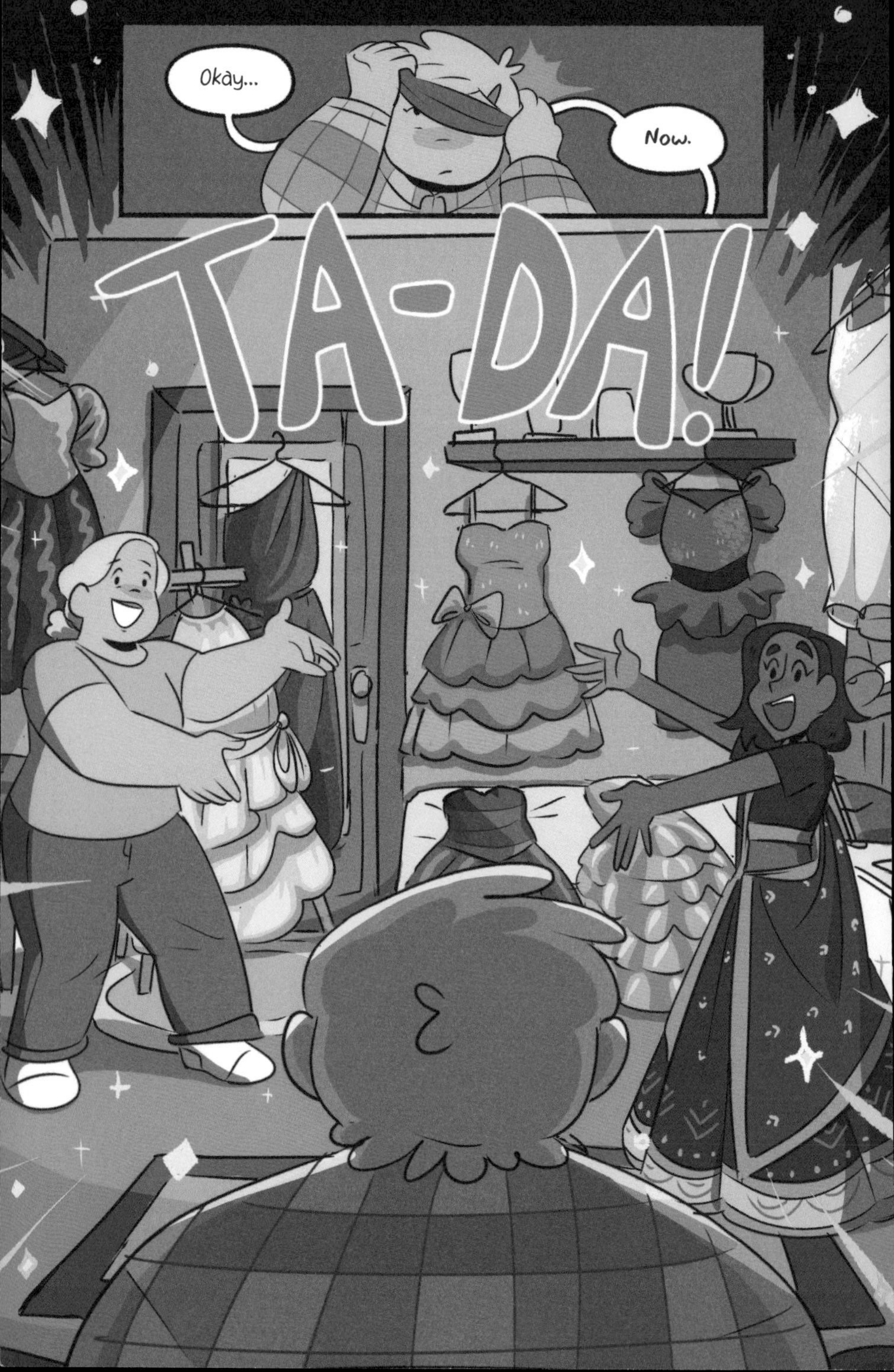
Okay...
Now.
TA-DA!

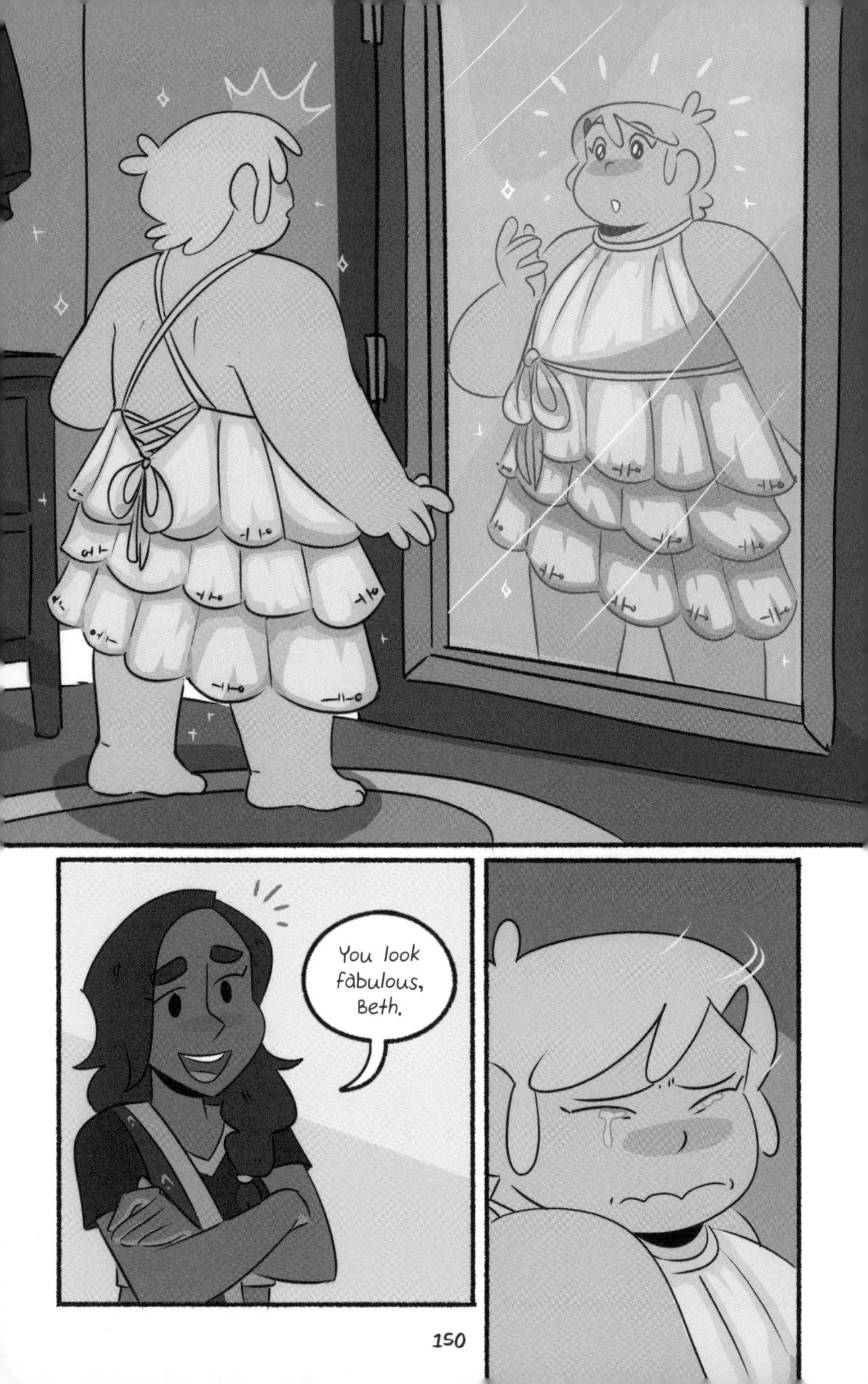
You look fabulous, Beth.

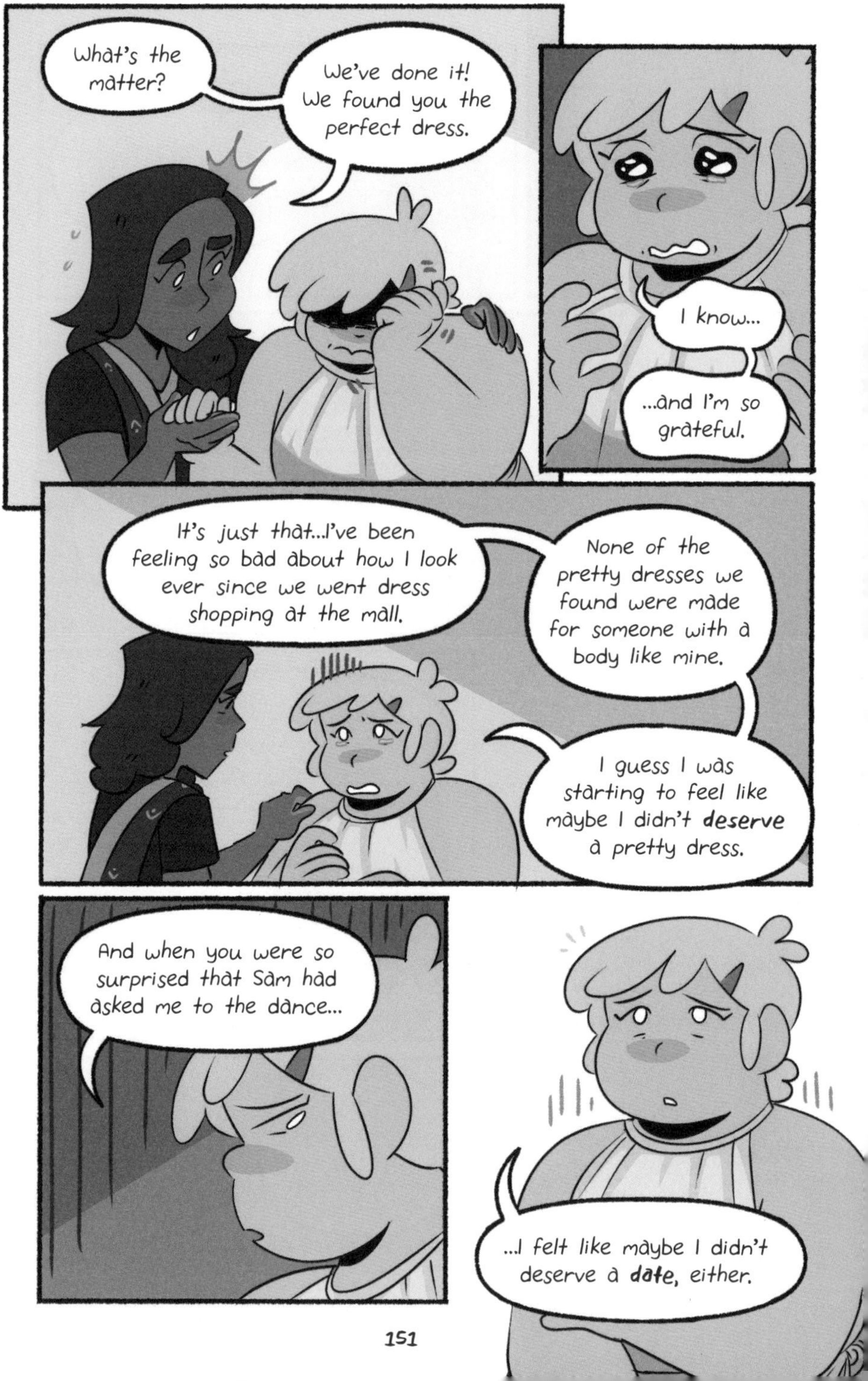
What's the matter?
We've done it! We found you the perfect dress.
I know...
...and I'm so grateful.
It's just that...I've been feeling so bad about how I look ever since we went dress shopping at the mall.
None of the pretty dresses we found were made for someone with a body like mine.
I guess I was starting to feel like maybe I didn't **deserve** a pretty dress.
And when you were so surprised that Sam had asked me to the dance...
...I felt like maybe I didn't deserve a **date,** either.

I'm so sorry I made you feel that way, Beth.

Me being surprised about you and Sam had nothing to do with you and everything to do with me being afraid I was doing something wrong.

Which I **totally was**, though I guess in more ways than I thought.

Of course you deserve a date.

You deserve everything.

And most of all you deserve to see yourself the way that **I** see you.

You deserve to have an amazing night at the dance and to feel good about yourself.

The way that everyone we know sees you...

As the strong, kind, and beautiful Beth we love.

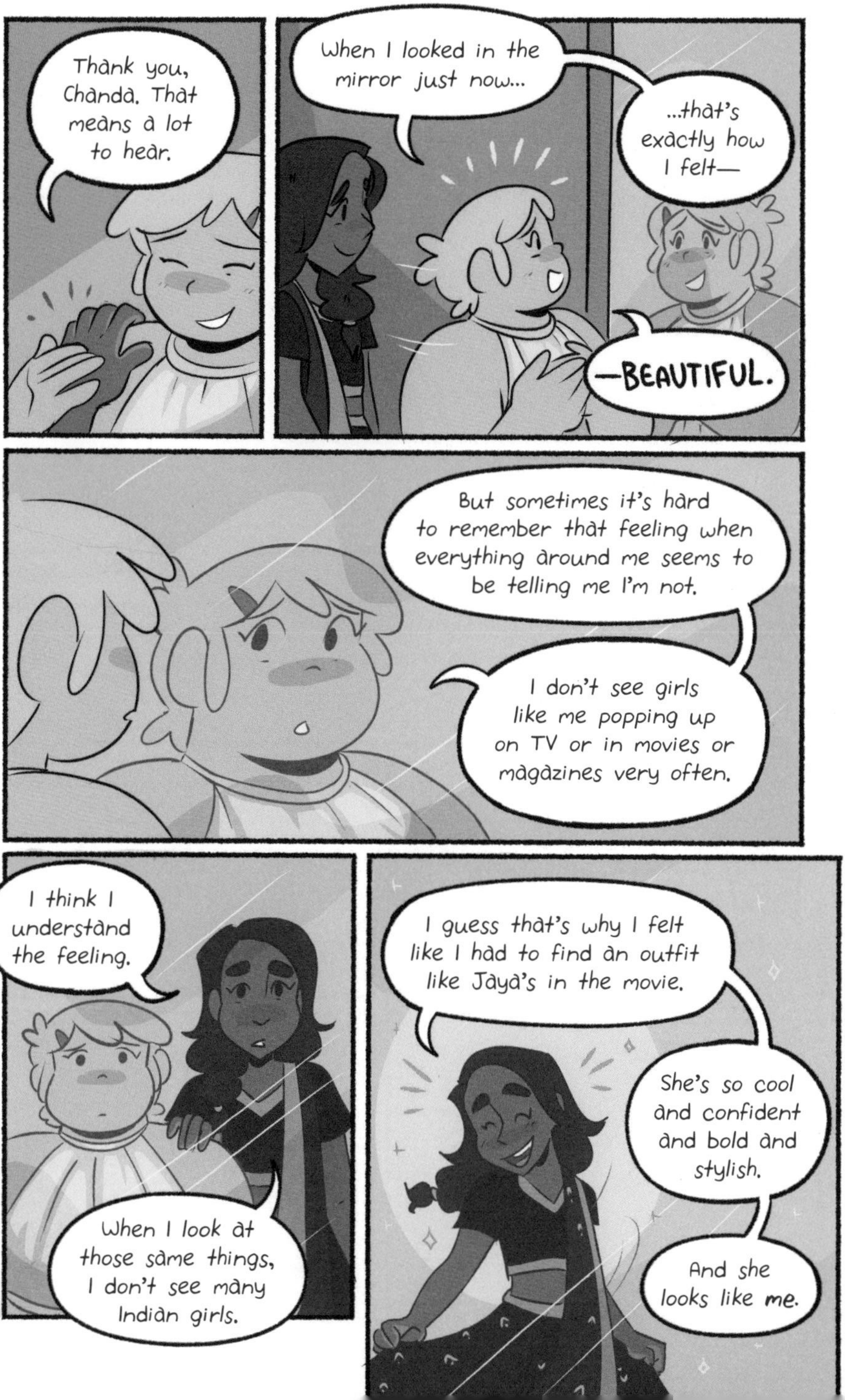
Thank you, Chanda. That means a lot to hear.
When I looked in the mirror just now...
...that's exactly how I felt—
—BEAUTIFUL.
But sometimes it's hard to remember that feeling when everything around me seems to be telling me I'm not.
I don't see girls like me popping up on TV or in movies or magazines very often.
I think I understand the feeling.
When I look at those same things, I don't see many Indian girls.
I guess that's why I felt like I had to find an outfit like Jaya's in the movie.
She's so cool and confident and bold and stylish.
And she looks like me.

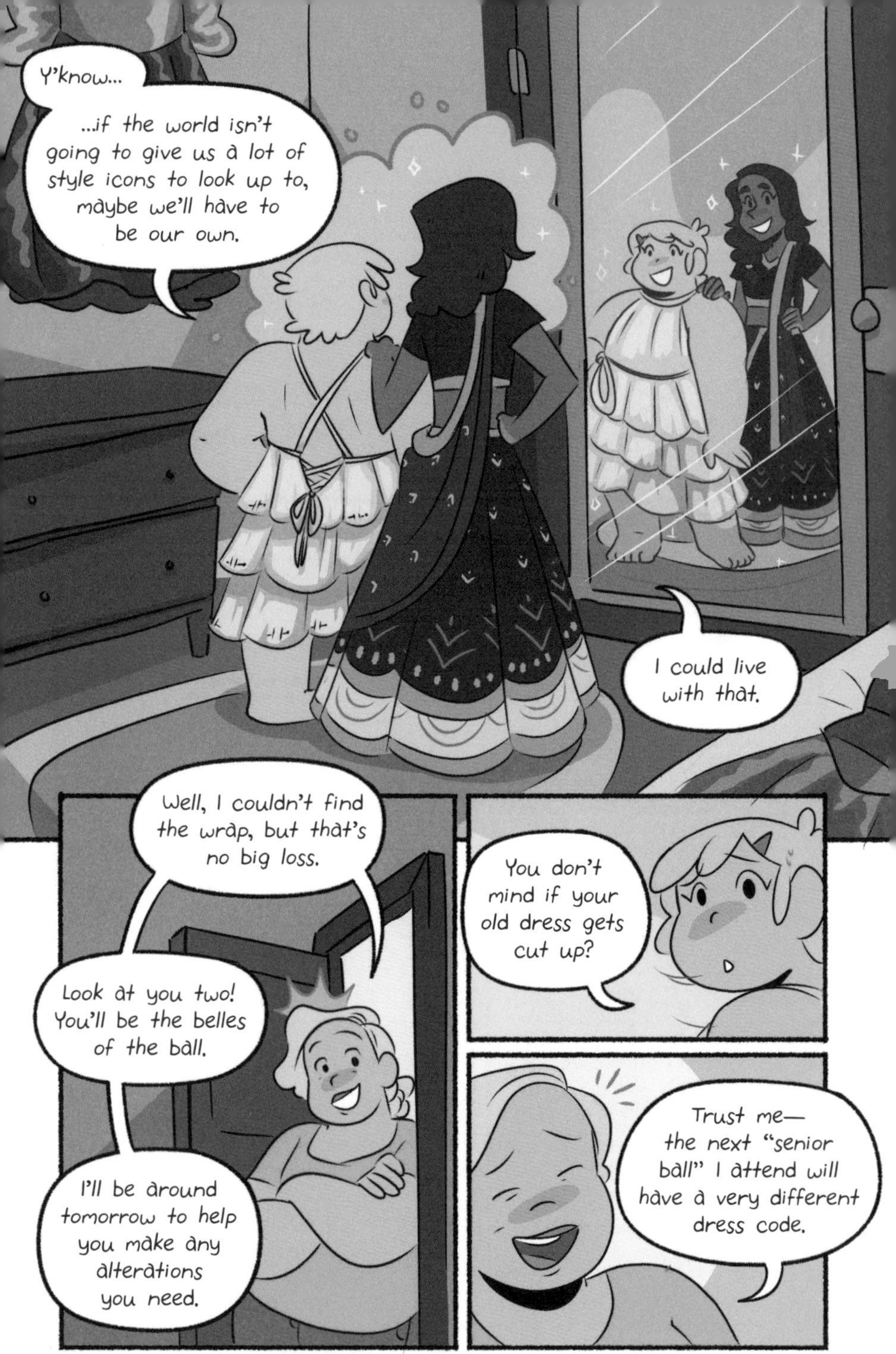
Y'know...
...if the world isn't going to give us a lot of style icons to look up to, maybe we'll have to be our own.
I could live with that.
Well, I couldn't find the wrap, but that's no big loss.
Look at you two! You'll be the belles of the ball.
I'll be around tomorrow to help you make any alterations you need.
You don't mind if your old dress gets cut up?
Trust me—the next "senior ball" I attend will have a very different dress code.

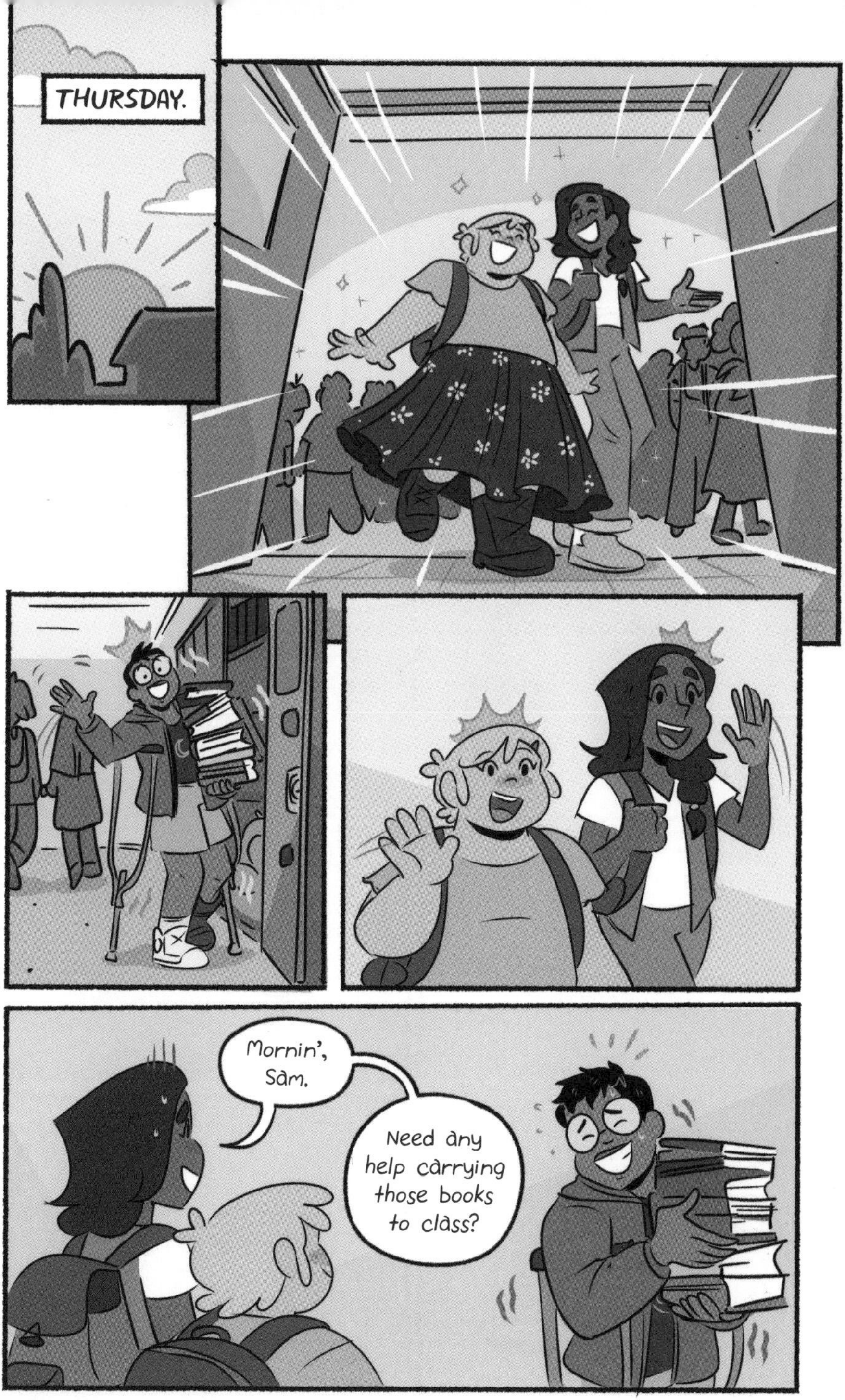
THURSDAY.
Mornin', Sam.
Need any help carrying those books to class?

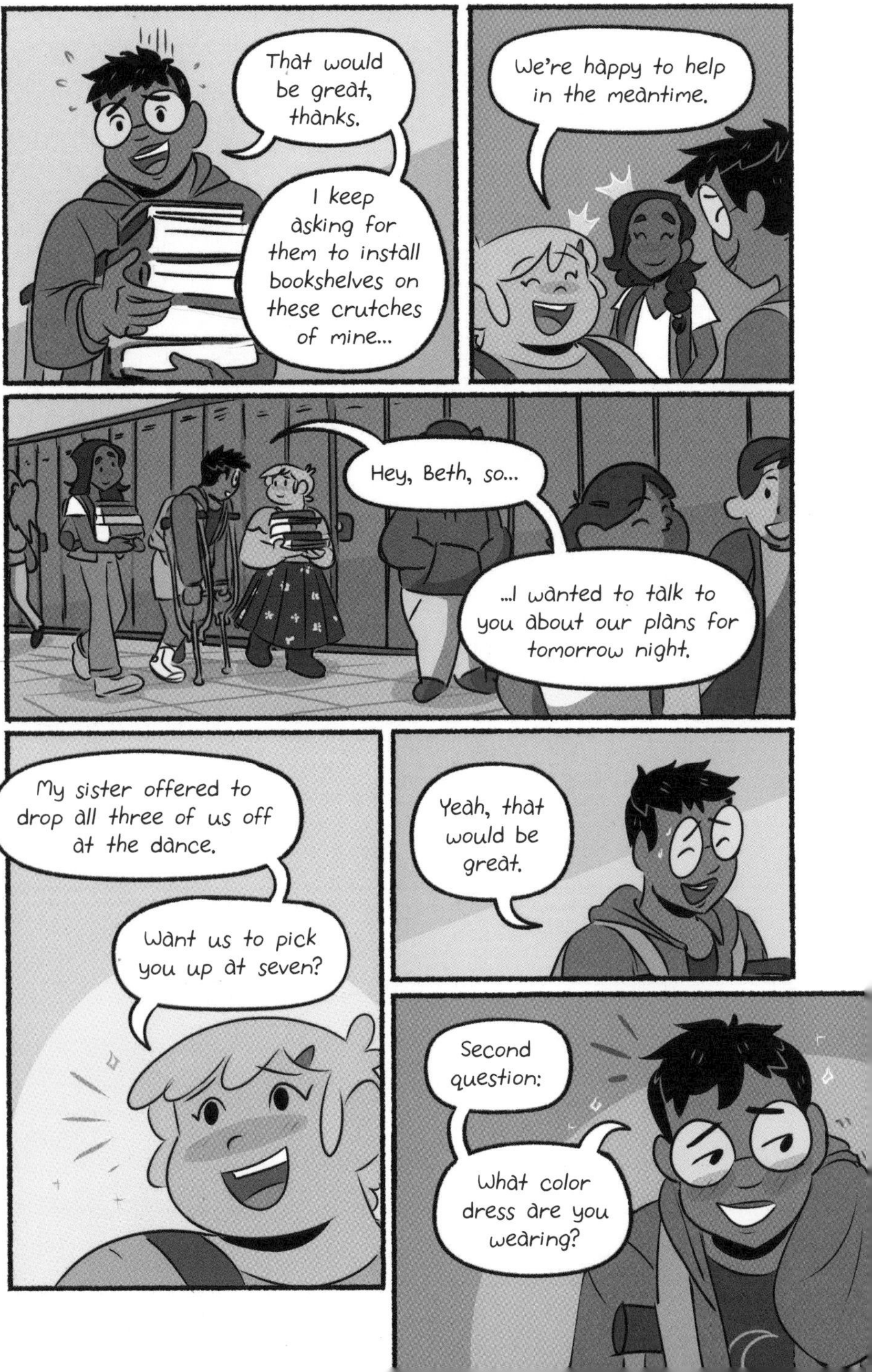
That would be great, thanks.
I keep asking for them to install bookshelves on these crutches of mine...
We're happy to help in the meantime.
Hey, Beth, so...
...I wanted to talk to you about our plans for tomorrow night.
My sister offered to drop all three of us off at the dance.
Want us to pick you up at seven?
Yeah, that would be great.
Second question:
What color dress are you wearing?

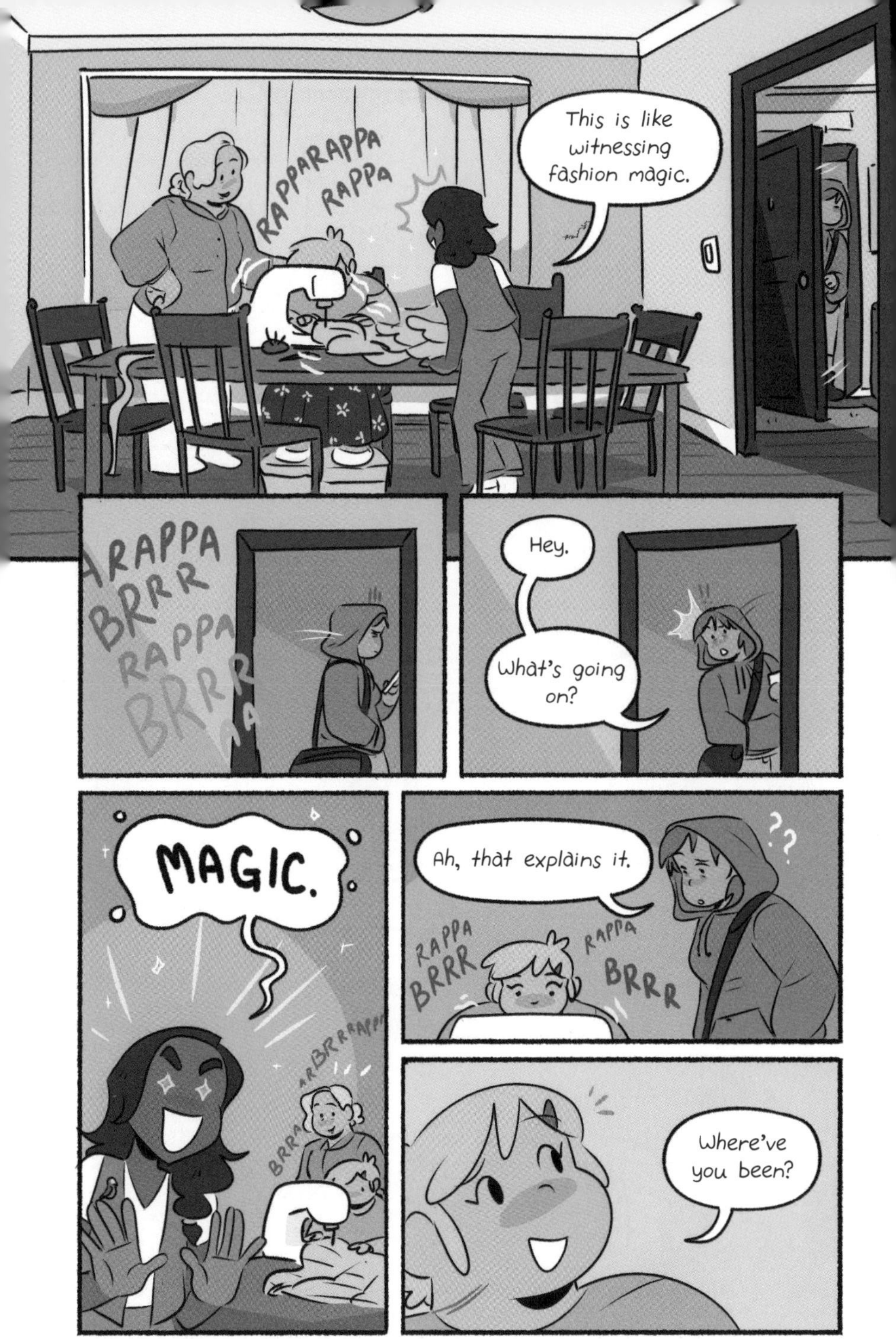
RAPPARAPPA RAPPA
This is like witnessing fashion magic.
ARAPPA BRRR RAPPA BRRR
Hey.
What's going on?
MAGIC.
ARBRRRAPPA
BRRA
Ah, that explains it.
RAPPA BRRR
RAPPA BRRR
Where've you been?

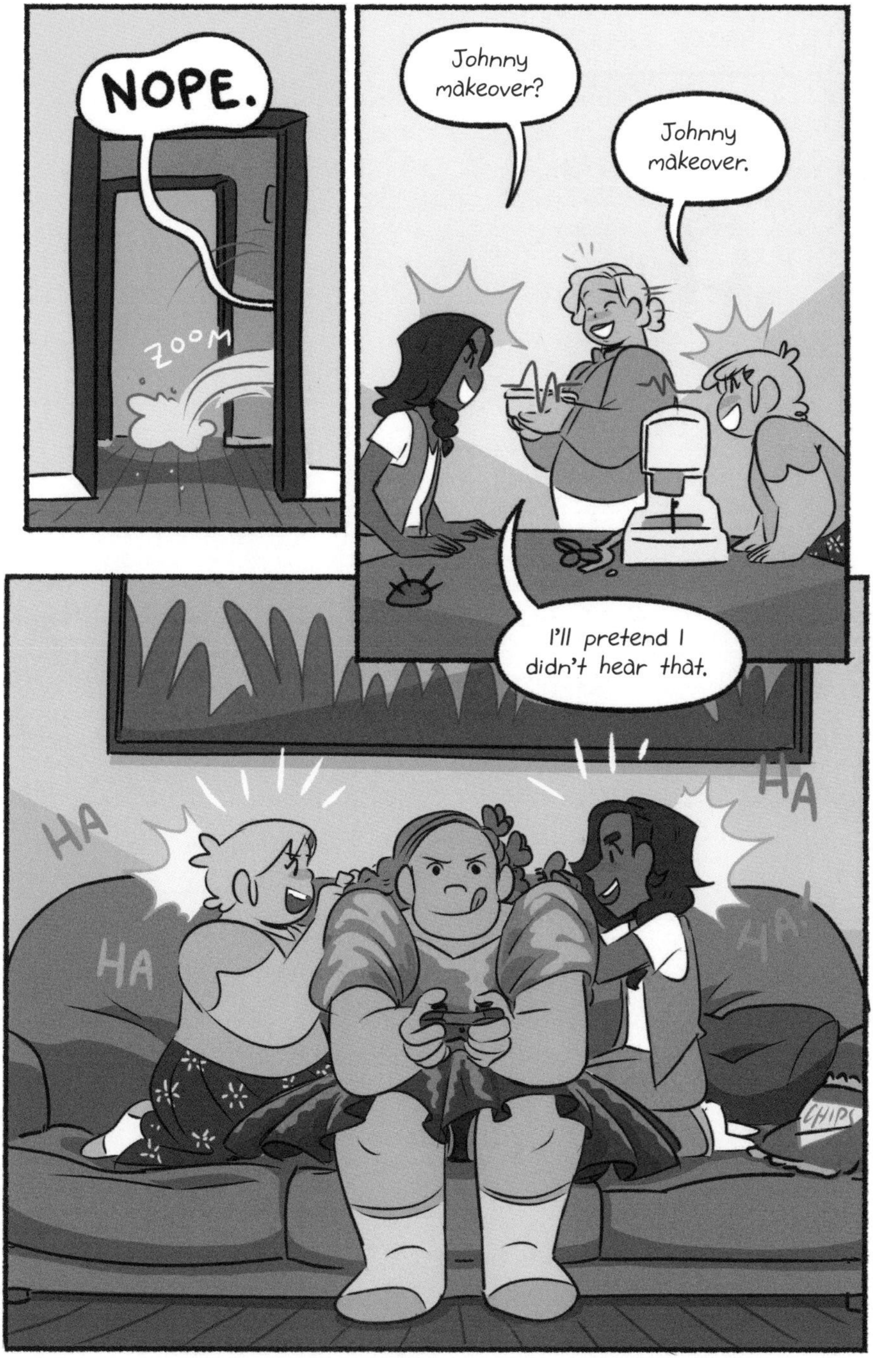
NOPE.
ZOOM
Johnny makeover?
Johnny makeover.
I'll pretend I didn't hear that.
HA
HA
HA
HA!
CHIPS

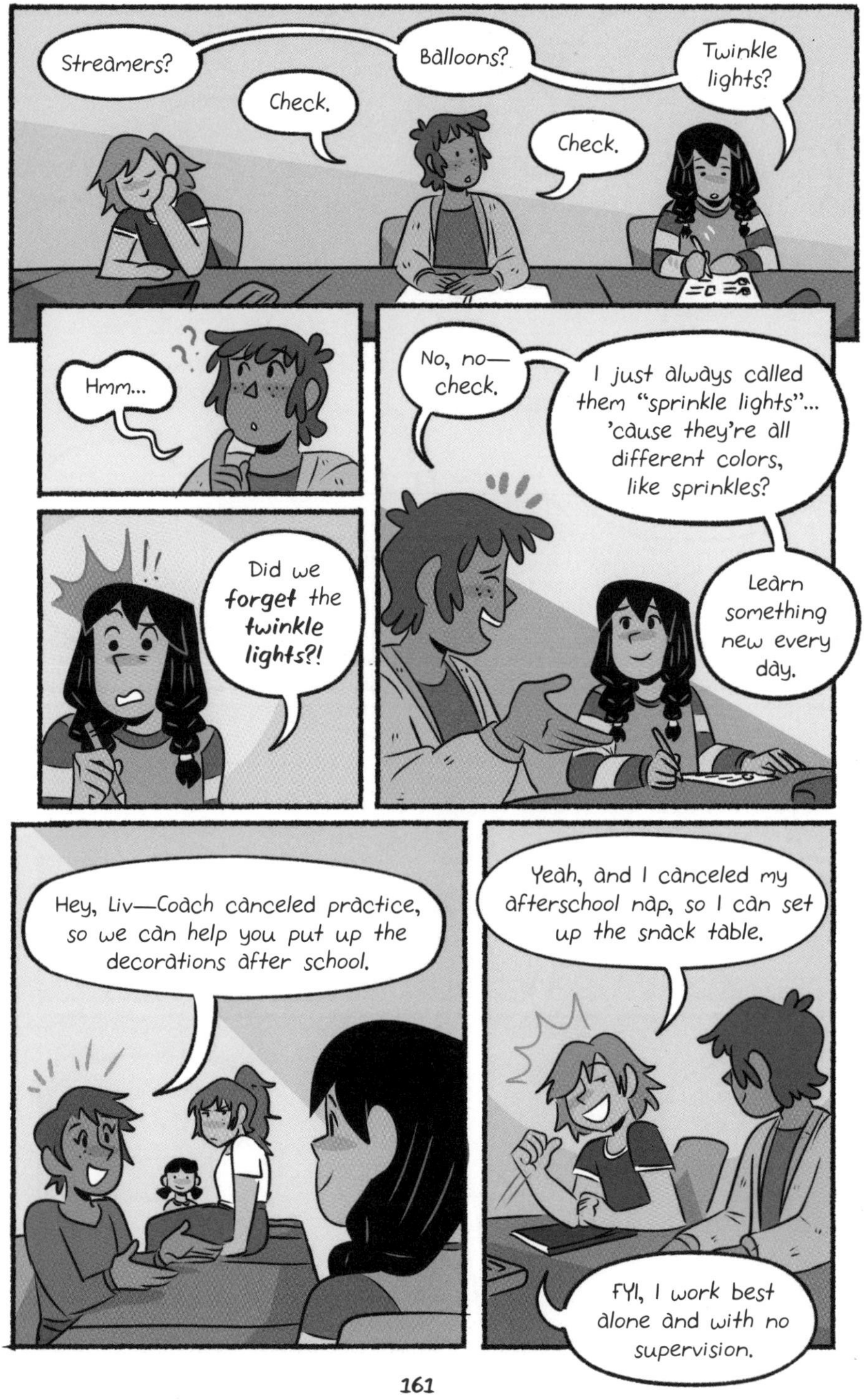

Streamers?
Check.
Balloons?
Check.
Twinkle lights?
Hmm...
No, no—check.
I just always called them "sprinkle lights"... 'cause they're all different colors, like sprinkles?
Did we **forget** the **twinkle lights?!**
Learn something new every day.
Hey, Liv—Coach canceled practice, so we can help you put up the decorations after school.
Yeah, and I canceled my afterschool nap, so I can set up the snack table.
FYI, I work best alone and with no supervision.

162

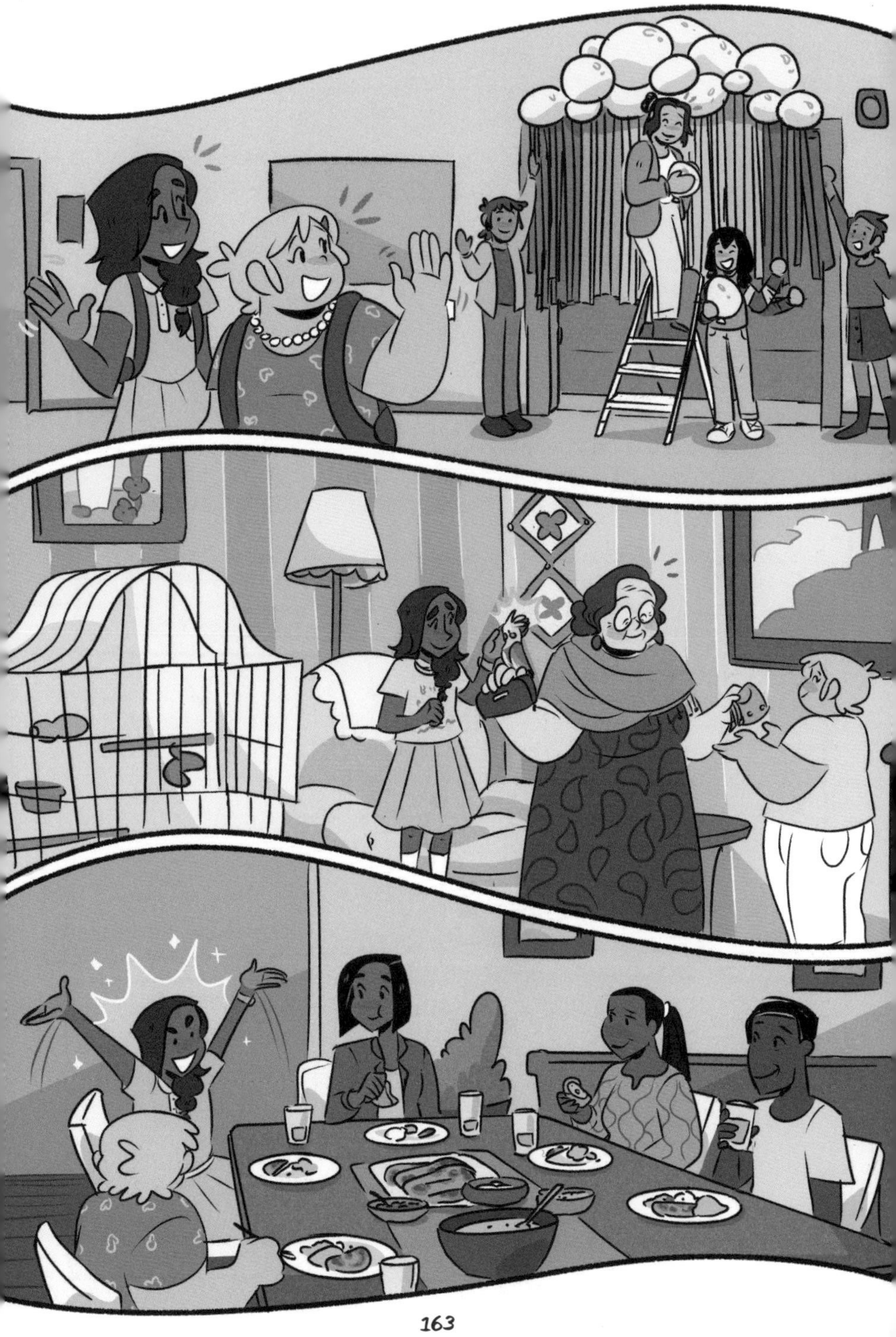

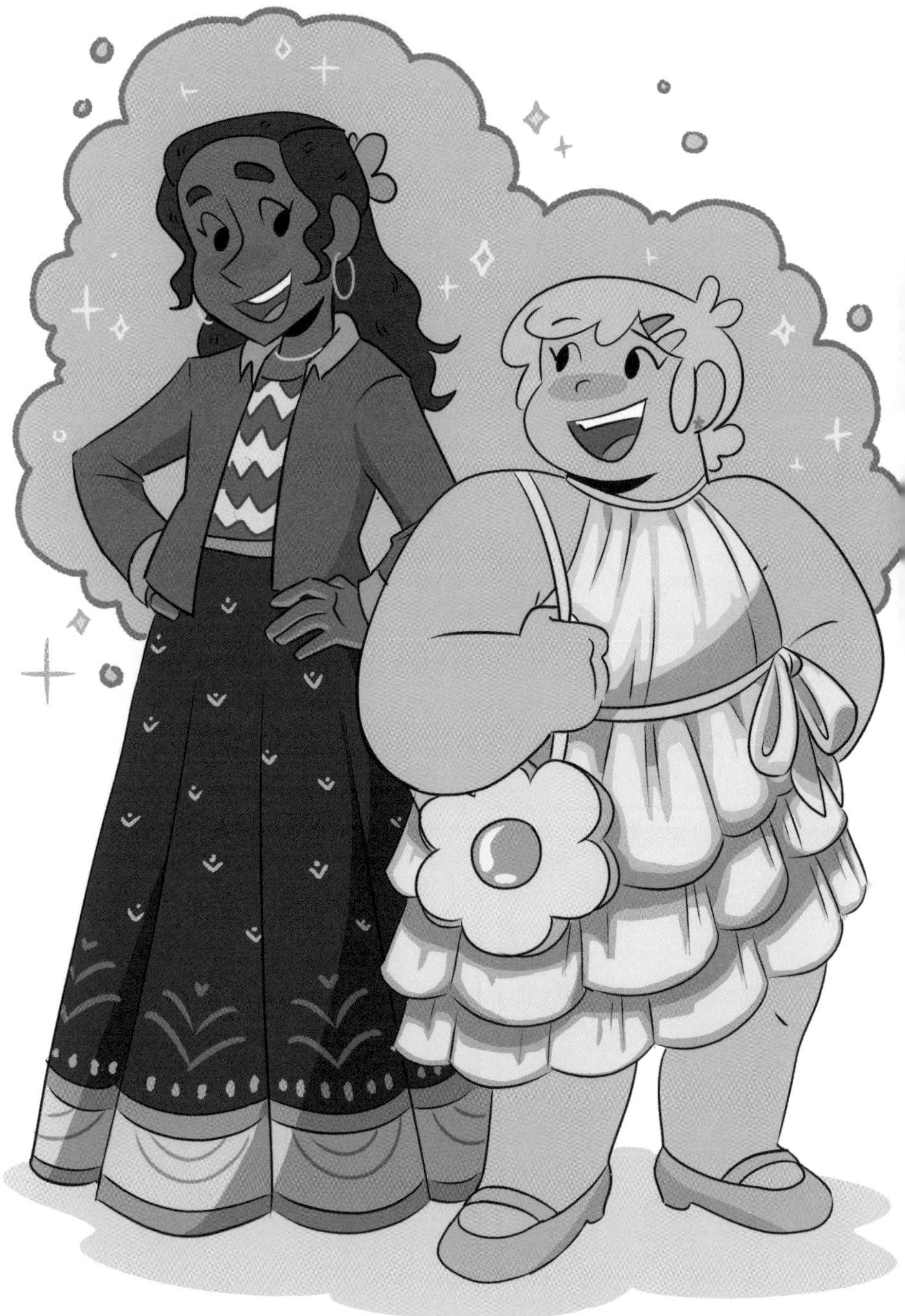

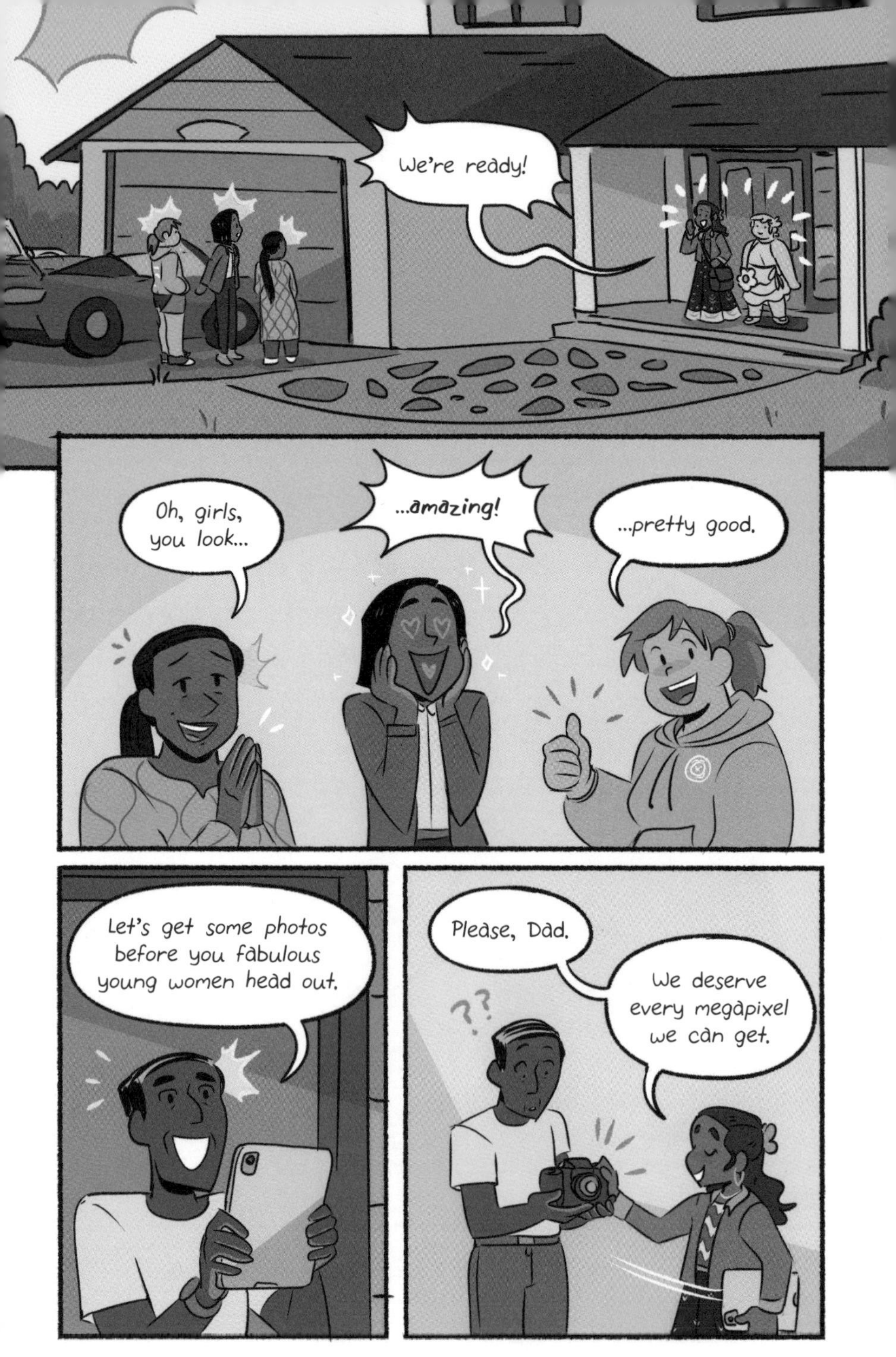
We're ready!
Oh, girls, you look...
...amazing!
...pretty good.
Let's get some photos before you fabulous young women head out.
Please, Dad.
We deserve every megapixel we can get.

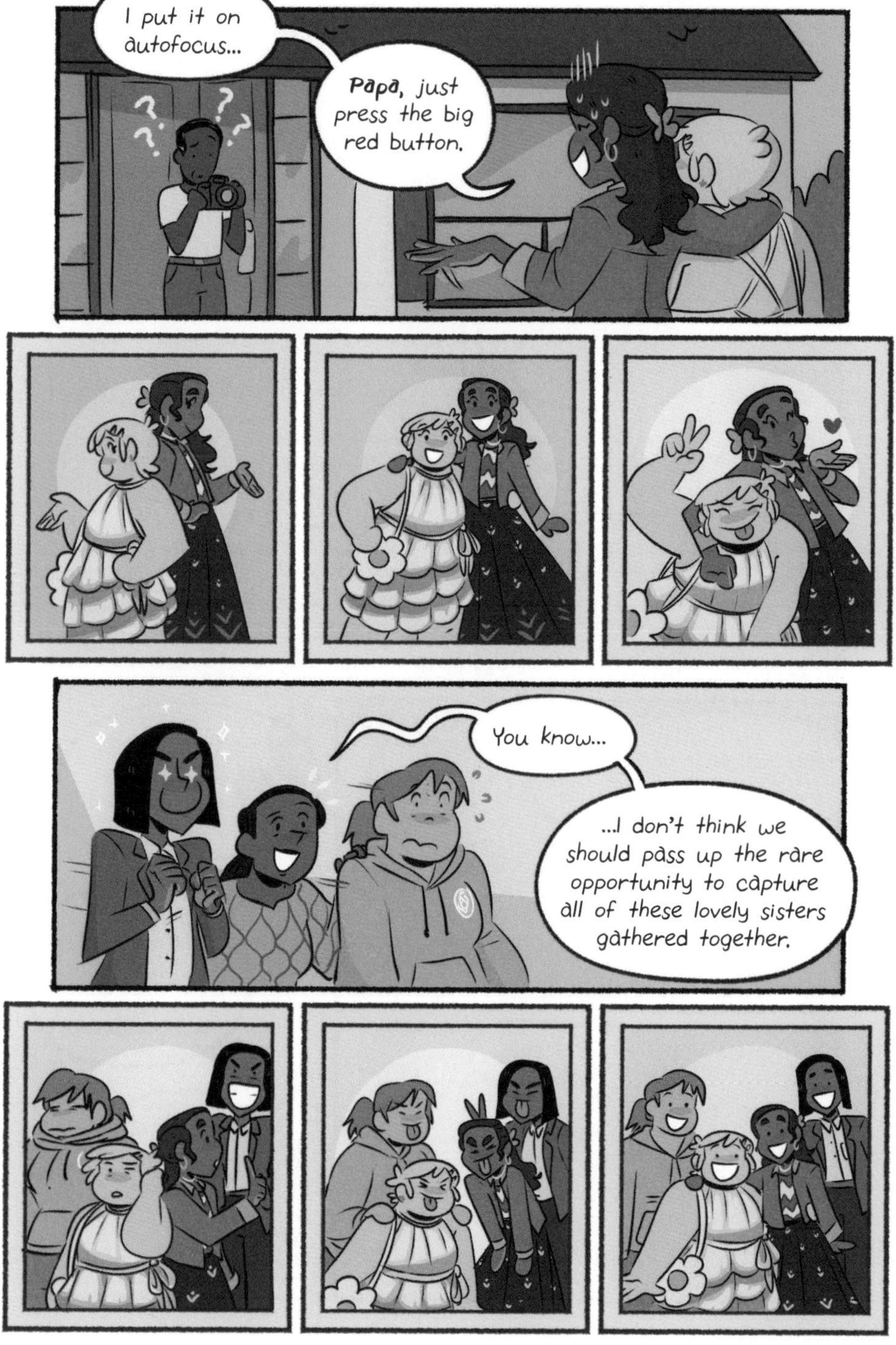
I put it on autofocus...
Papa, just press the big red button.
You know...
...I don't think we should pass up the rare opportunity to capture all of these lovely sisters gathered together.

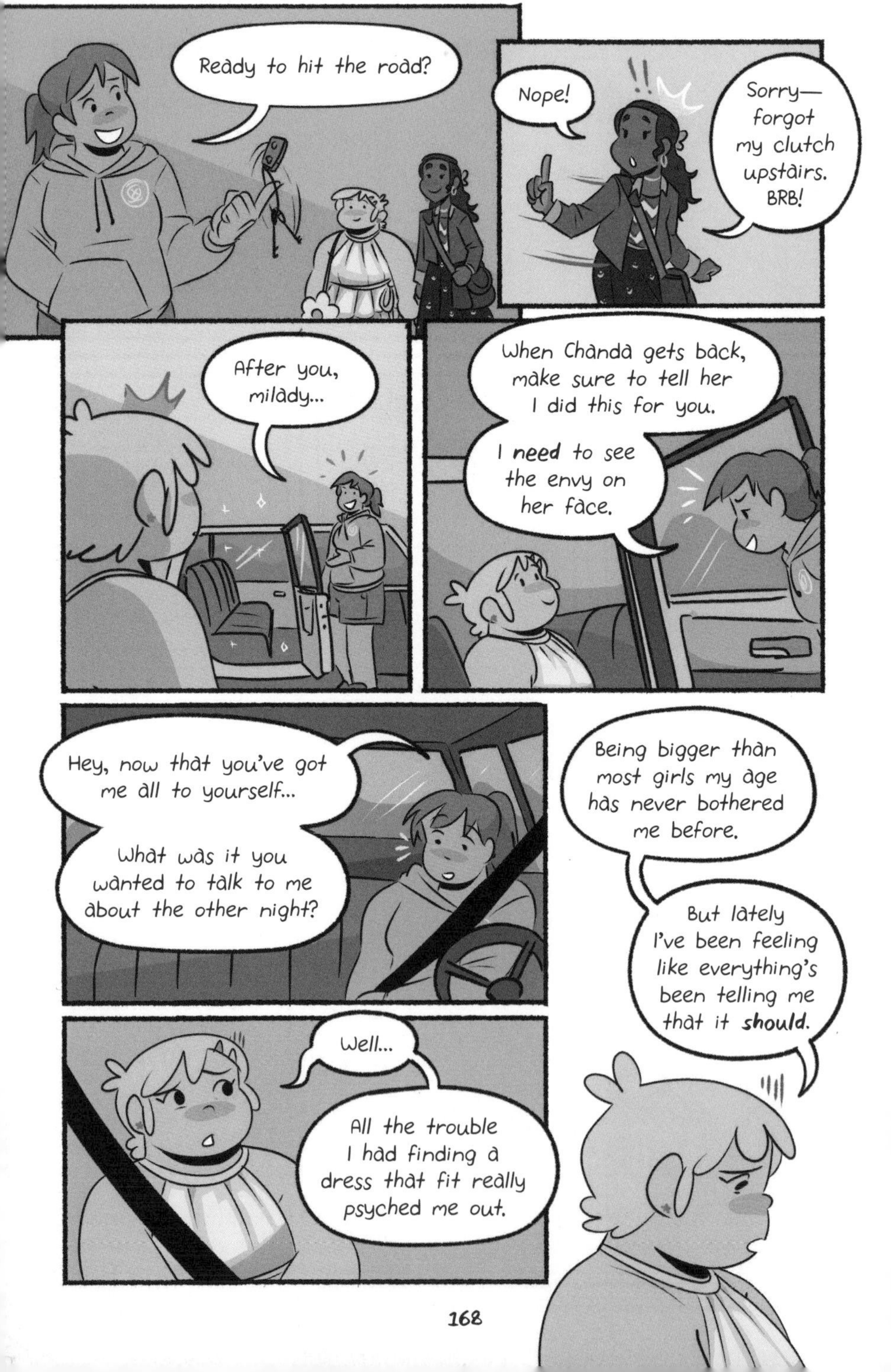
Ready to hit the road?
Nope!
Sorry—forgot my clutch upstairs. BRB!
After you, milady...
When Chanda gets back, make sure to tell her I did this for you.
I **need** to see the envy on her face.
Hey, now that you've got me all to yourself...
What was it you wanted to talk to me about the other night?
Well...
All the trouble I had finding a dress that fit really psyched me out.
Being bigger than most girls my age has never bothered me before.
But lately I've been feeling like everything's been telling me that it ***should***.

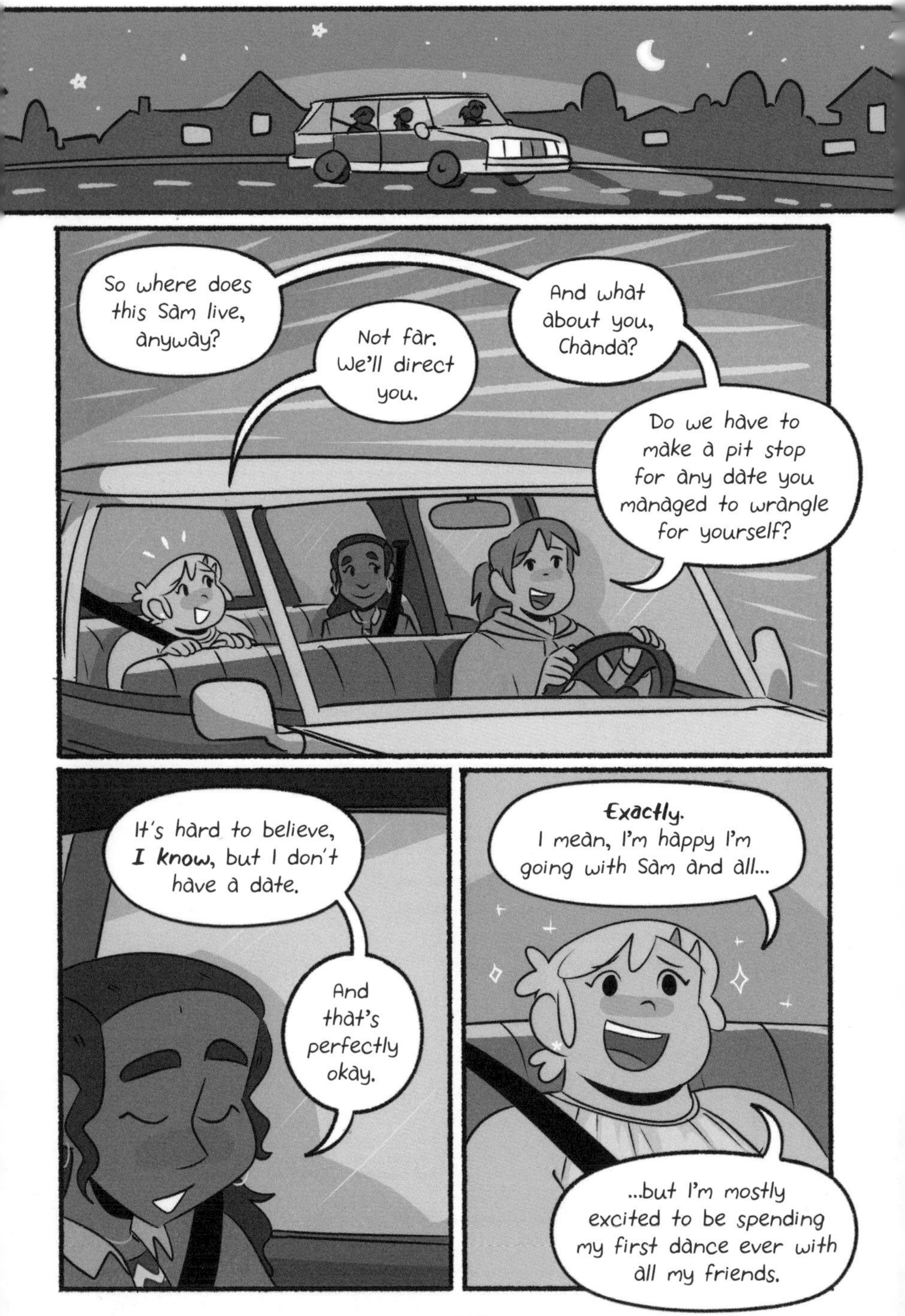
So where does this Sam live, anyway?
Not far. We'll direct you.
And what about you, Chanda?
Do we have to make a pit stop for any date you managed to wrangle for yourself?
It's hard to believe, **I know**, but I don't have a date.
And that's perfectly okay.
Exactly.
I mean, I'm happy I'm going with Sam and all...
...but I'm mostly excited to be spending my first dance ever with all my friends.

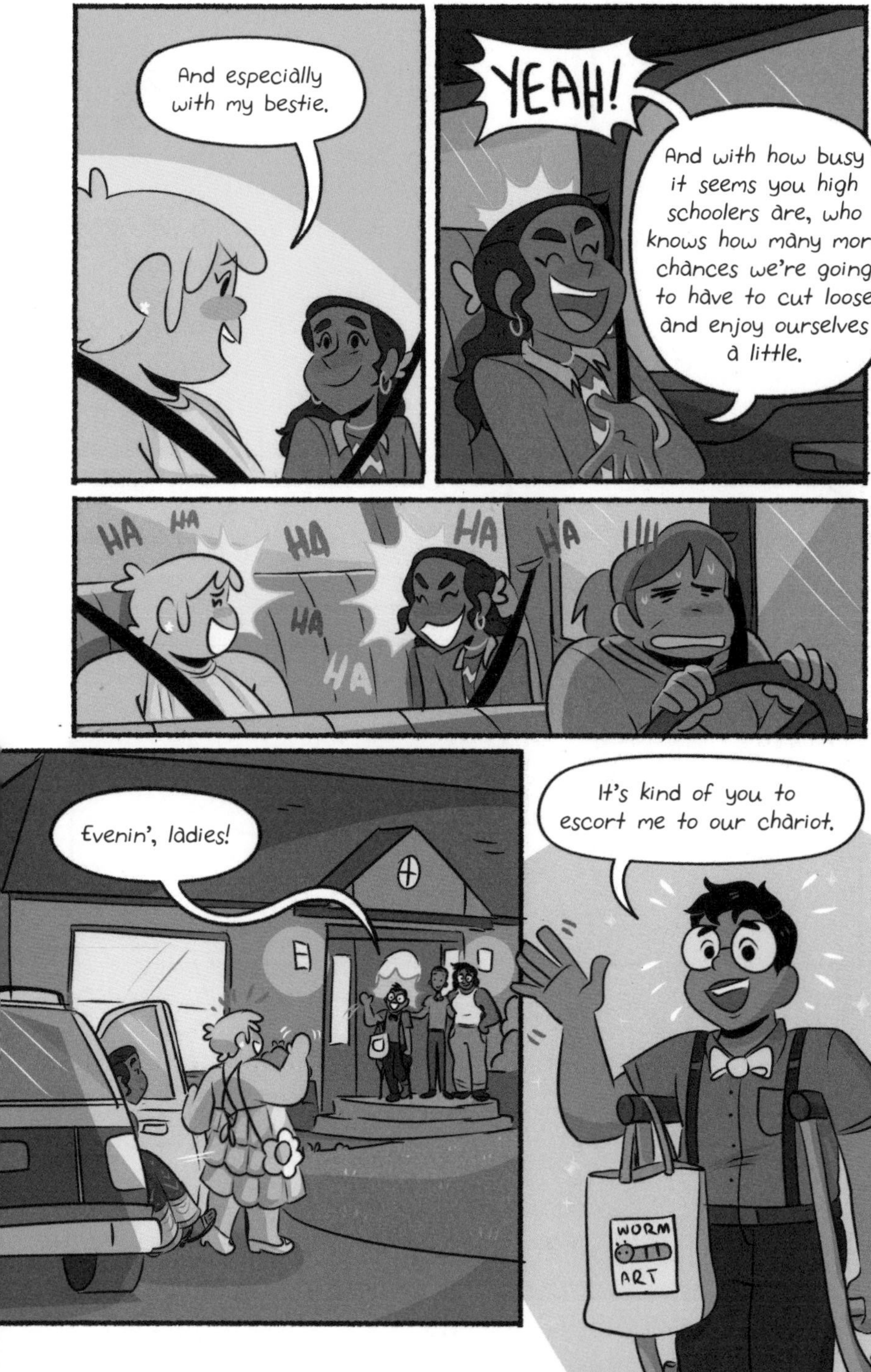
And especially with my bestie.
YEAH!
And with how busy it seems you high schoolers are, who knows how many more chances we're going to have to cut loose and enjoy ourselves a little.
HA HA HA HA HA HA HA HA
Evenin', ladies!
It's kind of you to escort me to our chariot.
WORM ART

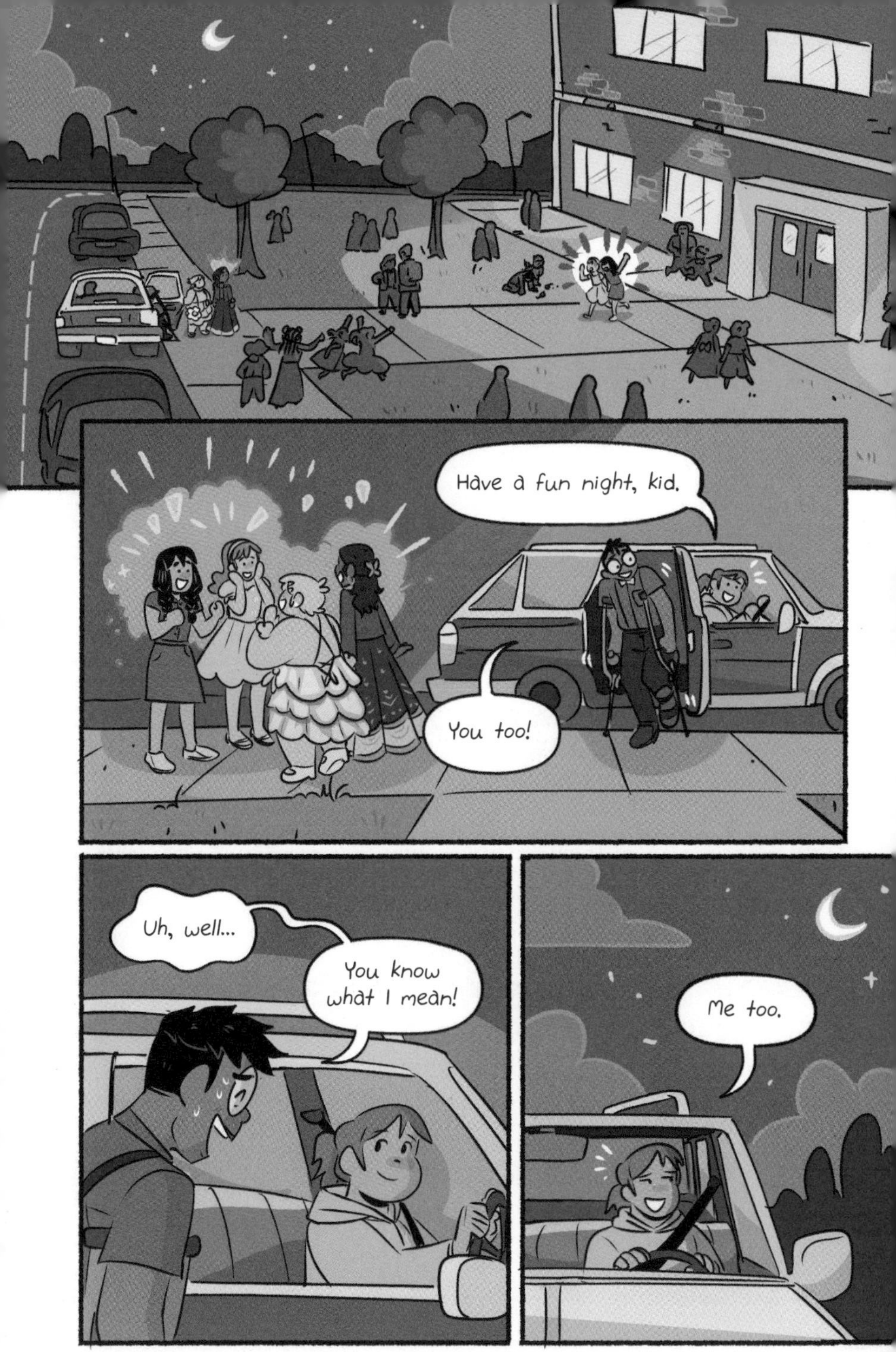
Have a fun night, kid.
You too!
Uh, well...
You know what I mean!
Me too.

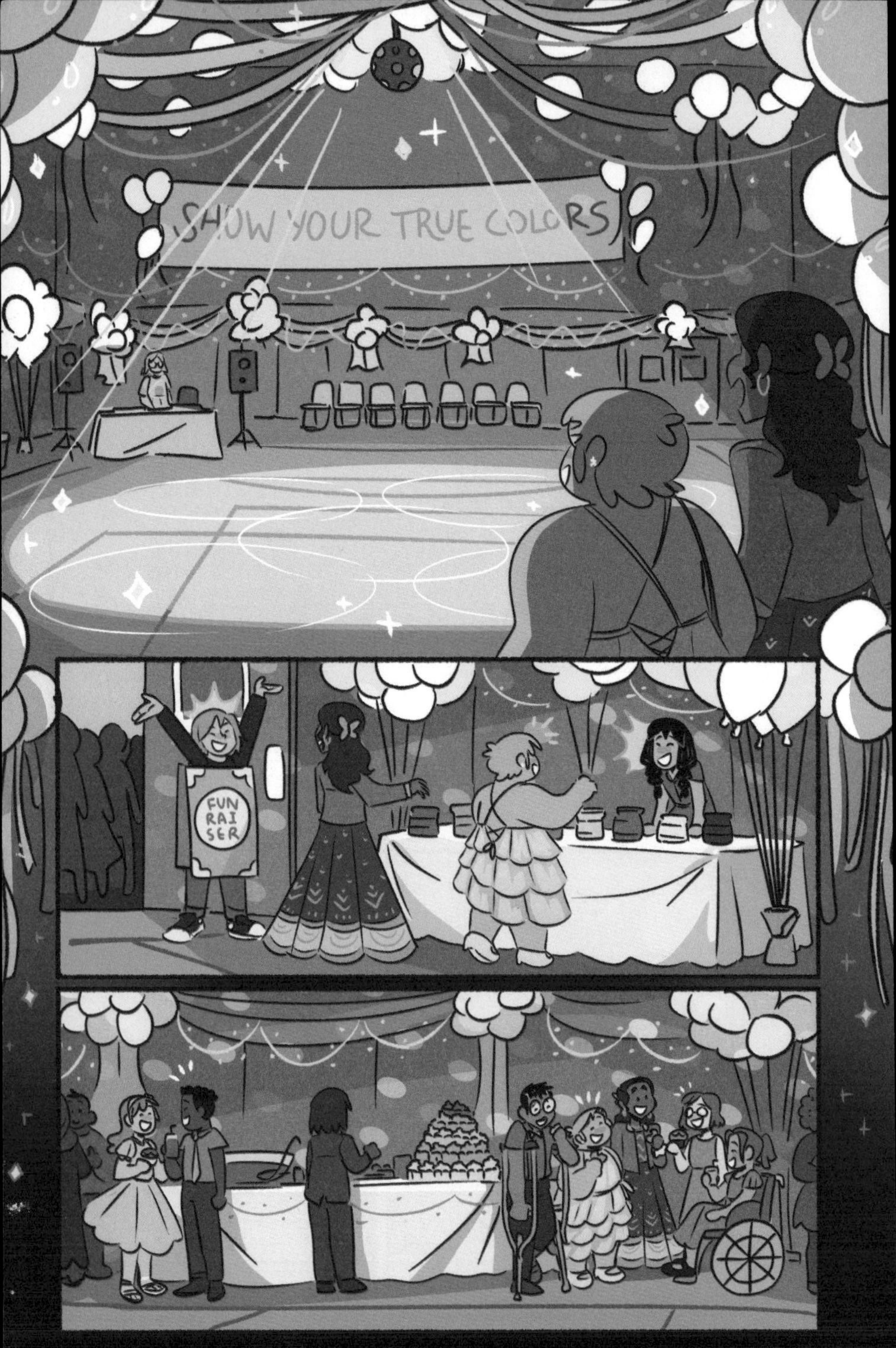
SHOW YOUR TRUE COLORS
FUN RAISER

179

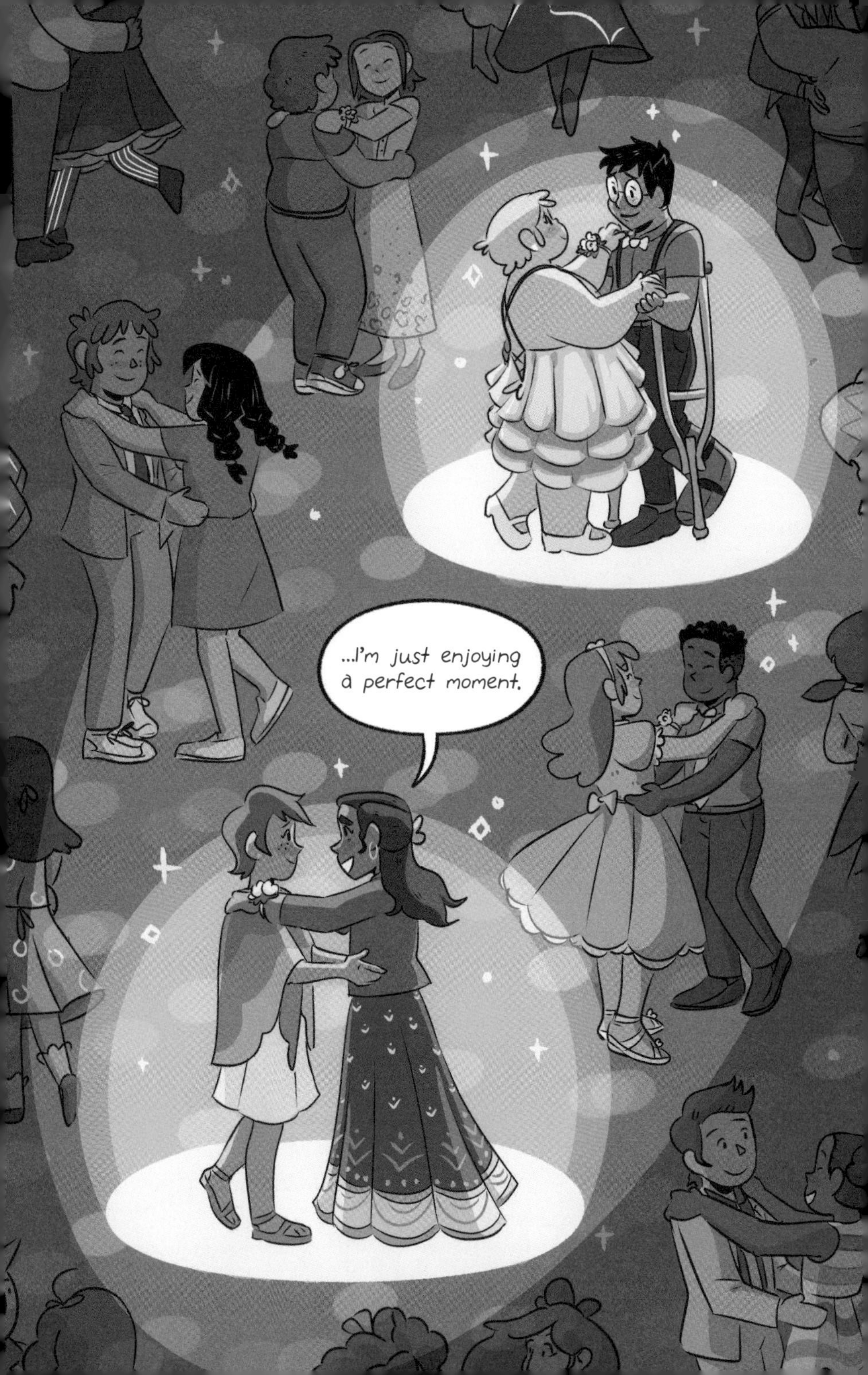
...I'm just enjoying a perfect moment.

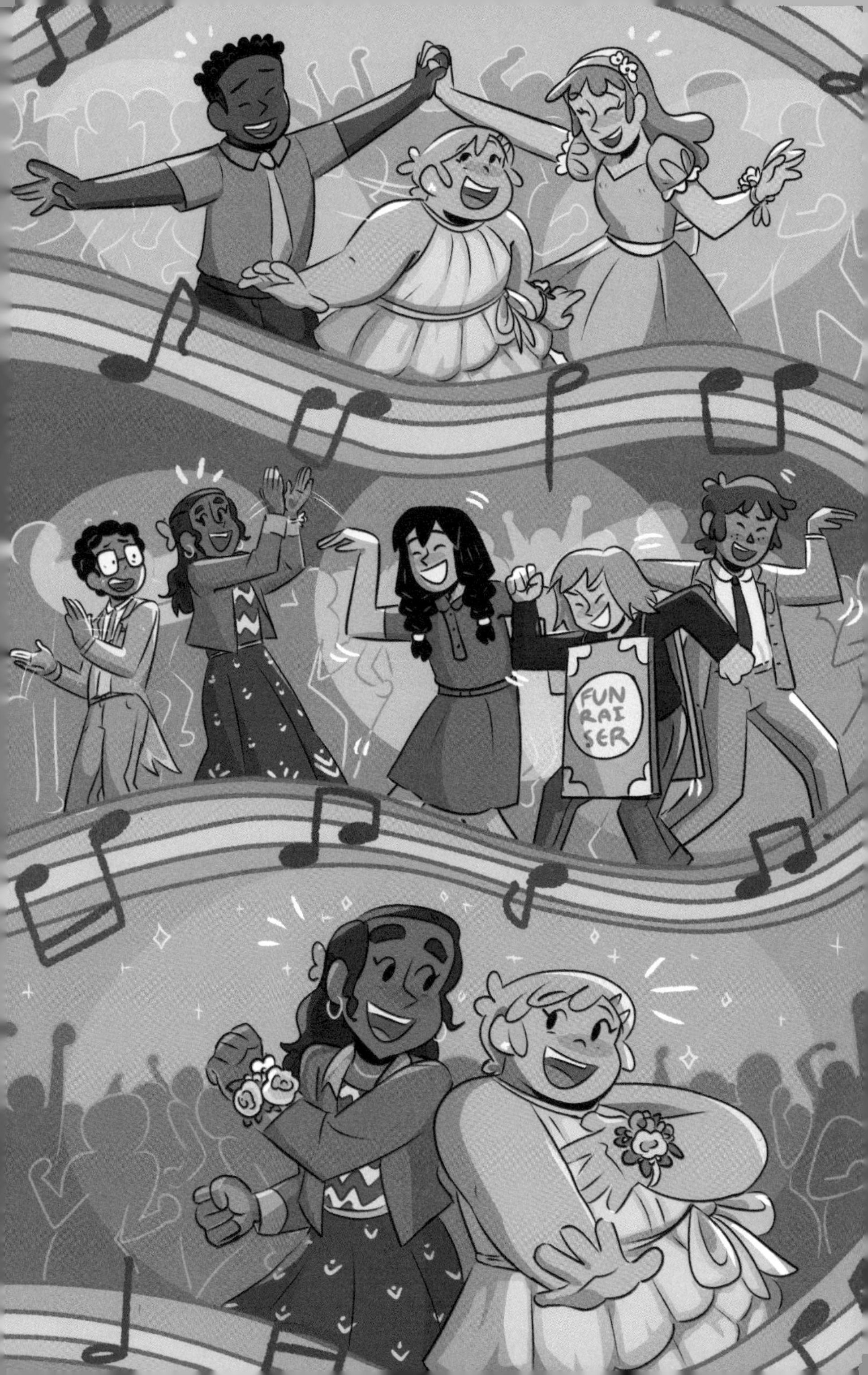
FUN RAI SER

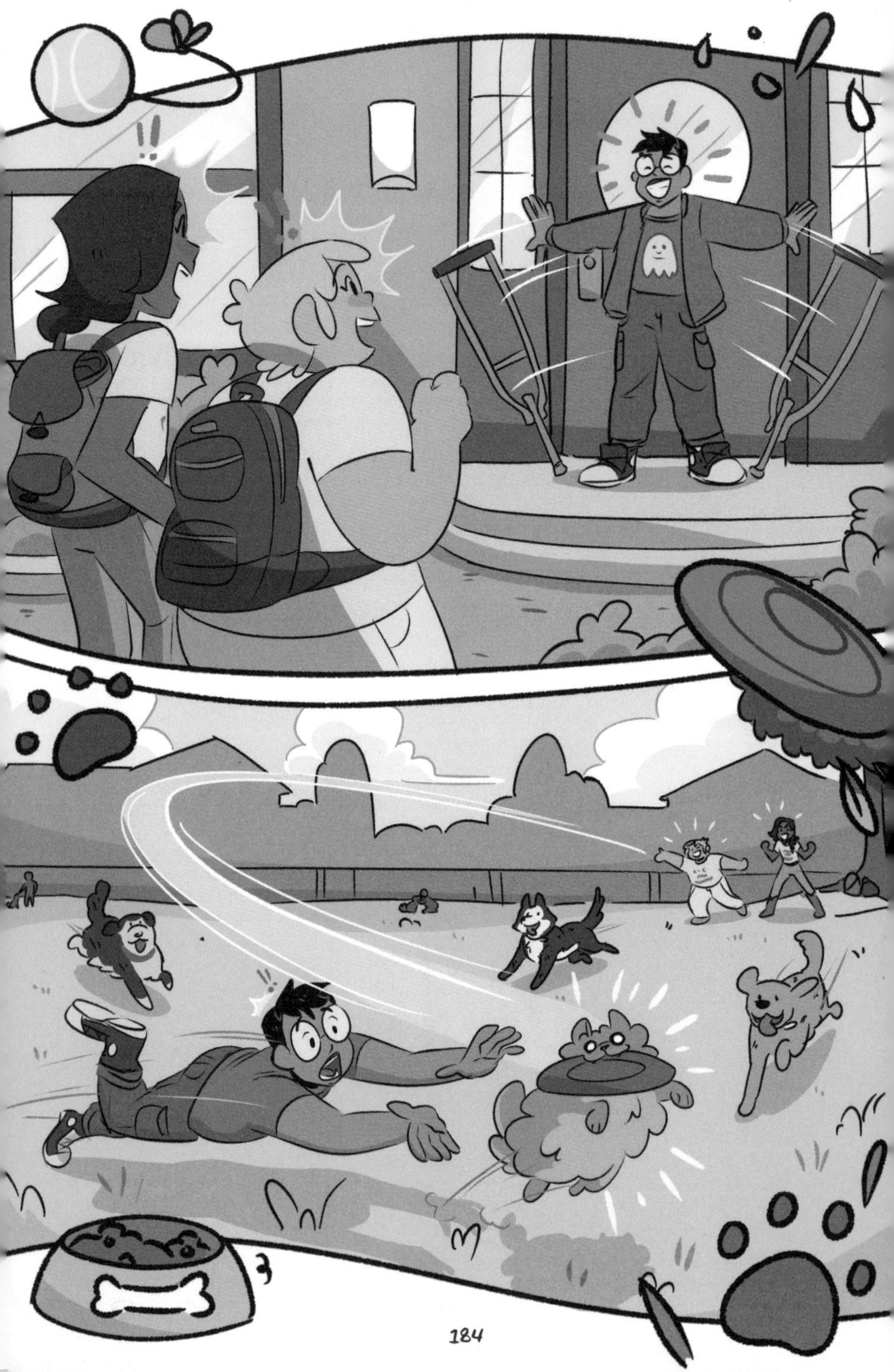

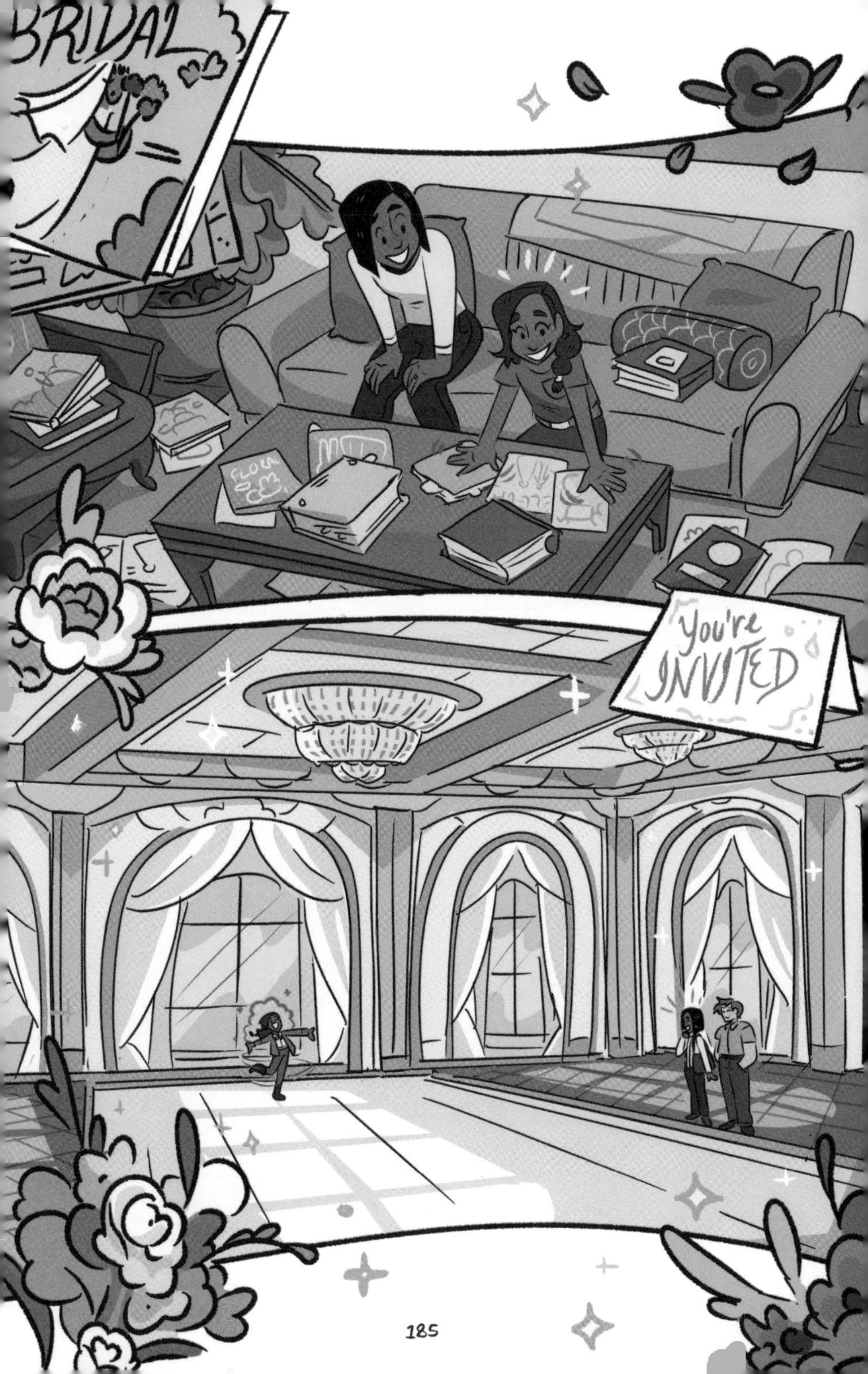
BRIDAL
FLORAL
You're INVITED

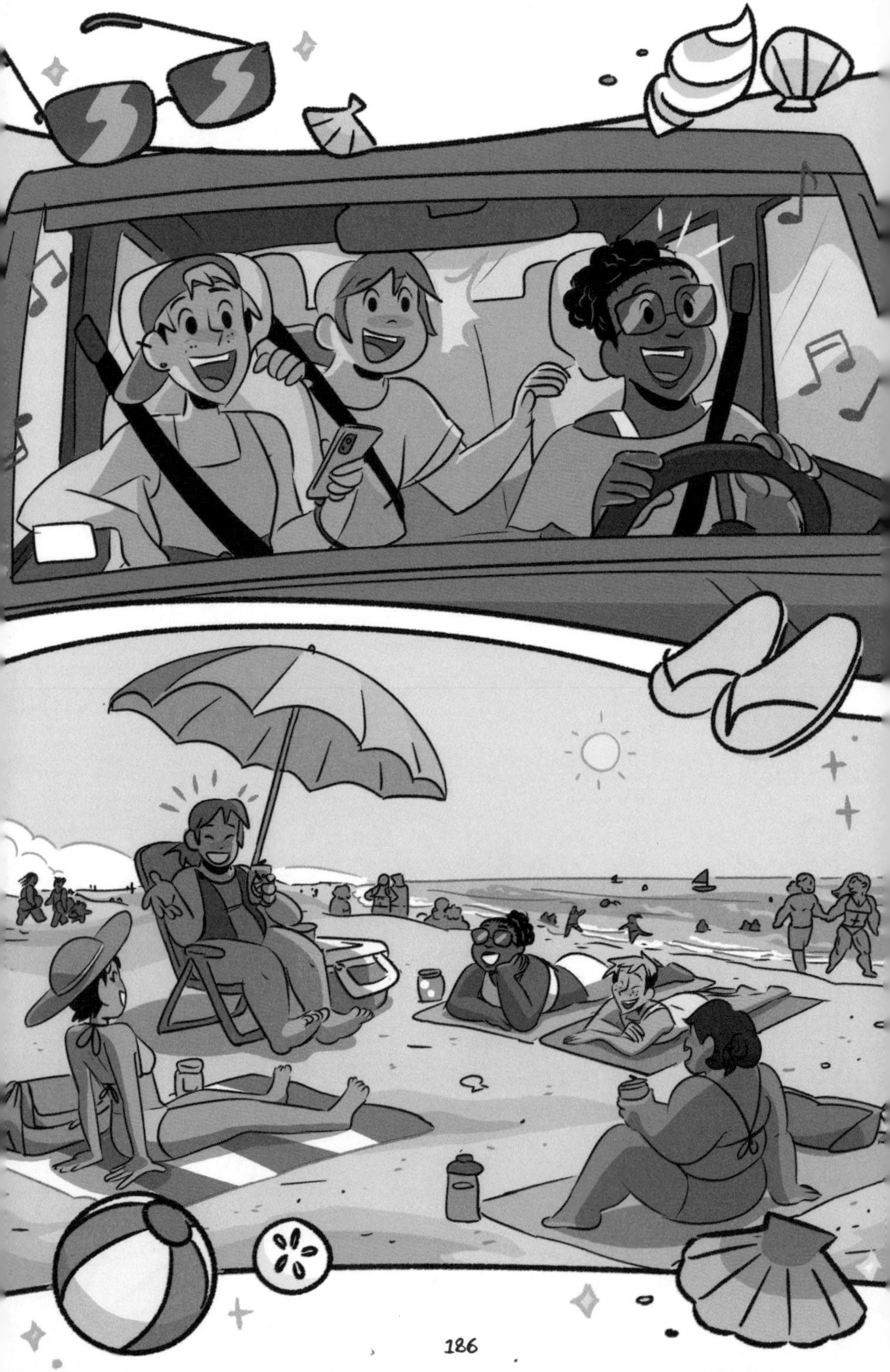

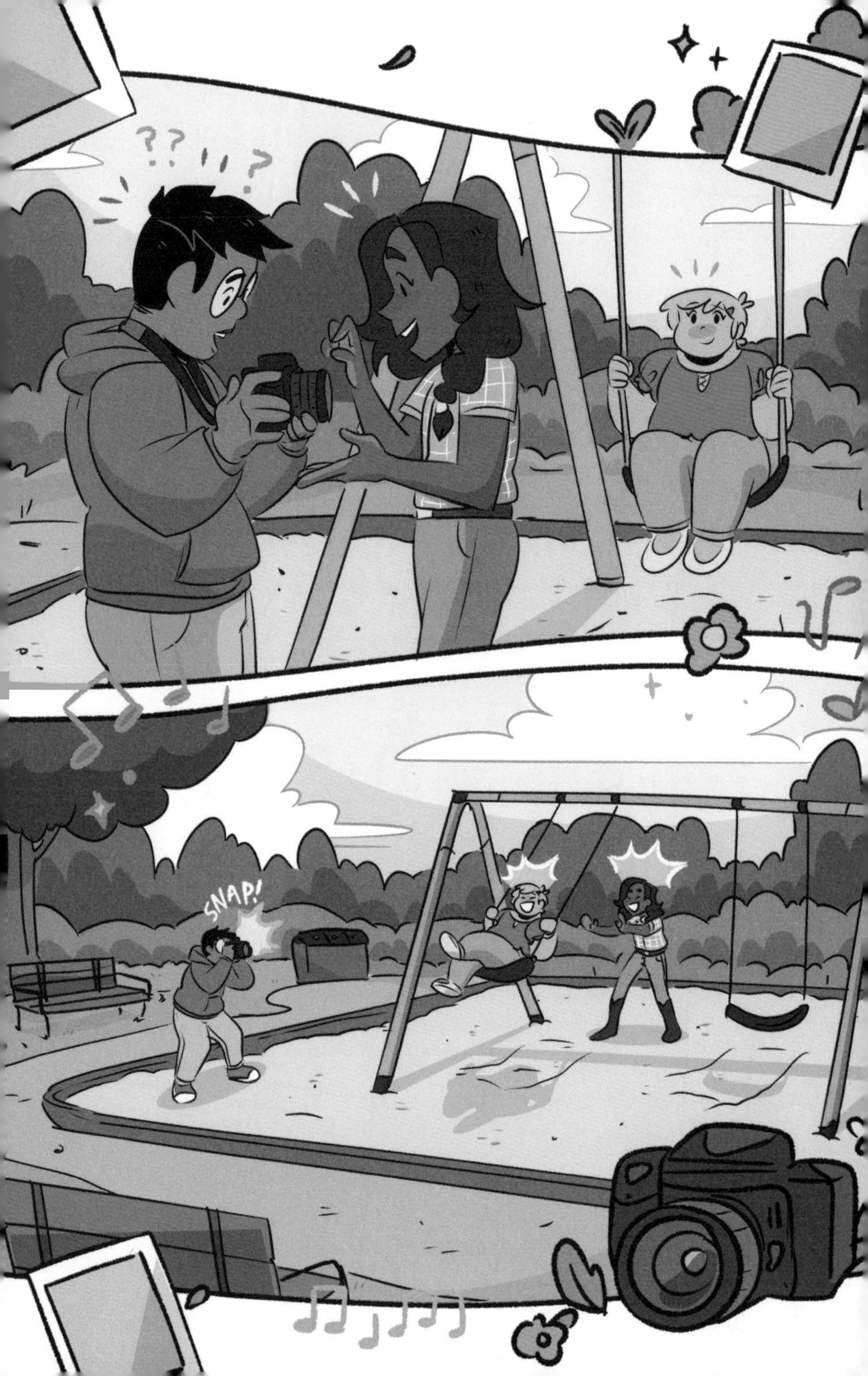
SNAP!

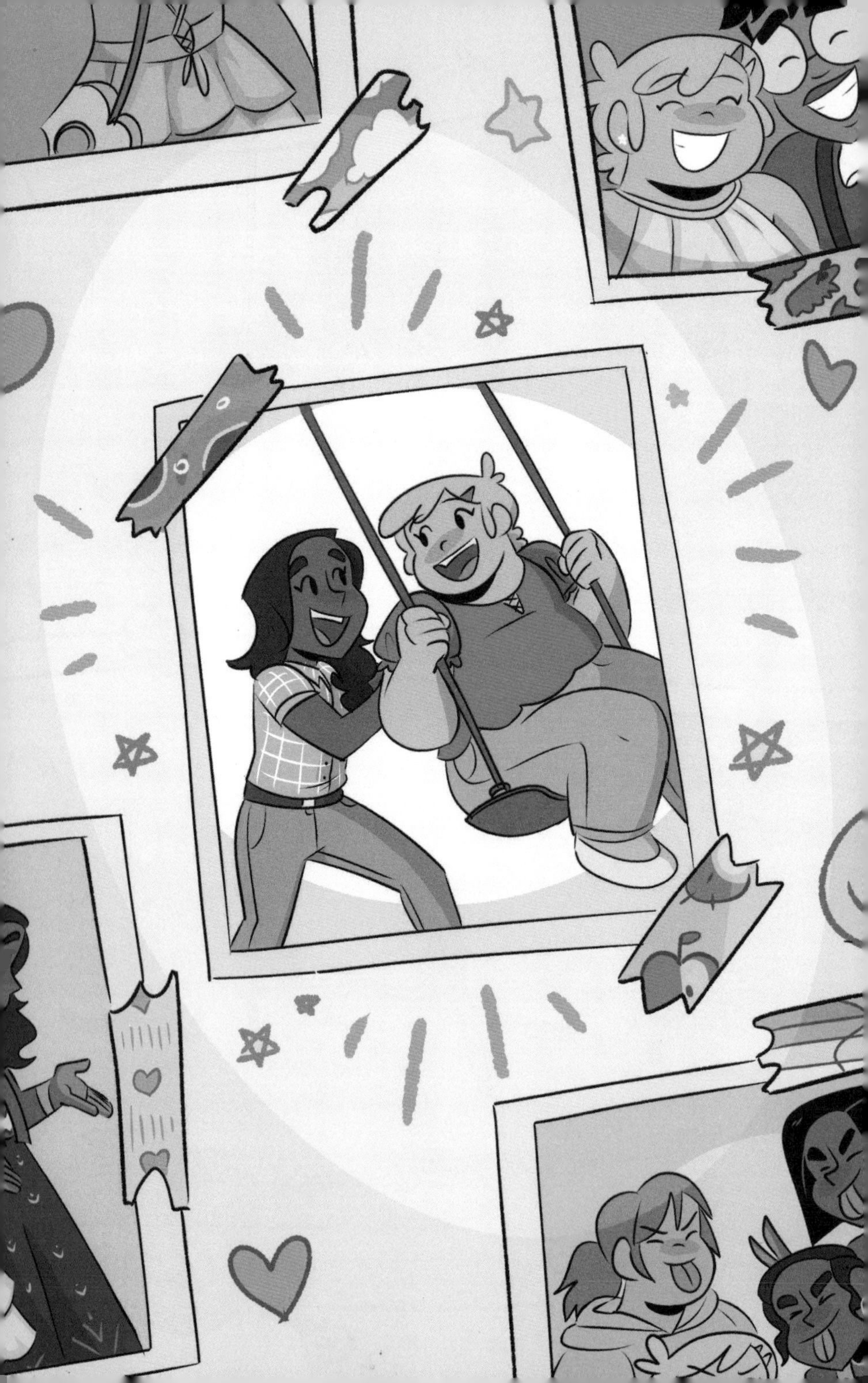

A Q&A WITH THE BESTIES TEAM

Q: What was different about working with your collaborators on book two versus book one?

KAYLA: Not to be too cute about it, but I think we "found our groove." Seeing the first book finished helped us picture what the finished art in this book would look like and allowed us to write scenes where we knew Kristina's art would shine.

JEFFREY: I must agree with Kayla. The biggest difference for me was having learned all of Kristina's strengths as an artist over the course of working on *Besties: Work It Out*. The script for book one was written with only a few samples of Kristina's art for the series in hand, so I largely pictured a version of Kayla's style in my mind when writing that script. But, after seeing all that Kristina brought to the table in book one, I felt confident going for more emotion, drama, and dynamic visual storytelling when writing *Find Their Groove*. There's nothing Kristina can't draw to perfection.

KRISTINA: By now, I think we all had a pretty good idea of what everyone's strengths were, and we just had to modify them to work even better together and to really shine. That's the best kind of collaborative work—when something is greater than the sum of its parts. This book was even more collaborative than the first. We also expanded the art team to include Victor, our inker. With three people on the art team, it really felt like a full-team effort, and I couldn't be more proud of what we accomplished. With Kayla and Jeffrey's whip-smart and heartfelt writing, Victor's beautiful background work, and Damali's lovely colors, I think we've made something really special. This book speaks to me on so many levels, and I think the love and care everyone's poured into it really shows.

DAMALI: Working on this book was different, but I can't really complain, because I feel like our workflow as a team got a lot smoother. Working on the first book was a bit tough, but coming back for book two was a bit like saying hi to a friend. I think the changes only made it stronger.

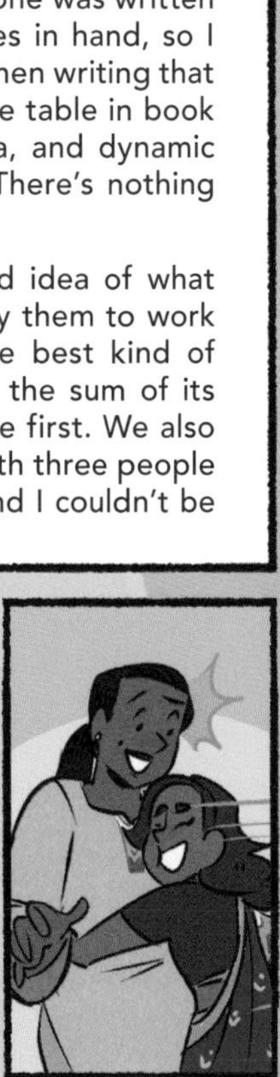

Q: What were the biggest challenges in creating book two?

KAYLA: This one felt more emotional than the previous book in that both girls are dealing with these situations that are extremely personal to them, so putting in scenes where they had to process these difficult emotions was hard—even if I knew things would get better in the end! Tapping into those old feelings of wanting to be accepted and struggling to accept yourself so that you can put that feeling on paper is always a little draining. I cried while planning some of the scenes!

JEFFREY: This book deals with some bigger and weightier issues than *Work It Out* did. The challenge we met was finding a way to maintain the high energy and atmosphere of fun that was present in the first book while also working in themes and situations that went into deeper, more serious subjects. So, when writing the script, I thought a lot about how to balance these two aspects of the story and do them both justice. Fortunately, Chanda and Beth are exactly the type of characters to make long, thoughtful conversations about meaningful issues entertaining!

DAMALI: Book two gets to show off a lot of new places like the mall shops, Ms. Foley's house, the surrounding neighborhood, and parks. Bringing all of these unique spaces to life was a challenge, but a fun one!

KRISTINA: This book had some pretty impactful emotional moments for the girls, so capturing the gravity and weight of those scenes was a good challenge! I have so many moments in this book that really resonated with me as a chubbier queer Vietnamese girl in a predominantly white school. I wanted to put in as much love and care while depicting each girl's personal struggles as best as I could. The insecurities we feel aren't always based on something tangible like cruel words or a school bully, it often runs so much deeper than that. And I feel so honored to have had the chance to make a story that really cuts into that topic with Kayla and Jeffrey!

Q: Do you have a favorite scene in the book?

KAYLA: I'm a sucker for dances. I wasn't a big fan of them as a kid, but when it comes to seeing them in graphic novels and movies, I love them. The outfits, the lights, the decorations, the drama—it's such fun!

In terms of the process, Chanda's "Boy Safari" was my favorite to write. I think it might have been the first scene I imagined fully when Jeffrey and I were coming up with the plot.

JEFFREY: I'm partial to the several heart-to-heart conversations that the characters have with one another throughout the book. My favorite is the big talk Chanda and Amaya have that brings their relationship to a better place and sets Chanda on the right path. Sister-sister bonding always hits me right in the feels.

KRISTINA: It's hard to have a favorite! But, if I had to pick, I absolutely love Chanda's "Boy Safari" scene. It's such a hilarious part of the book and so relatable! As someone who really didn't get "liking boys" at all as a teenager, Chanda's whole struggle really resonated with me. Trying to make yourself "have a date" or "be in love" when you just don't feel that way really feels like going through an equation: Me + Boy = Perfect? But life isn't like mathematics. Frankly, it's a lot more complicated and layered, and that's what makes it so interesting and unique to each of us.

DAMALI: I like the scene where Chanda and Beth find out about their classmates' dates. As everyone pairs up, the stakes are raised and the race is on. Olive has two dates! It's really funny.

Q: In the story, Beth and Chanda struggle to find a way to fit in that also lets them be seen for their individual awesomeness. What do you hope readers will take away from the book?

KAYLA: I hope readers see Chanda and Beth rocking their uniqueness and feel like they want to do the same in their own lives. Also supporting each other's individuality! Let your friends know what you like about them and why you love them! We all feel self-conscious and down on ourselves sometimes, but hearing something positive from a good friend can really help.

JEFFREY: I think the most important thing kids can do is embrace what makes them unique. There's a lot of pressure—from school, family, friends, society—to check off certain boxes and live up to certain expectations in a particular, predefined way. Chanda and Beth feel that pressure, and it fuels the conflicts in this book. But what if "fitting in" means giving up or trying to change something you love about yourself? The Besties learn to embrace who they are and what they want while tuning out all the feedback around them, and I think that's a mindset to aspire to.

KRISTINA: I had a pretty turbulent relationship with fashion and self-image for most of my youth. It's a misconception that being yourself and loving yourself is easy. It's a struggle for everyone. I really want readers to understand that it is okay to make mistakes, to not always be happy, to have moments of doubt and reflection. And you can rely on other people to be there for you. There is no ultimate form of self-love or self-expression. You'll have bad days that make the world feel like it's falling down. But you'll also have good days that make it all worth it. You're *supposed* to figure yourself out, not just have it all set in stone. So let yourself stumble and breathe the way Beth and Chanda do here. Try new things—don't be afraid to have fun and be weird and be YOU.

DAMALI: I hope readers can learn a little bit about patience through the story. It's really easy if you're feeling self-conscious to either want to fix your problem immediately, or to assume it can't be fixed at all. Chanda and Beth both struggle with this, but a lot of their problems were because they were looking at things the wrong way. By taking time, both girls found solutions that best reflected who they truly are and made them happy. I really think it shows how if we're patient with ourselves and others, things work out for the best.

Q: *Do you have a brief story or something to share about a school dance experience?*

KAYLA: I said earlier that I didn't like dances, which is true of formal dances—mainly because I *hated* shopping for dresses—but I used to love these casual dances in middle school where everyone would hang out in the municipal center's gym. There was a DJ and a snack bar and an air hockey table . . . and no one really worried about dates!

JEFFREY: I have vivid memories of my middle school dances. Only a few kids dressed up, and most spent the majority of the evening huddled around the lunchroom snack tables buying up all the candy and soft drinks that were for sale. (This is where I first learned the joy of drinking Dr Pepper through a sour candy straw.) The dance floor saw a little bit of action, but only when the biggest hits were played. No one could resist the Macarena.

KRISTINA: School dances can and should be fun! But the pressure surrounding them is very real, and I honestly avoided a lot of dances in my youth because of it. I didn't even realize I loved just dancing and how fun it was to go with friends until I was much older. To think I missed out on what could've been a fantastic school-days memory makes me so sad. I think my best dance experiences were ones I went in fully thinking, "I am here to have fun and dance to music I like," and that was it. Tune out the rest of the world and just be there with your friends and have a good time. Nothing else matters. The happiest people at a dance aren't always with a date. The happiest people are always the ones giving 100 percent to the music and just dancing the night away as if no one else is watching. As the book says, find your groove. :)

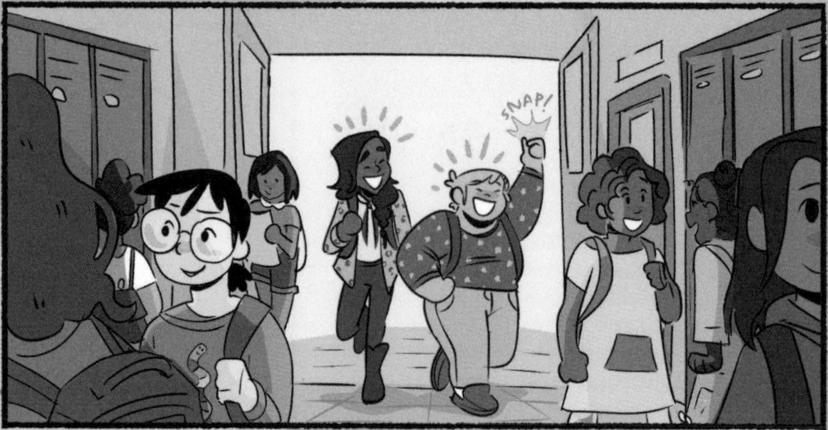
SNAP!

CREATING THE COVER

Sketches

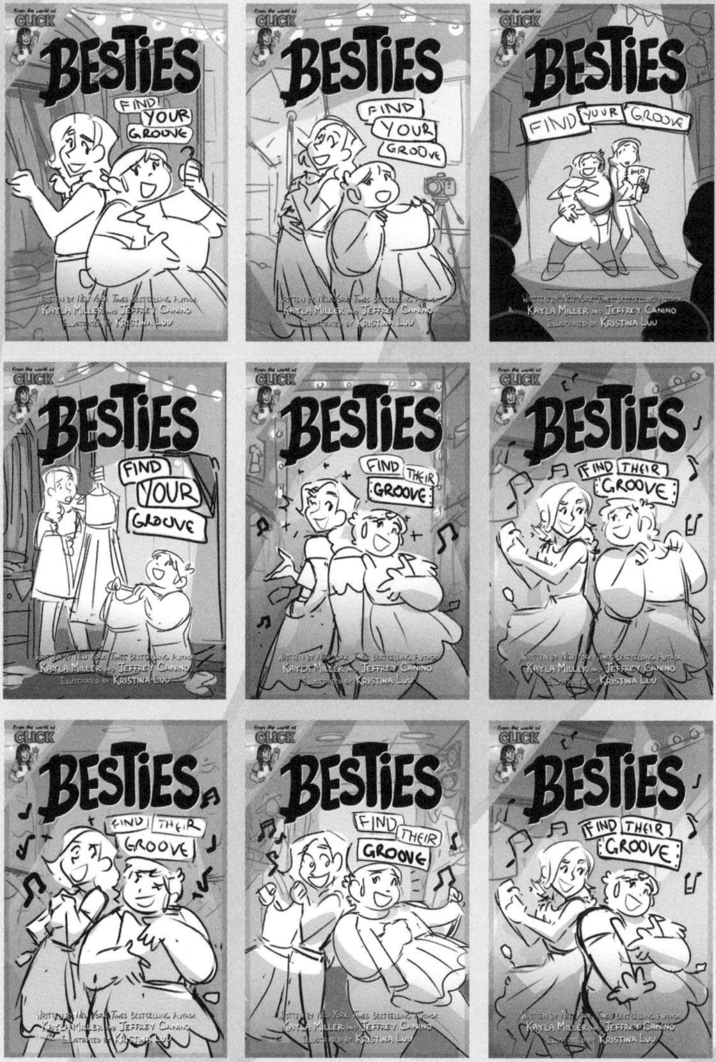
From the world of
CLICK
BESTIES
FIND YOUR GROOVE
Written by New York Times Bestselling Author
Kayla Miller and Jeffrey Canino
Illustrated by Kristina Luu
From the world of
CLICK
BESTIES
FIND YOUR GROOVE
Written by New York Times Bestselling Author
Kayla Miller and Jeffrey Canino
Illustrated by Kristina Luu
From the world of
CLICK
BESTIES
FIND YOUR GROOVE
Written by New York Times Bestselling Author
Kayla Miller and Jeffrey Canino
Illustrated by Kristina Luu
From the world of
CLICK
BESTIES
FIND YOUR GROOVE
Written by New York Times Bestselling Author
Kayla Miller and Jeffrey Canino
Illustrated by Kristina Luu
From the world of
CLICK
BESTIES
FIND THEIR GROOVE
Written by New York Times Bestselling Author
Kayla Miller and Jeffrey Canino
Illustrated by Kristina Luu
From the world of
CLICK
BESTIES
FIND THEIR GROOVE
Written by New York Times Bestselling Author
Kayla Miller and Jeffrey Canino
Illustrated by Kristina Luu
From the world of
CLICK
BESTIES
FIND THEIR GROOVE
Written by New York Times Bestselling Author
Kayla Miller and Jeffrey Canino
Illustrated by Kristina Luu
From the world of
CLICK
BESTIES
FIND THEIR GROOVE
Written by New York Times Bestselling Author
Kayla Miller and Jeffrey Canino
Illustrated by Kristina Luu
From the world of
CLICK
BESTIES
FIND THEIR GROOVE
Written by New York Times Bestselling Author
Kayla Miller and Jeffrey Canino
Illustrated by Kristina Luu

CREATING THE COVER

Color samples

final cover

DESIGNING THE CHARACTERS

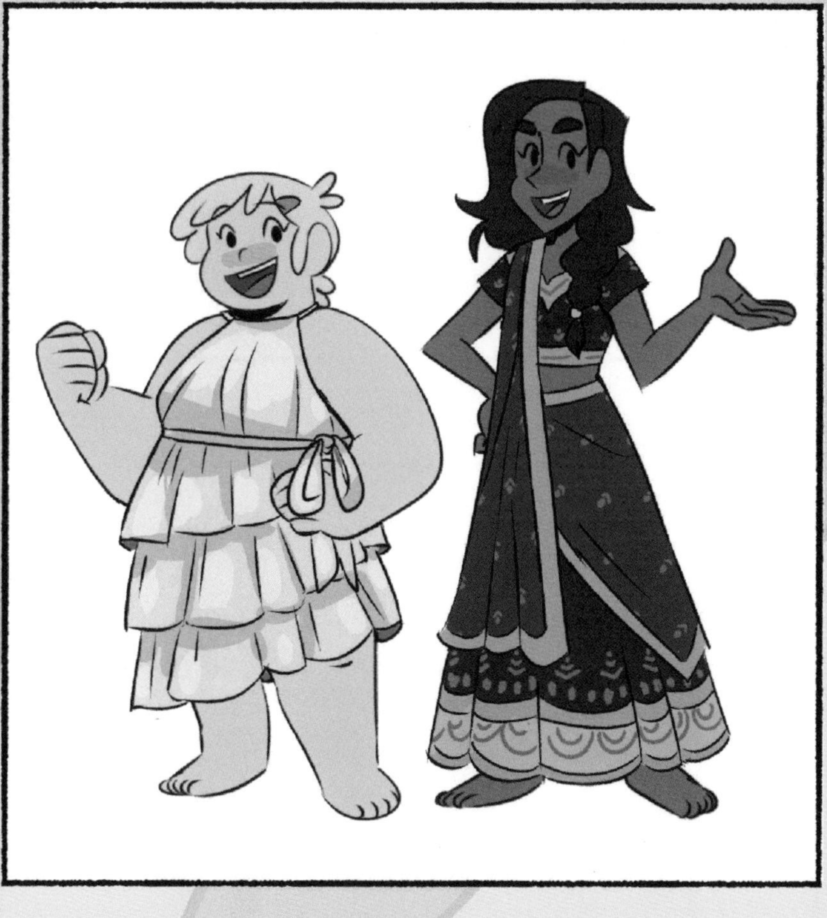

DESIGNING THE CHARACTERS

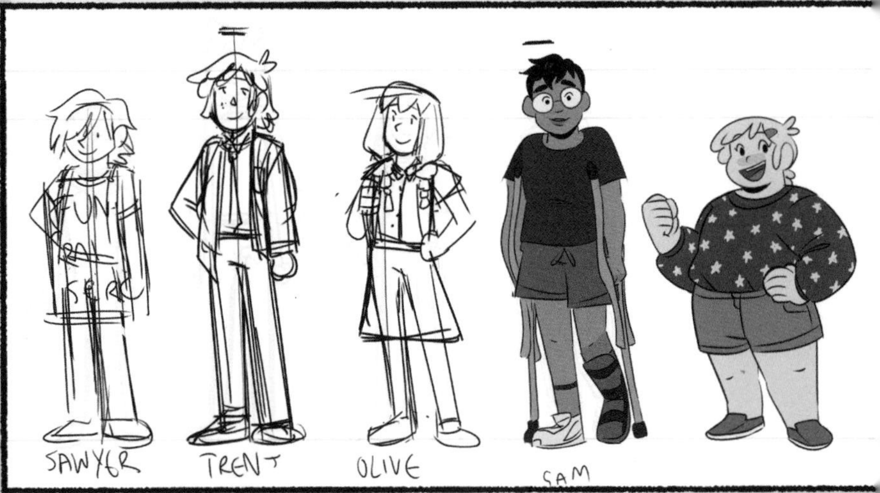
SAWYER
TRENT
OLIVE
SAM

Line-up of Sam, Beth, Chanda

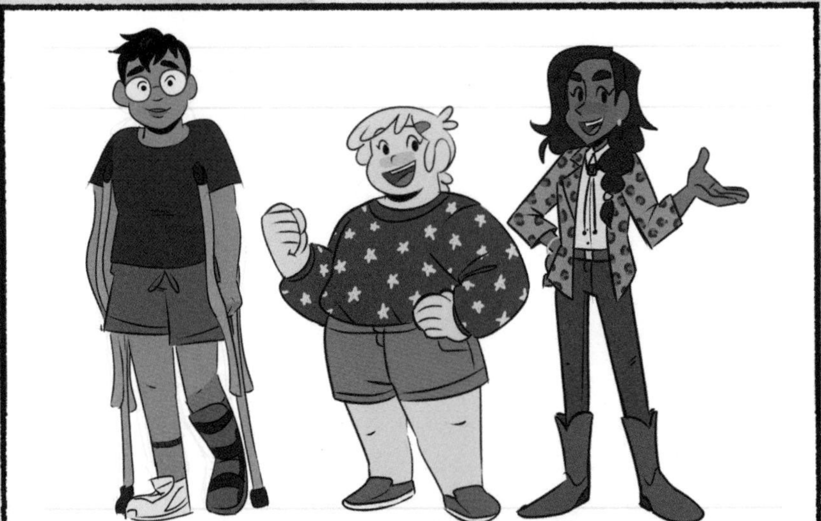

Line-up of Sam, Beth, Chanda, and all friends

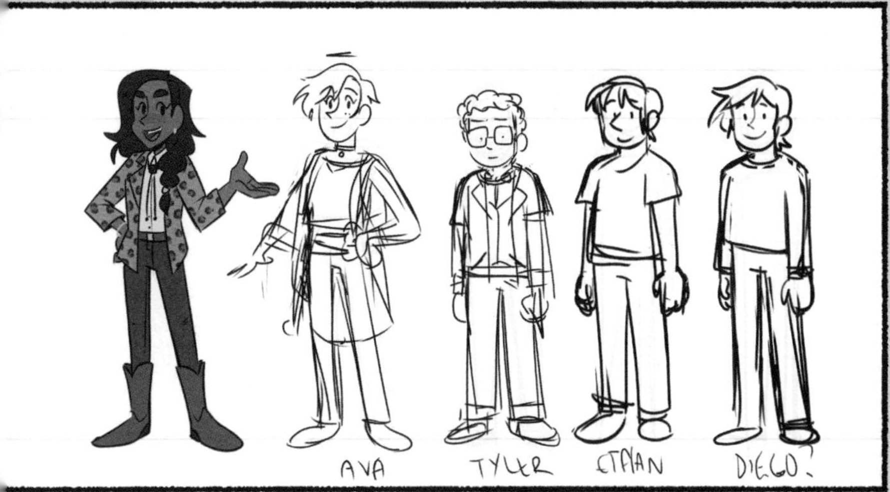
AVA
TYLER
ETHAN
DIEGO?

Beth, Chanda, Mr. and Mrs. Basu, Amaya, Seth

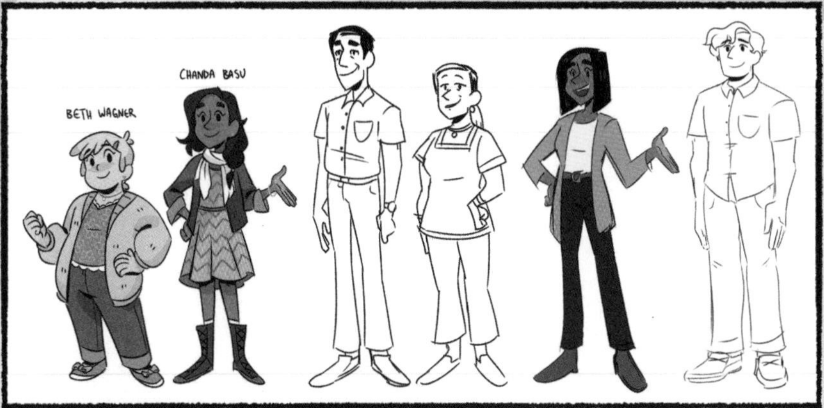
BETH WAGNER
CHANDA BASU

A PAGE FROM START TO FINISH

Step 1: panels

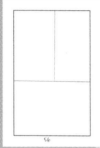

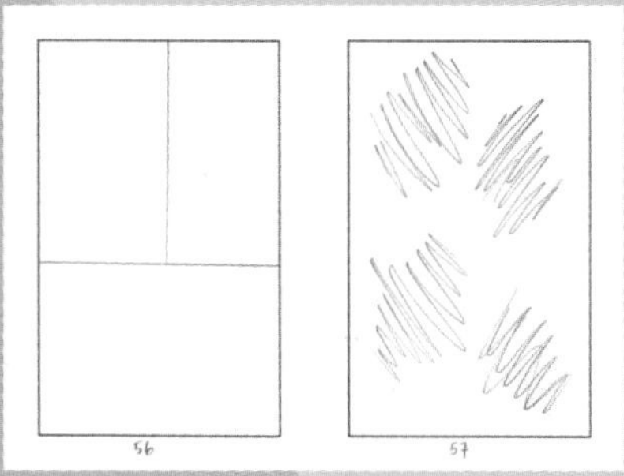

Step 2: thumbnails

Step 3: sketch

Step 4: initial inks

Step 5: final inks

Step 6: final color